BIG FLAT

BIG FLAT

HENRY OYEN

Introduction by Eric Kennedy

Hastings College Press | Hastings, Nebraska

Production Staff

Anna Bultman
Lyette Erin
Mae Heater
Blake Hessler
Eliana Hogan
Lilly Nelms

Emily Nevins
Sebastian Reese
Kierra Spurgeon
Reagan Weidemann
Renee Williams

Proofreader
Bruce Batterson

ISBN-13: 978-1-942885-90-0

Note on the text: This edition has been reset from the first (1919) edition. Original spelling and grammatical conventions have been maintained, except in the case of publishing errors in the first edition. The original punctuation has been maintained but updated using modern conventions (e.g., eliminating spaces around dashes).

Introduction

Eric Kennedy

When I was initially asked to write the introduction for this republication of Henry Oyen's 1919 novel about a community of timbermen in rural Wisconsin, I was eager at the opportunity. A book of class struggle and the complicated coexistences of communal class-consciousness and the individual entrepreneurial spirit embedded within American cultural constructs, *Big Flat* tells the story of a small community of settlers and timbermen-turned-potato farmers who fight back against the nefarious workings of the general manager of the Starin Paper Company, who desires to run them off the one thing they can call their own: their land. The novel includes themes of strife, fortitude, assertion of the ever-popular myth of the American Dream, concerns about ecological conservation, and surprisingly progressive female characters. For a text so loaded with popular themes, why this complex novel and its author have been forgotten by scholars and the general public is central to the new edition you now hold in your hands.

Henry Oyen

Sources list Oyen's year of birth as either 1882 or 1883 and his year of death as 1921. He was born in Christiania, now Oslo, Norway, and raised in Waupaca, Wisconsin, from where a neighboring farmer helped him get a job with Armour & Company, a meatpacking operation in Chicago. When he was 22, Oyen published a story in *Century Magazine*, which led to his six-year employment with the *Chicago Tribune*, shifting his income from $8

per week to $35 ("Henry Oyen, Novelist, Dies Suddenly at 38";
Oyen, "Writing a Second Choice"). When he found out Oyen had
become a writer, the befuddled farmer who helped him get work at
Armour questioned why Henry couldn't "make it go out there to
the stock yards" (Oyen, "Writing a Second Choice").

For the *Tribune,* Oyen published both fiction and editorials,
writing mainly for the paper's "Worker's Magazine" section. Oyen's
editorials focused on the lived experiences of workers and the lower
classes as well lifestyle pieces that lauded the growing "success
craze" and movements for clean living ("Success Craze Checking
the Drink Habit"; "Ruin and Death in Wake of Cigaret"), and
offered perspective and advice on how to conduct and present
oneself in terms of manners and success ("Dress Counts for Much
in the Business World"; "You Cannot Afford to Be Dishonest").
I will return to Oyen's work for the *Tribune* below, but it is of
interest to note here how his work in both the examination and
progressive cause of the lower classes clashes with the perspectives
offered in his lifestyle columns. This contradictory nature is at
work in Oyen's fiction, offering some level of complexity to his
characters and narratives.

On March 28, 1916, Oyen married Sara Goldsmith, a
"member of the staff of the Brooklyn Times" and daughter of an
attorney, in St. Louis. The marriage was apparently a "surprise" to
their friends ("Miss Sara Goldsmith Weds Henry Oyen of N.Y.").
In 1920, Henry and Sara had a son, Henry David, who later
anglicized his family name to Owen and became an accomplished
diplomat and political figure, serving as "ambassador at large for
international economic summits" under the Carter administration
(Vitello).

Outside of his life in Chicago, Oyen found some success in
the burgeoning film industry, adapting several of his works for the
screen. The most successful of his film projects appears to be 1915's

The Man Trail, adapted from Oyen's novel of the same name and directed by E.H. Calvert and starring Richard Travers (Calvert). *Variety* called the film "a real thriller from the start to the finish" and praised both the cinematography and the fight choreography (Fred). It is a shame, then, that like so many films of the earliest era of American cinema, *The Man Trail,* along with the five other films Oyen was associated with, has been lost to time.

In the midst of courting Hollywood and developing his skill and style as a writer of fiction, it seems that Oyen was also of some interest to the New York papers, in which his work was reviewed and his life occasionally reported on. This includes a visit to the city in 1915, the article about which claims that Oyen, who came for a week and left in two days, said he would never return. The article is not clear on the context, but it suggests that Oyen was commenting on the subjects of his writing, deciding to switch from noir-tinged stories of "sickly, pale, cocaine-sniffing misfits of the underworld" to writing "of the woods, of the husky lumberjacks, the great sinewed naïve children of the forest—men with hair on their chests" (McIntyre). Oyen did in fact return to New York, making his home on Long Island and/or in Forest Hills, Queens. It is reportedly in his home in Queens where Oyen, at the age of 38, died of a sudden cerebral hemorrhage on November 3, 1921 ("Henry Oyen, Novelist, Dies Suddenly at 38"). Oyen's body was taken to his hometown of Waupaca, Wisconsin, and buried in Lakeside Cemetery (*Lakeside Cemetery Report* 227).

Even with his widespread publications and notable successes over a short lifespan, Oyen is a ghost in the canon of American literary figures. Within literary scholarship, that most holy record of all things obscure and pedantic, there is no mention of his work or life, despite what ultimately proved a prolific literary career in a rather very short span of time—Oyen wrote, by my count, eleven novels within the span of twelve years after beginning his full-time career as a writer of fiction in 1910—and despite being one of the earliest examples of a writer entering into and adapting his work for Hollywood cinema. In the seeds and snippets of information I have stumbled across in my research for this introduction, my interest and intrigue for Oyen's work, life, and accomplishments have only grown.

Big Flat and Class

As I noted above, Oyen's work as a journalist and fiction writer is notably marked by a contradiction in the ways in which he presents a stark awareness and critique of class disparities in American society alongside lifestyle pieces that promote bourgeois values of culture, social mores, and business. A social climber from a distinctly working-class background, it is not difficult to see how these contradictory perspectives on social and economic order could be found in contentious coexistence within a person of Oyen's biography. Despite the relative success that Oyen found on the rungs of the American social ladder, his fiction never appears to abandon working-class roots.

In the August 22, 1919 edition of *The Palm Beach Post* there is an entertaining rebuttal to Oyen's story "The Plunderer," in which the author finds that "the implication of the story is grossly unjust" to those involved in the business and development of land in the Florida Everglades (Bussey 4). This amusing critique of a story that places its sympathies with those on the losing ending of capitalist industrial progress is as indicative of Oyen's fiction oeuvre as it is an exposure of the socioeconomic biases that dominated, and still dominate, popular media and cultural narrative constructions. This exposure is paramount to the power of the social commentary with which Oyen imbues the narrative and character of *Big Flat*.

There are no depressed social-climbing Daisy Buchanans or destiny-affronting Isabel Archers within the pages of *Big Flat,* and that is telling in the way in which Oyen develops his female characters, scant as they are, as rather refreshing-for-the-times subversions of gender politics. While Alice Demaree is eventually revealed to uphold some of the bourgeois stereotypes of her economic strata and gender, particularly as seen through the eyes of the country characters, *Big Flat*'s gender role subversions are most typified in the character of Hattie Lee, the daughter of Martin's closest neighbor and his life-long friend and love interest. Hattie's narrative arc may be the most intriguing of all of the characters in the novel, even Martin's, despite the relatively little time given to her within its pages. Hattie begins the novel as what we can assume is Big Flat's sole schoolteacher, running the one-room schoolhouse in which the settlers' children spend their days. But Oyen spends no time within the walls of the schoolhouse with Hattie. Instead, we see Hattie mostly at work with her hands, tying fishing flies, first for her father, whose storied and successful method she replicates, then for vacationing city folk, and finally as a full-fledged business for a company in Chicago.

Hattie's entrepreneurialism runs as a parallel narrative to that of Martin's ambition to make Big Flat a prosperous farming community. Where Alice Demaree seems content with her life of leisure and familial wealth, Hattie Lee demonstrates the striving for the American Dream typically exemplified by male characters in works of the late nineteenth and early twentieth centuries. It is Hattie's strong will and desire for a life of her own that acts as the driving force behind the moments of progressive gender politics in *Big Flat.* When Martin questions her desire to move to the city and focus on making flies full-time she responds,

It keeps me busy for one thing. And it makes me
independent. That's the main thing; it makes me
independent. I don't have to ask anybody for a single
thing I want. I don't have to worry about getting
somebody else to do anything, or get anything for me. I
can do and get things myself. I can do what I want, and
get what I want. I—I don't have to be a slave, like the
average farmer's wife. Yes, I like it. (176)

Hattie's declaration of independence is similar to claims from
other independent women characters in the literature of the first
part of the twentieth century, but it stands out in several ways.
One is her socioeconomic status—Hattie is no upper-middle
class woman "bartering [her] sexuality" (Hapke 155) in search
of wealth and leisure, nor is she suffering from having found it.
Her frankness is also unusual, holding back none of her joy for
her avenue of success and expressing no guilt for leaving her old
way of life behind. And, in spite of her comparison of the life of
a farmer's wife to that of a slave's, Hattie, throughout the novel,
gives no impression of disdain or scorn for working-class lives that
Alice Demaree does. And lastly, through her frankness, she affects
her male counterpart's thinking on the life of the women of Big
Flat:

He had never thought of that before. He was farm
born and bred, and the world to him was a man-world.
Women had their share in it, but the idea that they might
want to know the savour of independence; the idea that
beneath the patient exterior of the average subdued farm
wife there smouldered a spirit such as had dared to break
out in Hattie Lee, was revolutionary. (176)

Revolutionary! This epiphany of Martin's is quite comical in the context of the twenty-first century, certainly, but Martin's expression here is very likely an echo of many men living through perhaps the strongest moments of Women's Suffrage in America. A year before the enactment of the 19th Amendment, Hattie manages to give convincing voice to the struggle of all American women in the ear and mind of a hardened farm boy. Within the context of the novel, this seems quite the feat!

Of course, the novel's closing moments undermine Hattie's victory to some extent. Changing her mind about the move to Chicago at the last possible moment, Hattie chooses to stay in Big Flat because Martin "looked so—so awf'ly helpless" (271) and the two embrace in what Oyen declares a "world made a paradise through the miracle of love" (272). It is a scene that could induce sickness if it were not so expected.

Though *Big Flat* shares much with the strains of literary naturalism and realism of the time, its ending runs counter to the downbeat notes so characteristic of those movements. *Big Flat* avoids this, taking a sidestep from protagonists succumbing in the middle of the desert while clutching their bag of gold as does McTeague, or freezing to death on the New York streets while their estranged wife coldly prepares for her next performance as in *Sister Carrie;* neither are there crashing sleds or frozen corpses. Even in Frank Norris's *The Octopus,* which shares much narratively and thematically with *Big Flat,* the story ends with the corporate antagonist drowning in a silo of wheat. Not even the greedy antagonist of *Big Flat,* Keener, suffers terribly. After his efforts to destroy the land and profits of the settlers, he is simply relieved of his position. The settlers go on to another successful year of potato farming, and the boy gets the girl we knew he was meant to be with all along. Perhaps this is one of the reasons Oyen and *Big Flat* have been neglected until now. The novel's lack of a naturalist gut-punch ending that so defined major works of the era, acting as a reminder of the harshness of the natural and social orders humans exist and build within, keeps it from fitting nicely into scholarly categorization. The narrative of this novel does not align with the pessimism inherent in works from the heavyweights of American literary naturalism such as Norris, Dreiser, Wharton, and London.

Or maybe Oyen has been forgotten because of his association with pulp literature. Although references to Oyen are few, he is typically identified as a "Pulp Author" (S "Pulp Flakes"), saddling him with a genre signifier that goes largely disregarded as cheap and disposable and lowbrow. It is certainly true that Oyen published his fiction regularly in pulp magazines and newspapers, including in many editions of the popular *Adventure Magazine.* But then again, so did such lauded writers as Ernest Hemingway, H. Rider Haggard, William Faulkner, Owen Wister, and Ray Bradbury. And it is also true that his style of writing is punchy, littered with dialect and colloquial dialogue, and often fast paced and episodic in its construction. But, again, similarities of style and approach are echoed in the work of the same authors I just listed. And like those authors, Oyen was successful in his lifetime, so while his placement within the realms of pulp publishing may play some part in his absence from the literary canon, the ephemeral and temporary nature of the pulp magazines and the material from which they were made cannot be the only reason.

Perhaps the most obvious reason for Oyen's exclusion from literary scholarship is that *Big Flat* is *a novel about class.* Specifically, the *working class.*

I emphasize this point because, like Oyen's work, discussions of class and the working-class are largely absent from scholarly discourse, and even cultural discourse at large. Steve Fraser expresses the heart of this type of diversion and avoidance well when he writes:

> Class is the secret of the American experience, its past,
> present, and likely future. It is a secret known to all, but
> a source of public embarrassment to acknowledge. It lives
> on all the surfaces of daily life, yet is driven underground
> every time its naked self offends cherished illusions about
> how we deal with each other. (4)

We are, of course, keenly aware of the existence of class hierarchies, but so often choose to look the other way when the problems it causes—inequality, poverty, racial bias, gatekeeping, and so on— threaten the narrative of a classless society.

Even when we find works that are largely concerned with narratives that question and take to task American socioeconomic class strata, like *The Great Gatsby* or *The Jungle,* our academic focuses steer away from the critiques these works so desperately want our attention directed toward. *The Jungle* is a great example of this culturally. Though it was successful in changing the way food production and sanitary compliance were handled in America, Sinclair's goal of drawing attention to the poor treatment of working-class people and the awful state of their labor and living conditions went, and often still goes, entirely ignored. As Barbara Jensen reminds us, "Just as having to punch a time card or ask permission to go to the toilet can be an erasure of one's humanity, so too the invisibility of working class life erases the real lives of working class people" (22).

And yet, works that place class front and center, in all its sweat-stained, dirt-covered, tent-citied glory, often find themselves disregarded or placed on the fringes of the academic terrain. *Big Flat* places class front and center. Surrounding the tepid love story and the fights, fires, and floods is a story about a working-class young man and his community caught up in what Steve Fraser may call "an antipathy to the constraints, protocols, dependencies, and emasculations felt to be the psychic ransom of social stratifications and the submissions it commands" (6). Martin Calkins's story is one of a fight against the encroaching tentacles of Capital and the need of its proponents to own and control everything. It is also a story about the struggles of staying true to one's values while still managing to adapt to the sociopolitical conditions of the time in order to survive. The contrasts of the different ways to survive in a capitalist society (selling out, buying in, or communal investment) and the damage the wrong choice can do to the human spirit are the weights bearing on Martin's psyche from the novel's start.

Even Oyen himself seemed to have trouble balancing the antinomies of the American class structure. Though *Big Flat* depicts a community coming together to push back against the machinations of corporate power and greed, the novel also takes pains to examine the need of communities and individuals to adapt to changing technologies and marketplaces, and to social expectations. As I noted above concerning his editorial writing, Oyen's proffered perspectives on the likes of business, success, and working conditions proved a grouping of somewhat mixed messages when taken together. Many of Oyen's editorial columns provide insights on the nature of success and ways for the average worker to potentially achieve it. In total, the message of these pieces comes down to a few factors: work hard, be presentable, be honest, and avoid vice. "Drink, laziness, shiftlessness, these are the shoals [failure] warned of," Oyen tells us in one piece for the *Chicago Tribune* ("Success and Failure; Two Types"). Yet, in another piece, Oyen details a day in the life of a street beggar named "Flopping Ed." It is not clear if Ed is someone Oyen actually met and profiled or if he is a work of the author's imagination. Either way, Oyen demonstrates a kind of sympathetic admiration for Ed, writing of his panhandling tactics as Ed's "art—a subtle knowledge of human nature and the psychological

value of moments that had soaked into him in years spent living
by his wits alone. But it was effective" ("One Day as a Street
Beggar; the Story of 'Flopping Ed'"). What connects Ed's story,
then, to Oyen's other editorial pieces is the throughline of an
appreciation for ambition, enterprise, and skill. And it is these
three qualities that are central to the character of Martin Calkins
and the style of class narrative that Oyen communicates in *Big
Flat.*

The novel's complicated weaving of American values of
entrepreneurial spirit and the Alger-esque self-made man together
with a critique of capitalist overreach and corporate power,
though not uncommon in literature of the time, is nonetheless
impressive in the ways in which Oyen is able to couch those
critiques within a story that never obliquely pushes a political
stance. Where major literary works of the early twentieth
century like *The Jungle* (1905) and Ernest Poole's *The Harbor*
(1915), or even later works such as *The Grapes of Wrath* (1939),
would couch the political slant of the narrative and its author
within an extended speech by a character or narrator, usually
somewhere near the narrative's conclusion, *Big Flat* chooses to be
suggestive, avoiding overt political statements in favor of tracking
Martin's sociopolitical evolutions through his words, thoughts,
and actions. In doing so, *Big Flat* takes what I consider to be
a more actualized and relatable approach to the political lives
of the working-class and their true lived experience, then and
now. There are depressing similarities within the 2023 economic
structure of the United States with that of the early 1900s—and
in either period, and really, all periods, those in the working-class
are hardly convinced or desire to be bothered by posh elocution
and theory-laden political rhetoric. No, if the political landscape
since 2016 has taught us anything, it is that though the eloquence
of Jim Casy or the verbose speaker on Socialism in *The Jungle*

may speak powerfully in their way, their words will likely fall on ears deafened by exhaustion and truly felt economic struggle; and rarely is there a refined lady to jog us from our sleep and find success in telling us "If you would try to listen, comrade, perhaps you would be interested" (Sinclair 357).

Instead, *Big Flat* offers its reader—who, Oyen was most likely aware, would be in the working or middle class—a delicate, if sometimes flawed, balancing act of moralizing and ideological analysis across classes. I have lightly demonstrated this at work in the novel with Martin's revelation about the desire for agency that may be captive in the women in his life. This is just one instance of Martin's progressive development through the novel. Martin himself might call this "getting waked up," a wonderfully prescient phrasing for the reader of the "woke" age of the twenty-first century. When a neighbor who is having doubts about their part in the collective operation that Martin has organized and its purchase of a tractor in service of pulling stumps tells him, "The old hand-fork is good enough for me," Martin responds with humor:

> "No it isn't, Jim," laughed Martin. "And you know it isn't.
> If you really felt it was, you'd never have gone in with us
> on the tractor. You're getting waked up. It hurts at first,
> I know, but you'll get used to it and when you do you'll
> begin to like it." (99)

Martin's response serves multiple thematic purposes here. First, "getting waked up" speaks to the difficulty many of the Big Flat residences have in adapting to new ways of life, particularly the use of machinery and technology to conduct the business and work of farming. Second, Martin is speaking to the slow revelations each of the members of his collective is having in regard to the machinations of Capital and the power it exerts over those who fall behind, as the farmers of Big Flat were in danger of doing before Martin's plan to collectivize.

In both cases, "getting waked up" is a political awakening, and it is not necessarily one that takes any particular side of the aisle. Martin's awareness of the functions of Capital could have led him in pursuit of joining its ranks—that narrative may well have led to the failure and tragic end more suited for a Naturalist novel. But in getting waked up, Martin begins to understand the attempts at exploitation that Keener, as general manager of the Starin Paper Company, is enacting on him and the settlers of Big Flat.

In this understanding, Martin chooses to push back and works to bring his neighbors with him. We learn that even before the first scene of the novel Martin was attempting to rouse his community against the paper company and their offers to buy the settlers' land (32). However, talk seems to have fallen on uncertain ears, as Martin continues to scheme ways of convincing his neighbors to band together, modifying an old saw mill engine to pull multiple stumps at a time. Demonstrating this personal innovation in hopes of raising funds to buy a tractor like the ones used by the company, Martin finds just as little success in moving his fellow farmers. They are skeptical of their need for such technologies and content with their traditions. After all, "collective manual labour is by tradition a rather ritualized activity, deeply intertwined with the ritual structuring of personal lives and social collectives" (Hobsbawm 69). Put simply, these workers figure, "if it ain't broke, why fix it?" It is not until Martin mortgages his property with the bank to buy a tractor that the interest of the Big Flat residents is piqued.

Accomplishing this produces one of the funnier scenes in the novel, where Martin takes the tractor door to door, unannounced, and silently clears a spat of his neighbors' land of stumps before moving on to the next. The demonstration of the machine, the

action in action, with its tangible and realized results, is what
is needed to convince the farmers to break with tradition. This
scene is exemplary when it comes to understanding working-class
solidarity and how to achieve it. As Mark Fisher has suggested,
"An ideological position can never be really successful until it is
naturalized, and it cannot be naturalized while it is still thought of
as a value rather than a fact" (16). For the settlers of Big Flat, the
modernization of their farming techniques could never be a part of
their value system as tradition has dictated it—it is too impersonal,
too far away from working with one's hands. Seeing the machinery
in action in service of their needs, however, acts to spark a forward-
thinking process that reasons both tradition and technological
progress as beneficial for their personal and professional lives and
begins to reshape the potential realities of their lived experiences.
In other words, they are "getting waked up."

But that waking up has at least one additional side, as I alluded
to above, and it is from this third perspective that the complicated
nature of fighting against the machinery of Capital within a
system of survival dependent upon the capitalist model becomes
apparent. That is, even within a capitalist society, the fight against
Capitalism and Capitalists is at least in part dependent upon the
socioeconomic rules and structures of Capital. Ask anyone involved
in a Socialist/Communist/Anarchist collective business and they
will likely sigh in recognition of this. Thus, the waking up of the
farmers of Big Flat necessitates their waking up to the monetary
value of their property and goods: "They would awaken to the fact
that their land was full of dollars, would his neighbours, and it
would be harder and harder for Keener to buy them out" (99).

Martin's exuberance for the potential monetary value of and
produced by the land of Big Flat is positioned largely as his own
throughout the novel. Other characters may sway toward Martin's
way of thinking and certainly join in his planning, but the

expression of unrealized value is left to Martin. This is noted early in the narrative as Oyen describes Martin's economic vision for the land:

> [H]e saw the Flat not as it was now, not as others saw it, but as he wished it to be, as it should and would be—the stumps pulled, the burnings cleared, the swamps drained and dried, the land broken and divided into orderly fields and teeming with crops. He saw the river-road graded and straightened and lined from the northern horizon to the foot of the ridge with neat, rich farms, straight, taut fences, and houses and barns glistening with coats of paint, white and red. (29)

Martin's daydream here is one of entrepreneurial vision—he sees the potential of the land, the way it can be molded by will, and the social and, most importantly, economic gains that can be had by imposing that will. This is not uncommon in the protagonists of early twentieth-century American literature about rural spaces. Paul Lauter has argued that "this image of the independent American artisan, entrepreneur, and farmer has constituted and continues to constitute, the expression of a powerful, if not altogether distinctive, American ideology" (25). Taking Lauter's assertion about this idealized image of a wholly American figure into account, it seems right to read Martin's vision for the future of Big Flat as falling in line with the values of the American capitalist narrative. Martin wants to turn his community into an enterprise, and even in his movements to do so with those in the community, his desire is still acceptable within the value system of American business.

Martin thus perpetuates the fiction; an "idealized solution to a set of difficult questions having to do with work and class: why we work, when, for whom, under what circumstances, among other questions" (Lauter 25). Not wanting to sell off his land and go work for someone else, like the company or, even worse, in an office in the city, Martin must adopt the guise of the businessmen he is fighting against. Hence the demonstrations for his neighbors, hence the employment of workers to assist in jobs he is unskilled in, hence the risk of mortgaging his home to buy the first tractor, hence his holding out two years in a row for better prices on the crop of potatoes he has harvested on his land. Some of Martin's tactics, under scrutiny, may be seen as risky and shrewd, but the narratives of the "great" men of American industry are filled with tales of such risk and shrewdness. Martin's strategy differs from Keener's because, as another character puts it, he is not "the curse of business—the hog who wants everything in sight" (234).

Martin demonstrates sure capitalist tendencies through his firm desire for some measure of wealth, but his view on how to gain it diverges from the corporate ideology that was taking hostile hold over American economic practice at the time. For Martin, the profit should go to those who do the labor, not those who own the tools—a Communist thought if ever there was one, in spite of the absence of direct political reference in the novel. But it is a thought that is also infused with the American Dream mentality that speaks of labor and ownership in the same breath as pride and success. The dreams of Martin and the settlers of Big Flat are "animated by a sense of possibility in the creative relationship of body and landscape," that "there can be dignity in labor when it is performed on one's own terms, without harm to the land, and for the benefit of family and community" (Coles 217). To realize this dream of dignity in labor, the settlers must take control of the machinations of Capital wherever they can, and though their fight for control may be riddled with flashes of violence and danger, like any good pulp adventure story, it ends with treasure and the hero getting the girl.

There is much more I could and would like to point to regarding class perspectives and literary value in *Big Flat,* but I fear I may overwhelm the page count of the novel itself. So I will leave the engagement with the themes of technology and nature, land and property, lived experiences, and the role of violence in working-class lives for another space and time, or even to another writer. And I have not even touched on the potential issues at play in the narrative, not the least of which is the way the novel presents its immigrant characters—a plight common to literature of the time, especially within American literary naturalism.

However, to conclude this argument for the value of *Big Flat* and works like it within the canon of American literature, I would like to touch on one potentially negative critical reading of the text's ending. As I have noted, the settlers, in the face of great force and several setbacks, win their independence from the corporate machinations, and Martin and Hattie embrace in a "world made of paradise through the miracle of love." That criticism is, well, that it is all just a bit too clean, isn't it? Verbosely romantic. Almost utopian. After all, "literary utopias portray an ongoing cultural desire for greater equality and justice represented—and experienced—along varying lines of felt need or oppression" (Catano 130). *Big Flat* does just this, and without the overt philosophizing or sci-fi dalliances so common to utopian narratives. This is why I think this reprinting of *Big Flat* is appropriate and needed in the current moment of the twenty-first century. I argued here already that the issues facing the characters of the novel are familiar, too familiar, to our own modern moment. Those issues have worked on our social order so long and so intensely that, though many of us raise up fists in combat against the declining standards of our day, the specters of doubt and pessimism have shadowed our sense of hope and belief that something better is possible. To have a utopian narrative that does not simply describe the post-enlightened society, but rather explores the action of community effort and resistance toward a better way of life through the lens of working-class lives, is something invaluable in casting light on that shadow.

Works Cited

Bussey, H. L. "Unfair Propaganda Regarding the Everglades Being Disseminated by Country Gentleman." *The Palm Beach Post,* 22 Aug. 1919, pp. 1, 4. Newspapers.com.

Calvert, E. H. *The Man Trail.* The Essanay Film Manufacturing Company, 1915.

Catano, James V. "Utopian Labors: Work in Nineteenth- and Twentieth-Century Utopian and Dystopian Fiction." *A History of American Working-Class Literature,* edited by Paul Lauter and Nicholas Coles, Cambridge University Press, 2018, pp. 130–45.

Coles, Nicholas. "Working the Fields: Love and Labor in Farm Fiction from 1890 to the Dust Bowl." *A History of American Working-Class Literature,* edited by Paul Lauter and Nicholas Coles, Cambridge University Press, 2018, pp. 215–31.

Fisher, Mark. *Capitalist Realism: Is There No Alternative?* Zero Books, 2009.

Fraser, Steve. *Class Matters: The Strange Career of an American Delusion.* Yale University Press, 2018.

Fred. "Film Reviews: The Man Trail." *Variety (Archive: 1905-2000),* vol. 40, no. 3, 17 Sept. 1915, p. 25.

Hapke, Laura. *Labor's Text: The Worker in American Fiction.* Rutgers University Press, 2001.

"Henry Oyen, Novelist, Dies Suddenly at 38." *New York Herald,* 4 Nov. 1921, p. 11. Newspapers.com.

Hobsbawm, E. J. *Workers: Worlds of Labor.* 1st American ed, Pantheon Books, 1984.

Ivakhiv, Adrian. *Ecocultural Critical Theory and Ecocultural Studies: Contexts and Research Directions.* 1997, https://www.uvm.edu/~aivakhiv/eco_cult.htm.

Jensen, Barbara. *Reading Classes: On Culture and Classism in America.* ILR Press, 2012.

Lakeside Cemetery Report. City of Waupaca, 2021, https://www.cityofwaupaca.org/parksnrec/wp-content/uploads/sites/3/2021/03/LakesideCemeteryReport.pdf.

Lauter, Paul. "Why Work? Early American Theories and Practices." *A History of American Working-Class Literature,* edited by Paul Lauter and Nicholas Coles, Cambridge University Press, 2018, pp. 25–41.

McIntyre, O. O. "Sketches of Little Old New York." *The Morning News,* 27 Dec. 1915, p. 8. Newspapers.com.

"Miss Sara Goldsmith Weds Henry Oyen of N.Y." *St. Louis Globe-Democrat,* 29 Mar. 1916, p. 5. Newspapers.com.

Oyen, Henry. *Big Flat.* Hastings College Press, 2024 [1919].

———. "Dress Counts for Much in the Business World." *Chicago Tribune,* 25 June 1905, p. E6. ProQuest.

———. "One Day as a Street Beggar; the Story of 'Flopping Ed'." *Chicago Tribune,* 17 Dec. 1905, p. E1. ProQuest.

———. "Ruin and Death in Wake of Cigaret." *Chicago Tribune,* 16 Apr. 1905, p. F3. ProQuest.

———. "Success and Failure; Two Types." *Chicago Tribune,* 29 July 1906, p. E2. ProQuest.

———. "Success Craze Checking the Drink Habit." *Chicago Tribune,* 3 Sept. 1905, p. 33. Newspapers.com.

———. "Writing a Second Choice." *The Evening Missourian,* 12 Mar. 1911, p. 3. Newspapers.com.

———. "You Cannot Afford to Be Dishonest." *Chicago Tribune,* 19 May 1905, p. C13. ProQuest.

S, Sai. "Pulp Flakes: Henry Oyen - Reporter, Pulp Author." *Pulp Flakes,* 4 Jan. 2013, https://pulpflakes.blogspot.com/2013/01/henry-oyen-reporter-pulp-author.html.

Sinclair, Upton. *The Jungle.* Penguin Books, 1985.

Vitello, Paul. "Henry D. Owen, 91, Dies; Shaped Global Fiscal Order." *The New York Times,* 12 Nov. 2011. NYTimes.com, https://www.nytimes.com/2011/11/12/us/henry-d-owen-diplomat-of-economic-summits-dies-at-91.html.

Williams, Raymond. *The Country and the City.* 1. issued as an Oxford Univ. Press paperback, Repr, Oxford Univ. Press, 1975.

I

A great red spring moon was rising slowly above the black line of the tamarack tops across the lake as Martin Calkins came out of his mother's house and stood watching the glint of the dipping paddles of a canoe which was coming across the water toward the place where he stood. The night was very still. The man-made noises of the day had ceased and the natural nocturnal voices of the woods had not yet begun to speak. He could hear the methodical squeak of a paddle rubbed Indian fashion against the stern, and he judged it would be Frank White Pigeon paddling somebody across from Camp Bon Air, the Chicago folks' summer camp down on Clear Lake.

As the canoe emerged from the dimness into his field of vision he saw that his surmise was correct. The old Chippewa beached the craft noiselessly, lifting it cleanly upon the white-sand beach with a single flip of his paddle; and a short, compact figure stepped briskly out of the bow and came up the gentle slope toward the house.

"Splendid location you have here, Mr. Calkins," called the newcomer crisply as he drew near. "Beautiful shore, dandy knoll; splendid building spot." He held out his hand. "Keener's my name. I'm sort of a neighbour of yours, you know. Got a little camp down on Clear Lake. Bon Air. The women named it," he said with a chuckle. "'Hot Air' was my choice, but the women will have something fancy, you know. But you"—he looked around the small cleared plateau which commanded a view of the lake and the flat, low-lying country beyond—"Say! You've got us licked all to pieces for a building site, all to pieces!"

"Well, we like it," responded the young man doubtfully.

"I should think you would." Mr. Keener treated himself to another enthusiastic scrutiny of the clearing. "Should think you would," he said impressively; and, his manner changing sharply, he said: "I'm general manager for the Starin Paper Company, you know. Company that's bought out the old lumber company. Building a big pulp mill down at Rainy River Falls. Going to operate on a 200 section basis. I'd like to have a little business talk with you, if you've the time."

"Time is about all I have got," said Martin, with a slow smile.

"I know it," snapped the visitor significantly, tapping a sheaf of papers in his breast pocket. "I know all about it, my boy."

"Everybody knows it." There was no bitterness in the young man's tones, only a note of patience—almost too much patience for one of his years. "Yes, everybody knows that."

"Then I guess you're ready to talk business." Mr. Keener glanced suggestively through the open door.

"No," said Martin, moving away from the house, "there's no use bothering mother with any business; she worries enough as it is. Come on down to my room in the mill."

The old saw-mill was on the lake shore above the landing place; and in a small room partitioned off in one end Martin lighted a lamp and turned to inspect his visitor. The yellow light of the lamp illumined Keener as he stood in the doorway. Beyond him it cut a clean shaft in the gloom, in which moths and other insects could be seen flitting among the reeds at the shore; and farther beyond, at the landing beach, the light glinted upon the mahogany-like profile of White Pigeon, stolidly waiting in the stern of the canoe.

Martin Calkins saw before him a round-faced man with close-cropped silver hair, small shrewd eyes, and the well-nourished cheerfulness which comes from easily won success. Had his cheerfulness been a shade less obvious, and had he not mentioned his connection with the Paper Company, Martin would have been inclined to warm to him at once.

Mr. Keener carried the stamp of a man who knew things, and who knew how to get things done, but having been placed on his guard the young man looked at his visitor with critical and even suspicious eyes, and he saw that beneath the cheerfulness and good humour there was something about Keener which he could not like. There was cunning there, and the look of the opportunist who would accept ruthlessness as a matter of course; a man who looked as if he knew much, but who believed he knew, if not everything, at least everything worth knowing; whose set lips denied any serious value to anything outside of his own sphere.

Martin was disappointed; he had expected to find something big and fine in so important a man as the Paper Company's manager; but beneath Mr. Keener's assurance and cheerfulness he saw something that he would have described as "small."

Mr. Keener saw a tall, gangly youth with a lean brown face and unsophisticated eyes. That was all. "Green; slow; a rube." Such was Mr. Keener's swift appraisal. Had he been less impatient of matters not directly concerned with his affairs he might have taken the trouble to observe that Martin Calkins was of a type that is vanishing and all but gone from the streets of our large cities.

He was tall and wiry and thin. His arms and legs were long and the hands and feet at the ends of them were large. He toed in just a trifle and, bending down to regulate the lamp, he was as thin as a greyhound from thigh to ribs. His blue-grey eyes were almost simple in their unsophistication and in their expression of friendliness; and there were tiny wrinkles from sun and wind in the brown skin at their corners. The cheek-bones were high, and those of the jaw angular and sharp; and the nose, long and straight, sharp and bold, would have warned a careful observer of its owner's breed.

Mr. Keener's snappy mind said: "A rube," and he turned from Martin and peered swiftly around the room.

"What! Well, well! What's this? Book-shelves? Books? Turn that lamp a little higher, please. Where are my glasses? Ah!" He moved about with short, quick steps, swiftly reading the titles of the stiff calf-bound volumes on the shelves that lined the walls. When he had completed his scrutiny he removed his glasses and looked patronisingly at Martin.

"Hm. Where did you get them?"

"Most of them were my father's," was the reply.

"Well, well! A family library up here in the woods. Nice thing to have left a fellow, isn't it? But," continued Mr. Keener, swiftly spreading his papers on the table, "that's about all that was left you, isn't it? Let's see. Ah, here it is." He selected from his documents a typewritten page of foolscap and looked over it at Martin. "It's a report on your tract—on the tract you're holding here, I mean. Perhaps you'd care to read it?"

"I don't see why I should; I know every acre on the place," said Martin, puzzled.

"It's more than a cruiser's report on the tract; it's a sort of history of the whole business."

"Then it's the history of some pretty crooked business, Mr. Keener," said Martin quietly. "The men who sold to my father lied to him."

"They were sharp land agents," said Mr. Keener. "They were in business to find men like your father, and they found him. From this report it would seem that your father was not a good business man."

"He wasn't," agreed the youth. "He believed what folks told him."

"He bought badly, very badly. He bought on the word of the sellers. A poor way to buy. He put all he owned into a four-section tract of what he fancied was valuable timber, and which proved to be nothing but useless jack-pine and tamarack. To earn a living he built this sawmill and managed to scrape along by sawing lumber out of the scattered clumps of pine on the tract. The last pine was sawed two years ago, and then your father died, leaving the property—unencumbered, be it said to his credit—to you and your mother.

"Your conduct since then, Calkins, has indicated that you are a young man of exceptional character and ability. You have logged the hardwood, difficultly located on the tract, sawed and hauled it, and thereby made a fair living for your mother and yourself. Had your opportunities been more generous your industry and intelligence unquestionably would have won for you success. But the proposition which you are tackling is one which is entirely barren of good possibilities. It is entirely and absolutely hopeless, and"—he folded the paper and smiled patronisingly upon the youth—"I guess by this time you know it."

"I see," said Martin. "You want to buy us out."

"Entirely hopeless," continued Mr. Keener blandly. "No chance for a future at all. It's a shame for a capable young man like you to be wasting his best years on such a hopeless proposition. Your father tried, and it killed him. You are trying, and it's really too bad. A bright young fellow like you, with a little capital, somewhere where opportunity was right—where you had a fair chance—would make a real success. I've paddled over to-night to give you that chance, Calkins."

"A chance for what, Mr. Keener?"

"For a successful, happy life, my boy. The woods is no place for you. You're too bright, too capable to waste yourself up here. You belong in the city where there's a market for brains. That's where the opportunities are, and where the best that's in you will be brought out."

"I wonder?" said Martin thoughtfully.

"What?"

"I wonder if it is in the cities that what's really best in a man is brought out. I've wondered a lot about it, reading the newspapers, and these books, and roaming around by myself, and one thing and another. Sometimes I think it must be so, because all the important men seem to be city men, and then I think of what makes them important, and I have my doubts. For what is it that makes these big, prominent men important, Mr. Keener? It isn't anything but money, so far as I can see. And what's that, when you come to think of it?"

"Money? What—!"

But the young man continued in a way that would not be denied.

"Take Mr. Starin, now, the president of your company. I've read and heard a lot about him. He's one of the prominent men I'm thinking of. I've read how he began as an office boy; and now he's a power in this state, and even down in Washington, I understand. Well, I've always wondered about those big men and wanted to see one; so once when I heard he was down at the Falls I went down there to see him. His private car was on a side-track down by the river and he was walking up and down in it biting a cigar, and worrying about something. He was awfully worried. And there was the old Rainy River clucking by just as it always has and as it always will. Well—do you know how I felt, Mr. Keener? I felt sorry for Mr. Starin."

Mr. Keener recovered himself with great difficulty.

"We all go through something like that when we're young," said he with a laugh. "Later on we quit being soft-headed and learn to appreciate the things that count."

"That's it!" said Martin gratefully. "'The things that count.' That's what I wonder about. I wonder if Mr. Starin has them."

"Yes, indeed," laughed Mr. Keener. "Several millions of them." He leaned forward sharply, pointing a finger at Martin's breast.

"You speak of the river running along down there 'as it always will.' Now, it is not going to run always as it did that day; it is not going to run that way for many months longer. Why? Simply because Mr. Starin doesn't wish it to run that way. And having the things that count, he has the power to make the river do his will—specifically, to work for him through a dam."

He leaned back, mildly triumphant; but Martin merely said: "What does he do with all his money?"

The irrelevance of the remark drove Mr. Keener sharply back into the shell of business from which he had unconsciously emerged.

"Hm. Let us see. Yes." He busied himself importantly for a moment with his papers, and at last he lifted his gaze to Martin.

"And then, besides," said he casually, playing his trump card, "if you sell at a fair price, you see, you'll be able to take your mother some place and give her the comforts in her old age which you never can give her here."

After a long silence Martin said: "Why don't you buy the pulp-wood by the cord from people, the same as other mills do?"

"I can't discuss that with you."

"Then people would have their land left, anyhow, after the bush is cleared off."

"So they would, so they would. But it's a question if that would be an advantage to people owning land in this section. The less of this land a man owns the better off he is. You know what it is: swampland, jack-pine sand, lake sand. Such land is a liability, not an asset."

"In that case, why does your company want to buy it?"

"We don't want the land. We take it because we want the pulp-wood and complete control. The land isn't worth a year's taxes. Your tract especially. I've got a report on it, you know, right here. I know what you've got. Except for the pulp-wood your tract—and the whole region for that matter—is dead, useless waste."

Then, for the first time, Martin Calkins showed signs of resentment. His thin nostrils expanded slowly as he breathed. He had to clear his throat before speaking. The words came out clumsily, hotly.

"That isn't so, Mr. Keener—it can't be so. It isn't dead, it's alive—liver than anything else in the world—to me. You take and walk over it now, in the spring, when it's beginning to stir and wake, and you can feel that there's something there under your feet that wants to get out—into the sun—and do something. You can see it pushing up through the willows and breaking open the buds, and you can feel it pushing up on the ground when you walk. It's useless now, maybe, Mr. Keener, and it may be a waste—though I doubt that—but it isn't dead. It's as much alive as you and I are right at this minute. And after the pulp-wood is all cut and chewed up into paper, and the paper used and thrown away, the land will still be there. That's the way I feel about it, Mr. Keener."

Then Mr. Keener, too, showed signs of resentment. All this was very unbusinesslike. He gathered together his papers with an air of decision.

"We'll give you ten thousand dollars for your tract."

"I will take that," said Martin, "for the pulp-wood rights."

"For everything; for your title; for your land. Ten thousand dollars, cash. It's more money than you'll ever see up here if you don't sell. It would give you a good start where there are good opportunities."

"I am sticking right here, Mr. Keener."

Keener rose abruptly.

"That will spoil your life, my boy. It will ruin you. You'll be ruined in two years!"

The young man looked long and seriously at Mr. Keener's face, but his young eyes were unable to read that well-trained countenance.

"I wish I knew what you meant by that, Mr. Keener."

"I mean just what I say: accept our offer, or two years more will see you broke. I don't care to say any more now."

The young man continued his futile scrutiny, and giving it up, began to turn down the lamp.

"Well—if that's the way it is, Mr. Keener," he said slowly, as the wick went down little by little, "if you don't care to say any more now—I guess—I guess I don't care to say any more, either. No hard feelings, but"—Poof! The light went out—"this land isn't dead—or useless. Mr. Keener," he concluded cheerfully, "don't you forget that!"

II

He stood in the midst of his clearing after Keener had gone and
marvelled how a man could be so insensible of the soil's throbbing
vitality. Beneath the dark mantle of the warm spring night he felt
the earth pulsing. He stooped down, swinging his hands, and the
dew on the wild timothy, growing rampantly, brushed the tips of
his fingers. A faint gust of night-wind crept like a sigh along the
earth, crooning its way into the timber; and after it had passed
there was for a space only the silence of the softly breathing night.
The perturbation caused by Keener's final words seemed wafted
away with the passing wind. Hot, youthful resentment, evoked by
Keener's words—resentment springing from love of the land and
stubborn family pride—gradually disappeared. Keener was right—
partly. It was a hard, stubborn land—as it was now. But no matter
how hard or stubborn it might be he knew that he was bound to it
by forces too strong to be denied, even had he been so inclined, too
subtle for him to comprehend.

It was his land. Untilled and forbidding, it lay dormant,
waiting as it had waited through the ages for the coming of The
Man who was destined to release its mysterious forces for the good
of mankind. Through the silence of the pulsing spring night he
felt it challenging all that was best and strongest and finest in him,
challenging him to match his youth and strength against its latent
fecundity.

Far off a wolf wailed primitively; and from nearer at hand, from
the Lee farm down the road, came the sharp, serious note of a farm
dog's reply. Martin smiled, recognising the voice of Hattie Lee's fat
old Towser, and turned back to the house.

His mother was busy; as Martin reached for his hat he thought
how he could never remember her being otherwise; and Annie

Snow-Deer, the brawny Chippewa servant, was listening dutifully to the incisive exposition of the creed that cleanliness was not merely akin to godliness, it was necessary to godliness—especially in keeping house.

"Poor Annie!" said Martin with a grin.

"You hush up, Marty," retorted his mother promptly. "Annie knows that what I'm telling her is for her own good, and don't you try to get smart. Where are you going?"

"Oh, no place much. Just down to the Lees'. I'm starting for town before daylight to-morrow after Big Jud and the seed potatoes and some tools, and they may want something fetched back."

"Well, you tell Mrs. Lee that I'll be down and see her as soon as the road dries out a little; and you tell Hattie that when she closes the school this year she must not leave those curtains hanging during the summer for the sun to fade, but she must take them down and wash them and fold them and wrap them up and put them away, and then she'll have curtains good as new to begin school with next fall. And put nothing heavy on top of them when she puts them away or they'll be creased so hard that the creases won't come out. And she should—"

"Here," said he, producing paper and pencil, "better write her a letter."

"Now, Marty," said Mrs. Calkins, cuffing his hand away, "you remember that and do as I told you. Who was that man? What did he want?"

"Oh, that was just a man who came to see me on some personal business."

"Marty Calkins, you stop right where you are. Don't you dare go out of that door before you tell me who that man was."

"His name was Keener."

"Keener? Never heard of him. Who is he?"

"Oh, he's just the manager for the Paper Company."

"Huh! What did he want of you?"

"Oh, nothing much; just wanted us to sell the place to him."

"What did you say to him?"

"I said we were eager to sell, of course," teased the son as he departed.

And the wiry little lady said with a snap of her thin lips: "Well! I should think not!"

The road to the Lees' took him past the head of Clear Lake and that was how he came to hear the piano from Camp Bon Air. If it had not been spring the music might not have lured him. It was strange music that came faintly over the moon-reddened water there in the spring woods night; it was the second time in his life that he heard music which seemed to interpret his feelings toward the land about him. The first time it had come from the violin of Tori, the Finn with the long yellow hair, who had driven team for his father years before. He wondered who was playing down at Camp Bon Air.

As he went down the dark road past the school clearing he strove clumsily to whistle the tune, and he was still trying when he came to the Lee place, which lay a short distance beyond the school.

Simon Lee's house had been planned and begun one summer when lumber and help were cheap and plentiful. It stood well back from the road, a large, foursquare, two-story house, which, had it ever been completed, would have been a credit to its builder. The trouble was that Simon had proceeded to finish his house from the top down. Thus the large, ornate cupola enjoyed the distinction of being properly sided, painted, and ornamented with the proper fret-work at the eaves, and a lightning rod at its peak; but with that progress had ceased. The big house itself was quite innocent of siding; tar-paper took its place. A great porch, or rather the top of a great porch, hung across the whole front of the building. The roof of the porch had been built into the house and properly shingled and finished; and eight dignified but futile pillars hung from this roof with something of the effect of eight colossal, permanent icicles. Tradition had it that Simon Lee had heard of a new trout creek on the day he was to lay his porch floor, and he had never since found time to complete the task.

Hattie Lee was sitting alone at a table in the front room, working at some gaudily coloured feathers, but as Martin came whistling to the screen door she laid down her work and looked up curiously.

"Hello, Marty," she greeted casually. "Trying to be a whippoorwill?"

"What's the name of that tune, Hattie? Do you know it?"

"Tune? Were you whistling a tune, Marty? Let's hear it again."

She listened unmoved for several seconds. Then she folded her arms against her slender figure and began to smile. The smile first appeared in the right corner of her mouth. It spread slowly to the left, until at last it reached such proportions that in a boy it would have been called a grin. Tiny wrinkles began to appear about her grey eyes; they spread to the bridge of her freckled snub nose; and finally she doubled up and giggled outright.

"I don't see anything to laugh at," said Martin coldly. "I guess you don't know the tune, do you?"

"If I did I'd be a mind-reader," replied the little teacher. "Try again, Marty; I won't laugh."

"You won't have a chance to laugh again."

"You looked so awfully serious," she apologised. "I shouldn't have laughed, but you were making such hard work of it."

"Of course if you don't know the tune you can't say what it is," he said. The trouble with Hattie was that just because she was a school teacher she thought she knew it all. "What are all those feathers on the table?"

"For trout flies," said Hattie, picking up the dainty work she had been engaged in. "See, I'm copying the ones the trout like best."

"They'll be striking soon, you know, Mart," called her father from the kitchen. "We'll have to get after them one of these days."

"I haven't got any time to go trout fishing," replied Martin curtly. "I'm going to town in the morning. Is there anything you want me to get?"

"Oh, no, I guess not, Mart," drawled the old man. "Yes, there is too, b'golly. Get me half a dozen three-foot gut leaders, will you, Mart? Tell Jeffers to put 'em on the book."

"Gut leaders," repeated Martin. "Is that all?"

"I guess so, Mart; double leaders, you know."

"Father," said Hattie after a pause, "weren't you expecting some seed potatoes?"

"Yes; yes, that's so," came the contented drawl. "Yes, you might fetch them along, too, Marty, if you don't mind."

Martin rose impatiently.

"Sure you want them fetched?" he called from the doorway.

"Why, yes. Why d'you ask, Mart?"

"I thought they might interfere with your trout-fishing."

Trout fishing, he mused as he picked his way out to the road, was all right if a man didn't have anything to do, but it was a poor way to spend time in the spring if a man was trying to make a farm. Simon Lee wasn't trying, that was the trouble. His section was one of the best on the Flat, flat land mostly, and easy to clear. Simon had cleared twenty acres, and he was content. No wonder the country wasn't amounting to anything with such men in it! Trout flies! Stump-puller would have had more sense to it!

He came to a stop in the soggy road as his mind took up the problem which he had been struggling with of late. The old stump-pullers were too slow. They were all right where the stumps were large and few or on a small piece of land; but his immediate problem had mainly to do with forties of small jack-pine trees and stumps, much of it burnt-over land. Later on he could tackle the hardwood sections of big stumps; at present he must devote himself to the flats that might be most swiftly cleared. It would be like pulling a sheep's wool one strand at a time. Dynamite would do it quickly; but it would be too expensive. Absolutely out of the question. He must hit upon some new way, something that hadn't been tried around there, something quick and not costly. He must do it soon, too; if he didn't he would not, could not, succeed. He thought again of what Mr. Keener had said about his being ruined in two years. What could Keener have meant? He turned toward the camp at the other end of the lake, and so he again came under the lure of the music from the piano.

The camp was so far away that only the loudest notes came over the water to him, and he began to walk toward it slowly, the better to hear. It was wonderfully living music. Only when he approached so near that nothing was lost did he begin to truly appreciate how clearly it spoke to him. He halted when the lights of the camp came into view and leaned against a tree at the edge of the clearing to listen, spell-bound. The moon had risen high and had lost its redness, and after awhile something white came slipping out of the silvered water into the obscurity of the shore-line. Then, in a moment, out of the darkness at the water's edge, into the shaft of light from the open door on the piazza, came walking a tall young woman arrayed in a bathing suit which clung to her as she moved.

The music inside ceased. The tall girl stood in the doorway and laughed.

"Alice Demaree!" cried a woman's voice from within. "What do you mean by swimming alone out there in the dark?"

A low, laughing voice answered provokingly:

"À la Nature, Aunty Keener, don't forget that: absolutely à la Nature."

"But—but why did you do it?"

"Oh, I don't know." The swimmer stepped inside out of sight. "The moonlight—Grieg—and all that. I thought it might be a new thrill, but—ho hum!—it wasn't—as usual."

When Martin entered the house that night his mother called from her room:

"Land sakes! Where have you been? Is this a time o'night to be coming home? Now you get right to bed so you'll get a night's sleep."

"All right, mother," was the reply; and he obeyed the first part of the behest, but perhaps his land problem weighed too heavily upon him, for the sleep would not come.

III

It drizzled a little during the night, and the stretch of hard-packed
sawdust which composed the single short street of Rainy River
Falls was steaming odorously in the warm May sun when Martin
came driving into town and tied his team to a ring in the huge
pine stump before the old Company Store.

He tied with great care. The team which he drove was a
pair of big-headed black logging horses, which moved with the
deliberation of bodies of great weight. The clay of the crude road
had muddied their hairy legs to the knee-joint, and they came to a
stop by the stump with a finality which told of intention to stand
perfectly still until commanded to start again. Yet Martin tied
them carefully, devoting to the simple task of fastening them to the
stump a concentration and absorption which caused Jeffers, the
little weazened store-keeper, to grin.

"Martin," he said, "I can't get over the way you always go tying
that team. You tie 'em, and you try 'em, and you never look up
until you know they're fastened like they were a span of runaway
drivers."

The young man methodically tested the snap on the neck-rope
and the knot on the hitching ring without replying. He braced
a foot against the big stump and gave a sharp heave on the rope
to assure himself that the ring was still well fastened. Then he
turned around and unsmilingly regarded the grinning man in the
doorway.

"Well, Mr. Jeffers," said he, "what's the use of tying at all unless
you tie to hold?"

"Yankee!"

"Have my seed potatoes come?"

"Ho! you're all business, ain't you, Mart? Yes; the spuds have come. Two bushel for you; and Simon Lee's, too. Expensive seed, Martin: four dollars a bushel."

"Four." Martin regarded the sawdust thoughtfully. "Yes, that is dear. But we've got to begin raising good stock. Where are they?"

At that Jeffers' chuckle rose to the height of a mild laugh.

"All business, all business! Come to town; load up; go home. Why—look around, Mart, look around. Don't you see there's doings in town to-day?"

Then for the first time Martin looked around and took note of the scene presented in Rainy River Falls on this bright spring morning.

A goodly crowd was gathered on the store side of the street. There were tall, gnarled Scandinavian settlers and their wives, as reserved and stoical, almost, in their attitudes as the moccasined Chippewas who padded noiselessly about; and there were thin, long-faced Yankees who looked proud and poorly fed. Before the saloon, known as "The Bohunk's," were gathered a group of the newcomers in the district, the Austrian labourers, who had been brought in by the Paper Company, and from whom the settlers held themselves well apart. The leader and interpreter of the Austrians was a heavy, sleek man with stiffly upturned moustache who brought short, barking laughs from his countrymen by his sneering comments on the women before the store.

The focal point of interest was a crowd of men lounging about on the generous porch of the Hemlock Hotel, across the way; and between these men and the people about the store there was a line of demarcation much more emphatic than the sawdust street. They were lumber-jacks. They carried the marks of their calling in the reckless poise of their bodies, in the glint of their humorous, devil-may-care eyes, in their apparel. Swarthy Canuck descendants of the old courier-du-bois, rollicking Irish, Viking type of Norsemen,

Anglo-Saxon, Scot. They belonged no more in that region; they were adventurers.

A locomotive tooted impatiently at the modest boxcar station, and the lumber-jacks, squinting humorously up at the sun, bellowed:

"Toot, toot! All aboard for the West!" and tumbled boyishly off the porch into the sawdust street. Some gathered to themselves suit-cases and sacks; some had tied upon their backs the woodsman's "turkey" or "war-bag"; some stood ready to go in the clothes they wore. There was a medley of mocking farewells. A waitress in the hotel peeped out from an upper window, shading her eyes with her hand, and a dozen men solemnly assured her they were going away solely and wholly because she had broken their hearts. An Indian squaw, waddling stolidly across the street, was bidden a tender farewell from men whom she had never seen before.

Out on the carpet of logs, riding placidly on the waters of the mill-pond, men leaned on their long pike-poles and cheered faintly. The musical pnn-nn-nng of the saws, in the mill across the pond, stopped momentarily as the dusty mill-hands came out to join in the cheer, and the men in the street replied mockingly:

"Good-bye, you high-bankers, good-bye!"

A dark, broad-shouldered man appeared in the doorway of the hotel, and at the sight of him Martin said, "Mr. Jeffers, isn't that Mr. Royle?"

"Yep. That's him; that's Black Jack Royle."

"I thought he'd gone logging out in Washington state."

"He has. Struck it rich out there, too, they say. He's come back to get the old-timers to go with him out there."

The veteran camp-boss was running his sharp eyes speculatively over the men who still lounged idly upon the porch.

"You've got about fifteen minutes more to think it over, boys," he said crisply. "This country was good while she lasted, but she's no place for shanty-boys now. It's a new boiling out in Washington. There's real logging left out there. Real timber. We skid with a donkey-engine and haul with a locomotive. No forty below weather, and no snow up to your pants pockets. What's the use of staying in this country? She's done for. Pulp-wood choppers and city sports can have what's left. It's no place for shanty-boys. You'd better come out to the limber country."

His attention had become fixed upon a huge block of a man who squatted Indian fashion on his heels on the porch.

"Well, Jud, how about you? Have you made up your mind? Going to stay here and chop pulp-wood? Or flunky for city sports, eh?"

A gale of contemptuous laughter swept over the loggers, and the giant began tugging perturbedly at the hair-tufts in his ears.

"Only one thing pestering me 'bout that new country, Jack," he drawled.

"What's that?"

"Can I get Standard Chewing out there?"

"The wannigan's full of it," replied Royle without the trace of a smile.

"Sure?"

"Sure."

The giant heaved his huge body up slowly.

"All right, then, Jack 'y golly! I'll go with you. But if I can't get my chewing, Jack Boyle, you move when you see me coming."

IV

Martin Calkins came walking across the street straight toward the new recruit. He walked slowly, his feet seeming to take hold and grip the earth, yet springing him swiftly forward, and the slight movement of his shoulders swung his long arms at his sides. Royle admiringly appraised the lithe figure as it approached the porch, then, a smile of recognition flashing upon his face, he held forth his hand.

"Hello, Martin! You ain't coming with us, are you?"

"How do, Mr. Royle. No, sir, I'm not coming with you. I came to see Jud there."

Jud had begun to shuffle uneasily at the sight of Martin, and had drawn away until now, unable to retreat any farther, he stood with his back against the hotel wall, hanging his great head and pulling slowly at his hairy ears.

"You hired out to me for the summer, Jud," said Martin. "Are you going to break your word?"

"I don't aim to," said Jud, shamefacedly. "No, sir, I don't never aim to break my word."

"Are you going with Mr. Royle?"

Jud left off tugging at his ears and devoted himself to scratching his vast jaws.

"Well—well, you see it's this way, Marty: you was to come after me, and here I'm in town doing nothing and along comes Black Jack Royle that I run the Wiscons' with in the old days, years ago, and he talks mighty high about this new country, where the timber's big and tough to handle, and I'm blamed if I don't forget all about hiring out to you, Marty."

"You don't want to take Jud away after he's given his word to me, do you, Mr. Royle?"

"Why, no. No. If he's promised to come to you I don't want to take him away."

"How about that, Jud?"

"'S all right with me, Marty. Whatever is all right with you boys is all right with me."

Martin hesitated.

"He hired out to me fair and square, you know, Mr. Royle."

"Go ahead!" laughed the logger. "He's your man. No hard feelings."

"All right, then," said the young man, relieved. "I've got some potatoes and tools over in the store, Jud; you can load them if you want to."

Glad to be under orders and with work for his immense hands to do, Jud plunged like a bull off the porch toward the store. Martin turned hesitatingly to Royle.

"Mr. Royle, was that right what you said about skidding with a donkey-engine?"

"Eh?" said Royle. "Why, yes; certainly. Why?"

"How do you do it?"

Royle smiled.

"You haven't got any timber around here that you need a donkey-engine on, Martin."

"No, sir; I know that. I'm not thinking of logs. But if it isn't taking up too much of your time I wish you'd tell me how you put your engine to work."

The logger looked straight into Martin's eyes for an instant and, digging a pencil stub from his pocket, drew a crude diagram on the white-painted wall of the hotel.

"Suppose your chute or narrow-gauge is here. Your logs are out here in the brush. Set your donkey up here, far side of your chute or railway. You've got to anchor her well because there's an awful strain on her. We've got a big drum of wire-cable on her, enough cable to reach to the logs. Understand now? Just hitch your cable onto your logs and start the donkey and along they come, right onto your chute or flat cars. It's just a question of power. Enough power and you can snake a dozen at a time. See?"

"I see," said Martin slowly as he studied the diagram. "A dozen at a time, if you have enough power. Thank you, Mr. Royle."

Black Jack Royle laughed and held out his hand.

"Good-bye and good luck to you."

"Good-bye."

Martin turned to cross the street, but Limber Tim Cooney, merriest and toughest of the lumber-jacks, would not have it so.

"Mis-ter Calkins," said he, barring the way and bowing low, cap in hand. "Mis-ter Calkins, won't you give me a job on your crew?"

"I've got no crew."

"Hear that, boys, hear that: he ain't got no crew. What you hiring Big Jud for then? Going to pull stumps with him?"

Martin replied slowly: "Well, I don't know as that's any of your business, is it?"

"Mis-ter Calkins—please, Mis-ter Calkins, can't a poor lumber-jack even speak to a man like you? I was jest asking. Hey! Where you going?"

With a swift long step to one side Martin had passed his tormentor and was crossing the street.

"Won't even talk to a feller. All stuck up. Going to flunky for the city sports and all stuck up about it." Cooney's bantering tone swiftly gave way to one of challenge. "Hey, you farmer; come back here and I'll put a little sawdust on your back."

To the surprise of every man who heard, Martin continued on his way as if the words had not reached his ears. Jud was already emerging from the store, carrying in each hand a two bushel sack of potatoes. He casually tossed the sacks into the wagon, and Martin began untying the team.

"Hauling four bushel of spuds all at once!" cried Cooney. "Must be a big crew." He slapped his thigh at a new idea. "Hey, boys, I've got it; he's going to start logging the Calkins tract!"

A shout of laughter greeted this sally. Even Royle smiled and Martin laughed. And then the big, moustached leader of the Austrian gang interpreted the scene to his fellows and laughed jeeringly in Martin's face.

Martin went on untying the team. When the rope was free he began coiling it up on his arm. When the coil was done he stopped and looked at the Austrian, and the Austrian sneered. Martin slowly undid the coil, carefully snapped the rope about the horse's neck, and slowly and deliberately retied to the stump. This done he removed his cap, laid it upon the wagon seat and stepped out into the street. There were little ridges of muscle at the corners of his jaw. He cleared his throat.

"Cooney," he said seriously, "what was that you said about putting saw-dust on my back?"

"Shucks, boy!" laughed Royle from the porch. "Let it go. Don't you go scuffling about a little thing like that."

"Help yourself, Cooney," said Martin.

Cooney smirked in false apology.

"Why, I didn't mean—" said he ingratiatingly, and like a flash he dived for a leg hold. He was in a bad way the next second, for Martin stooped swiftly to meet him and caught his head in chancery. The exhibition of agility and suppleness with which Cooney then entertained the crowd would have done credit to a trapped wild-cat. He twisted and writhed incredibly. He butted, rushing his opponent around in a circle; he lifted him off the ground with sheer strength of his neck; he pulled backward, dragging his load with him.

Martin held on. He was tossed and tumbled about, but he held on. He jerked his man face down in the saw-dust, but the supple lumber-jack struggled back to his feet. He twisted. But Cooney's strong neck met every move. So Martin hung on.

"I believe I'd get a new holt, Marty, if I was you," said Big Jud judiciously. "You can't put him on his back with that grip. Get a fresh one."

"This is good enough for me," replied Martin.

Cooney stopped his gyrations. They had been wrestling for ten minutes now and neither was even breathing hard.

"How long can you keep it up?" roared Cooney.

"Don't know yet," said Martin.

Cooney now began hopping and bucking in a circle of which Martin was the grim centre. At the end of another ten minutes the tussle was halted again.

"How d'you feel about it now?"

"Same as ever, Cooney."

Once more the lithe logger tried to writhe free, to trip his wiry opponent, to better his position, and all in vain.

"I'll be damned," said he deliberately, coming to a final halt, "if I rassle any longer with a man like you. You ain't no fun atall."

"How about putting my back in the sawdust?"

By a great feat of contortion Cooney managed to scratch the top of his imprisoned head.

"Jack," he called to Royle, "ain't that train leaving pretty soon?"

"Right away," laughed Royle.

"Well, then, Marty, I guess I won't have time to do it. Leggo."

Martin did not let go. He did not join the spirit of jocularity evoked by Cooney's clowning. He held onto the logger's head, and the set of his lips grew tighter. Big Jud's humorous eyes lighted up with an old fire as he understood.

"'Y golly!" he chortled contentedly, and placed his colossal body between the crowd and the wrestlers.

"What d'you mean?" bellowed Cooney. "Can't you hear?"

"When I set up a post I aim to paint it," retorted Martin.

"Stay right where you be, boys," drawled Jud, as the crowd moved forward impatiently. "He's got a post to paint and I reckon he'll be allowed to do it right."

"What's the ideer?" growled Cooney. "What d'you want?"

Martin's response came gruffly:

"What's the matter with the Calkins tract?"

"Nothing," said Cooney after a pause.

"It's a good tract, ain't it?"

Cooney deliberated a moment but the arms on his head were like steel.

"Sure."

Martin let go his hold and stepped back warily. But Cooney first rubbed his neck anxiously and then held out his hand.

"You're—a corker—Mart," said he as they shook hands. "Guess if a fellow had you down putting the caulks to you you'd really start fighting."

Martin had turned away and was recrossing the street. He walked straight up to the sneering Austrian before the saloon.

"Friend," said Martin, "I don't like the way you laugh."

The newcomer bared his teeth in a contemptuous smile.

"No 'stand," he grunted.

Martin's long left arm rose slowly from his side and his hard brown fist came to a stop a scant inch from the Austrian's nose.

"Understand that?"

"Whoop!" cried Tim Cooney, and came leaping to Martin's side. "Give it to 'em, boy; I'm with you. Show 'em they can't look cross-ways at a white man."

"Go away," said Martin; "it's me and him."

"Should say not. Bohunks won't fight man to man like white men. They knife you in the back. Come on, boys!"

The lumber-jacks came tumbling joyously across the street, and the Austrians retreated sullenly into their saloon. The last man to enter was the leader. He snarled and glared menacingly back at Martin as he disappeared.

"Old sock," said Cooney, hooking his arm through Martin's, "we'll go right in and make 'em buy us a drink."

But now Logger Royle's countenance took upon itself the expression which had earned him the title of "Black Jack."

"Drink nothing," he snapped. "Come on, boys; train's leaving."

The lumber-jacks cheered as they tumbled into the single passenger car of the combination local. They threw open the car windows, kicked out the glass of refractory windows, and leaned out and cheered some more. They cheered so their voices drowned the locomotive's whistle as the train started, and they continued to cheer, to howl and to sing, while the train went puffing on to westward out of hearing and out of sight.

The little town, once the scene of the Homeric and Rabelaisian play of these reckless men, seemed very small and old and forsaken when they were gone.

"Hey, Calkins," called the station agent as Martin leaped onto the seat of his wagon, "I got a couple of trunks going out your way. Big heavy fellows, the kind city women pack their dresses in. They're marked for Miss Demaree, Bon Air Camp, Clear Lake. You go past there. Want to take 'em along?"

"Might as well," said Martin curtly, and he pulled his hat down over his eyes and sat looking straight ahead so no one might see the flush he felt rising upon his face.

V

The road that ran northward from Rainy River Falls was an old
tote-road, and the loggers who had slashed it through the timber
had built only for the swift, reckless days of their harvest. It ran
like a sword gash straight up the cruel grade of the high ridge that
sheltered the town from the north and separated it from the Big
Flat region beyond.

As he drove upward slowly, with the reins held taut to prevent
the heavy horses from hurling themselves impatiently toward the
top, Martin resolved, as he always did when breasting the ridge,
that one thing he surely would get his Big Flat neighbours together
on was the task of raising the gradeless river-road, now knee-deep
under water, to a height which would make it available for all-year-
around use. As it was now the road along the river could be used
only during the winter and; occasionally, during the dry, low-water
spells of mid-summer.

The Big Flat country, he knew, would never develop and
flourish until it had a better road to town. The ridge shut it off
from the world; and the task of crossing it, which was presented
with each trip to town, gave the Flat settlers a sense of isolation.
There would be another great advantage in raising the river-road—
solid embankments in the low spots would prevent the flooding of
many fine fields during the high-water stage of the river in spring.

On the top of the ridge he halted to breathe his team and to
feast his eyes upon the country that now came into view.

The great flat district, of which the township of Big Flat was
the heart, lay spread out like a panorama below the ridge. Its
eastern boundary was the straight, swift-running Rainy River; to
the west and north it lost itself in the hard, blue mists of the north.
Perhaps the most salient features of the landscape as one stood

on the ridge were the regiments of stumps where the loggers had left their mark; the black patches where forest fires had done their work; the tree-tops of the few unlogged sections; and the lakes and rivers, silvery in the distance. But here and there in the rugged scene there appeared small, orderly clearings of ploughed land, and in these openings the soil was dark and rich.

That was what attracted Martin's attention and quickened his vision. The soil was black. He could see the sun glistening on the fatness of the freshly turned furrows; and he saw the Flat not as it was now, not as others saw it, but as he wished it to be, as it should and would be—the stumps pulled, the burnings cleared, the swamps drained and dried, the land broken and divided into orderly fields and teeming with crops. He saw the river-road graded and straightened and lined from the northern horizon to the foot of the ridge with neat, rich farms, straight, taut fences, and houses and barns glistening with coats of paint, white and red.

"Look at it, Jud!" he cried.

Big Jud, who lay comfortably sprawled in the box of the wagon, his head pillowed upon a sack of potatoes almost beneath the seat, his feet, at a greater elevation than his head, resting heavily one each upon the trunks which lay against the end-board, lifted his head grudgingly and looked over the box.

"Looks the same as ever to me, only worse," he drawled. "She was a good country once, Marty, but she's done for now."

Martin smiled and started slowly down the far side of the ridge. Down on the Flat he pulled up at Nels Borg's clearing, the first out of town, where the stocky Norwegian settler and his rosy-cheeked wife were at work with a stump-puller.

"It takes too long, Nels," he exploded as he estimated the time required to start a stump from the ground. "Two men and a team; and what do you get done in a day? You'll be grandparents before you get a forty broke."

The woman laughed, leaning back on the reins and stopping the team she was driving.

"Geddup!" cried the man; and as the team resumed its slow round he looked up for a moment.

"Yah? Mabbe so. Ven you gat som'ting kvicker you tal me, eh?"

"Dynamite, you Squarehead, dynamite!" roared Jud.

"Dinnamite? Cost hoonderd dollare acre."

"We've got to get something new," said Martin.

"Oll right." Borg sank his axe deep in the root of a stump. "Ven you gat it you tal me, eh?"

"I will get it," mused Martin as he drove on. "I must get it."

Jud stirred his head on the potato sack. There was something on Jud's mind. Martin had sensed it for some time but he did not wish to appear curious.

"Times change," volunteered Jud as the wagon jolted and shook through the pitch-holes. "Hauling seed-potatoes and trunks! 'Y golly!"

Above him Martin swayed with the rise and fall of the spring seat and appeared not to hear, so Jud drawled on.

"I remember one time in the old days I drove out this road. Lessee, 'tain't so long 'go, neither. But, 'y golly! how things do change. It was one of the Old Comp'ny's tote-teams that night. The tote-teamster lay about where I be now, and I was up on the seat with the ribbons. There was about twenty of the boys piled into the sleigh-box, Marty, and every last mother's son of 'em was feeling good—'cept those who was sound asleep—and old Black Jack Royle—him that jest took the boys away—was setting on the end board with a peavy in his fist to keep 'em from grabbing the lines and turning back to town. Once in a while one of the boys would get thrown out, jest in fun, you know, and then he'd stand there in the snow and make a fair and square offer to lick the wadding out of them that did it; and then they'd pile out to tussle, and me'n Black Jack, we'd have to get down and load 'em.

"Well, 'bout three o'clock in the morning we came to where we swung onto Clear Lake to cross over on the ice, and there was a little clearing there where there'd been an old Indian camp, and Black Jack, he sez: 'Pull up, Jud.' 'Now, durn you,' he sez to the boys, 'pile out and have all the fun you want.' So they piled out, about a dozen of 'em, and fit all over that clearing, not ornery, you know, but jest for fun—and me'n Black Jack smoked our pipes and set watching 'em. When a man'd get knocked out we'd get down and load him nice and careful, and when any tried to sneak back to town Jack'd ketch him a kick and snake him back by the seat of his pants. Well, sir, it took those boys so long to have their fun out that by the time we got started again, and across Clear Lake and into the timber to camp, the boys had to set right down to eat breakfast and get out to work.

"But what I got thinking about was how times change. Now that Indian clearing where the boys fit, Marty, is the same one on Clear Lake where that high-mucky-muck, Keener, has got his fancy shanty, and where we're a-hauling them two big trunks."

"Eh—yah? What of it?"

"Nothing. Nothing 'tall. Jest happened, you know, to be the same clearing where this Keener's got his camp. Where we're going, you know?"

Jud half closed his eyes as he concentrated his hearing faculties to catch Martin's reply, but no reply came. After a long wait the old logger drawled:

"I hear'n tell he was a big mucky-muck with the Paper Company, Marty. Fact is I hear'n it from Keener himself. It was jest this way, Marty: Jim Jeffers comes up to me in the hotel and sez he: 'Jud, there's a man wants to see you over 'n the Comp'ny office.' So I went over there, having nothing to do but kill time, and Mr. Keener is setting there with a lot of papers, and he hands me an A.No.I ten-cent cigar and tells me to set down. 'Mr. Hart,' sez he, 'they tell me you know this country 'bout as well as any man living,' sez he. 'Calc'late I do,' sez I, 'unless you count Indians. Logged 'round here for nigh onto twenty year. Ought to know something about it,' I sez. Well, sir, he set right there and asked me questions for two hours hand running. Didn't need to neither, 'cause he had maps there that showed every forty and every bayou along the river jest as she is; but he wanted to be sure. Then when he was done he looked me over and sez: 'Mr. Hart,' sez he, 'you look like you'd make a good gang-boss on our job.' They're going to build a dam down there, Marty, that'll make a lake of the river for ten miles upstream. 'I can give you a note to the chief engineer,' sez he. Said they wanted a man who knew the river to take charge of a crew they're going to do some work with up on Big Squaw Island—up there near Simon Lee's you know."

"Why didn't you take the job?"

"Bohunks!" drawled Jud. "But what I was thinking about, Marty, was that he was asking about you, too. 'Was it so that you was trying to make a farm out of your tract?' sez he. 'And was you the one who was trying to get the settlers together and stirring 'em up to pull stumps and hang on to their land?' Course I set there dumb as a porkypine and said I didn't know but I guessed you'd kind of got the rest of 'em 'round here woke up a little. 'Guess I'll have to go up and see him,' sez he, meaning you. Did he come?"

"Yes. He wanted to buy us out."

"Wanted to buy the land, didn't he?"

"Yes."

"Well, that's what gets me, Marty. Why in Sam Hill don't they jest buy the pulp-wood? What do they want of this God-forsaken land, anyhow?"

"Don't know. Have many of the settlers sold?"

"No. They ain't offering more'n the pulp-wood's worth, I hear. But they want the land, too. Fact is, they want all the land 'round here. What they after, Marty; reckon they found there's min'rals in her?"

"No, it isn't that kind of soil."

"Ain't it, now, Marty? Well, now, since you can speak up and tell me that, what kind of soil might it be?"

"It's good farm-land," said Martin slowly.

VI

There was a period of heavy silence.

"'Y golly!" Jud shook his head, pulling at the tufts in his ears. "Don't think I want to doubt you, Marty; but, when you call this good farm-land"—he raised his great head above the box to assure himself that the nature of the land had not altered—"when you call this played-out logging country good farm-land—" He shook his head. "Marty, where'd you get that notion, anyhow?"

"Right there."

They had reached the open spot where the old tote-road branched off the main road for Camp Bon Air. Marty brought the team to a stop. Years ago the tote-teamsters, slowly hauling huge loads of supplies for the camps, had chosen this opening as a noon resting place, to feed their horses first and then themselves. Sometimes the loads they hauled had consisted of baled hay, and occasionally they had opened a bale there and spread it out upon the snow for the horses to muzzle and chew contentedly.

The big tote teams were gone from the road now, and so were the men who had driven them, but the timothy hay had remained to record the tale of their passing. Its seed had found fecund soil in the ground where it had been so carelessly scattered and its rapidly spreading roots had usurped the spot for their own. No brush grew in the old resting place, nor in the road that Martin now followed to Keener's camp. The roots of the timothy covered the cleared ground with a web through which no brush-sprout could force its way, and the tender spring-green shoots of the grass rose like a carpet about the horses' fetlocks.

"Played-out logging country," said Martin dryly as they drew near Clear Lake. "Jack pine sand and swamp. Won't grow anything."

"She'll grow hay, all right," admitted Jud. "But sand—"

"It isn't sand—except in streaks. It's mostly silt loam—Kenan silt loam—if that means anything to you."

The water of Clear Lake, glinting through the trees, had warned Martin that they were nearing Camp Bon Air, and a feeling of apprehension suddenly rose in his breast. He wished that he had let Jud drive in alone with the trunks; but had he done so, he knew he would have been tortured by regrets, for he had desired to go to Camp Bon Air since the evening before.

He sat up very straight on the seat, his countenance Indian-stolid with assumed indifference as they entered the Camp clearing, and saw a red-haired maid peering at them from the kitchen door.

"Trunks," said Martin.

"Trunks? Yiss. Jist a second and I'll ask Miss Demaree what she wants done with thim."

Jud was out, letting down the end-board when Alice Demaree came around from the front of the cottage. She was arrayed rather for the porch of a popular summer resort than for an isolated camp in the woods. Her white duck skirt and shoes were immaculate. Her silken shirt-waist, with a frill at the collar, might have come but a moment before from the modiste's. She was a tall, fair girl, and her abundant light hair was dressed to the last golden strand.

The giant figure of Big Jud caught and held her attention and she came toward him slowly.

"The trunks? Oh, dear! What a nuisance. You may take them back at once, Mr. Expressman."

In the presence of such exquisite femininity Jud was stricken with confusion, yet he strove to be pleasant.

"Expressman!" he repeated. "Haw, haw, haw!"

Then he blushed and tugged wildly at the end-board.

"Don't unload them, please," said Miss Demaree with a slight frown. "I have no use for them here, as I shall be leaving in a few days. You may take them back to town."

"'Y golly!" said Jud with a shake of his head, and as he looked appealingly up at Martin Miss Demaree followed his gaze. Martin was looking at her. He was looking at her with his clean eyes alight with frank admiration. For he had never before seen any girl quite like her; never any being of such worshipful—almost appalling—femininity.

As she returned his scrutiny Alice Demaree knew that she had never before seen a man quite like him. She saw a profile lean and brown from a hard outdoor life, yet unmistakably stamped with the lines of a superior race type. His clothes were rough and much worn, but they could not hide the graceful lines of a hard, slender body. The tigerish litheness with which he vaulted down from the seat startled and thrilled her a little. It also shocked and piqued her. This tall backwoods youth had taken charge of the situation, regardless of her wishes. With men her wishes usually were law.

"We just hauled them out as a favour to the agent down at the Falls," said Martin, moving swiftly past her to the end of the wagon. "I'm sorry, but if you want them to go back I'm afraid you'll have to get somebody else. We're on our way home. Where do you want them?"

"I want them to go back to town."

"I know. But where do you want them put—until you can get somebody to take them back?"

He had helped the confused Jud to free the end-board, and with one brown hand gripping a trunk handle he turned to her expectantly. They faced one another again, and again she wondered at the contrast between his rough clothes and the lines of his face, the look in his eyes. Up to that moment she had never imagined that such men existed save in stiff white collars and well-tailored, carefully pressed clothes.

"You may charge what you like to take them back," she said. Then she saw her mistake and added: "It would be such a favour to me."

Martin paused with a trunk half out of the box.

"No," he said after a moment's thought, "I'm sorry, but I can't do it. I would if I could, but I've got too much to do at home."

Then she turned upon him the full power of a dazzling smile.

"You're Mr. Calkins, aren't you? Well, Mr. Calkins, don't you see what a distressing fix it puts me in? I may want to leave at any moment, and how can I find any one to take them back for me? And then what shall I do?"

Martin looked away, but he did not falter.

"Sorry, but I can't do it," he said. "Would if I could, but can't spare the team. How'd they do on the porch?"

After another look at his eyes, she gave in gracefully, skilfully, though her cheeks were flushing angrily. She would not let him have all his own way, however.

"Oh, dear. The porch? Let me see. Could you carry them into the front hall?"

It was over swiftly then. Big Jud, greatly relieved at the chance for action, took a trunk under each arm and stalked after her around the front of the cottage. When he reappeared Martin was up on the seat with the reins in his hands.

"My purse, Maggie," called Miss Demaree coldly to her maid; but before she had secured the purse the team was going out of the clearing at a clumsy trot.

<h1 style="text-align:center">VII</h1>

As he drove back to the main road Martin knew that something important had happened to him since he had driven in a few minutes before. He did not know what it was; he was not at all sure that he was glad that it had happened; he only knew that he was in some fashion considerably disturbed. As near as he could explain it, his thoughts and interests seemed suddenly to have become divided.

Now there was a new influence in his life. It evoked thoughts of a nature strange and inviting to him; it seemed to broaden the expanse of existence. He sensed, too, that this new influence conflicted directly with his thoughts of the soil; but for the moment he was under a spell and, viewing his circumstances through this new vision, the life which he had planned on the tract of land which had been all in all to him seemed for the nonce poor and barren, indeed. Then he felt that he had been guilty of treachery to something sacred, and, rousing himself, he hurried the horses toward home.

He had recovered his usual frame of mind by the time he reached the Lee clearing, and the sight of Simon Lee sitting idly in an arm chair outside the door, with spring work fairly crying to be done, drove other thoughts from his mind.

"Waiting for your gut-leaders, Simon?" he called. "Don't worry; I didn't forget them."

Simon Lee looked up from the brown study in which he had been sunk.

"Hello, Martin. Hello, Jud," he said abstractedly. "Gut-leaders? Got 'em, did you? No. No, I wasn't exactly thinking about leaders just now."

"No?" Martin was briskly handing out potato sacks to Jud. "Here are your seed potatoes, then. You weren't by any chance thinking of them, were you?"

"Not exactly," said Lee, eyeing the sacks indifferently.

"No; I thought not."

"I was thinking"—began Simon Lee as Martin climbed back on the seat—"that maybe I ought to sell."

"You see," he went on, thinking aloud rather than addressing his hearers, "it ain't as if me'n ma was alone. We're getting old and we're satisfied here, anyhow. But have we got a right to stand in Hattie's way? That's the question. Smart girl like her, with her schooling, don't hardly belong up here in the bush, and I don't scarcely feel we're doing right by her here. There ain't much for a girl like her 'round here. Now if she was in a big town some place, where there are big schools and things like that, why, she'd have something to look forward to. Young folks are entitled to have a good time while they're growing up—that's the way I look at it. We could keep the twenty we've got cleared, ma and me, and live on it nice, and the money for the rest could go to Hattie right now while it would do her most good."

"When was Keener up to see you?" asked Martin.

"Eh?" Lee started in surprise. "How'd you know—? Oh, last night; last night jest after you left, Marty."

"He was pretty busy last night, then; he was up to see me early in the evening."

"He was? After you to sell, too, was he?"

"Yes."

"He's after everybody 'round to sell, Simon," volunteered Jud. "But what they want with this played out, logged-off, God-forsaken land's more'n I can see."

"You ain't selling, I s'pose, Mart?"

Martin shook his head.

"Well, it's different with you, a whole lot different. You're young and you're fixed different than I be. Care to say what he offered you, Marty?"

"Four dollars an acre."

"Four. Well, he did a little better by me—better'n five his offer was. Funny, too; I've skinned the timber off worse than you have."

"Keener isn't buying just pulp-wood; he's after land, too."

"Yep. He wanted the land, all right."

"I hold to it that they've found there's min'rals in her," said Jud.

"Gold, mebbe, Jud?" chuckled Lee.

"Iron or copper, more likely."

"Gold," said Martin firmly. "But it will take lots of elbow grease to make the crops that will bring it out."

"Yes," sighed Simon, "an awful lot of elbow grease."

"What else did Keener say? Did he make any threats to you?"

"He did just that thing, Marty. He was talking away, trying to get me to say, yes, I'd sell, and I was trying to find out why he wanted the land, and I reckon I was a little too slow for him and he got a little irritated."

"You didn't promise to sell then?"

"Well, no, you couldn't say I did, Mart. I was pretty near going to, because three thousand dollars is a powerful lot of money, and I'd begun to figger on what it could do for Hattie, and I was jest about to give him my promise, and then he said something that I didn't like. He said I'd *have* to sell in a year or two and then I'd come and beg 'em to buy. Beg! So," chuckled Simon Lee comfortably, "I just up and told him to pick up his papers and get right off my place."

"'Y golly!" bellowed Jud. "You old heller, Simon! Reckon he got, too?"

"Well," said Simon, swelling a little, "I'll say he did, Jud."

That was too much for Mrs. Lee, who had been listening behind the door.

"'Tain't no credit to you, Simon Lee, if he did," she snapped, popping forth. "You could have told him to go jest as well without swearing. And you, too, Jud Hart, you needn't come swearing and cussing 'round here. How's your ma, Marty? Tell her I'll be up to see her as soon as the road gets dried out a bit. And you didn't have needed to bring them silly fishing lines for Simon, either. Reckon he's got plenty to do without thinking of going fishing. Fishing! Huh! There you set with those seed potatoes to go into the cellar; and not a furrow turned yet, and your harness needing a hull new britching before you can do a lick—Well, I should think it was about time you were moving. Won't you'n Jud stop for a cup of coffee, Marty? Only take a minute. Well, I'm glad to see somebody in this country doesn't feel they've got time to loaf all day. And tell your ma I'll be up to visit her soon; and if you see Hattie up to the school you say I said she should come right home after school's out and not set up there reading 'zamination papers all alone."

"All right—if I see her," called back Martin.

But he did not see Hattie this day.

The little school house stood back from the road a short distance beyond the Lees' in a clearing the heart of what once had been a stretch of noble white pine. Probably with no appreciation of the solemn beauty of the thing they were creating the loggers had left standing, for a wind-break, a fringe of the old pines around the clearing. The tall, serene trees walled the school ground in on three sides. Red squirrels chattered impudently in the solemnity of their lofty branches, and during the recesses the school children romped noisily on the dark, needle carpeted aisles between the great trunks.

It had been Martin's custom to sound one loud shrill whistle upon his fingers while driving by and to wave back in response to Hattie Lee's greeting from door or window. He did not whistle to-day.

Hattie Lee heard the rumble of the wagon and looked out of the window. But the wagon had passed the clearing and all she saw of Martin Calkins was his back.

VIII

"Land sakes! Where you been all this time?" greeted Mrs. Calkins when he pulled into his own yard. "I thought you were getting an early start this morning so you could come back quick. Hello, Jud. What took you so long?"

"Well, I tell you, mother," teased Martin, "Mr. Royle was in town taking a bunch of the boys west with him so of course Jud and I had to have a few drinks with them to see them off."

"Marty Calkins! If you go telling me such lies—What were you doing? Land sakes! I've had the awfullest time. First squint I took out of the door after daylight this morning who d'you suppose I see but three men, and one of them's this Mr. Keener; and what d'you s'pose they're doing but measuring with some instruments over on the low flat by the lake. So I said, what did they want on our land, please? and Mr. Keener came up and introduced himself and said what a nice building spot we had here and was very cute and polite, but he didn't fool me bit; so when he got through trying to pull the wool over my eyes and said too bad that nice flat was lying so low 'twas like to flood in high-water I was ready for him and I said the water'd been mighty high sometimes but 't never had touched the Flat yet.

"'No,' he said, 'but suppose the water went two feet higher'n high-water mark?'

"'It won't,' I said. 'If it did half of Big Flat township would be a lake.'

"'Oh!' he said, laughing, 'we won't let it get to that.'

"'Thanks,' I said. 'The Almighty's got something to say about that and He never let Crooked Lake go over its banks yet and I reckon He won't now.'

"You jest bet that shut him up for a while. Then he said: 'Mrs. Calkins, will you take some good advice?'

"'Will if it agrees with me,' I said.

"'Sell your land,' said he; and then I did lay him out. Told him the Calkins's didn't need any advice on what to do with their land, and he didn't need to come trespassing 'round either. What kept you so long, Marty?"

"I told you," said Martin. "A lot of the boys were going west with Mr. Royle and we just stopped and saw them off."

"Well, the more of them he takes away with him the better for all concerned, that's what I say. Young devils like that Tim Cooney, that's what they are. Of course he wouldn't be took away by any chance. Now what are you laughing at there like a crazy loon, Jud Hart? I'll have you know that if you're going to stay around here you'll have to behave like a Christian creature, and don't you ever forget to wipe your feet when you come into my house, either."

"Marty," said Jud, as he led the horses toward the stable, "your ma and Susan Lee ain't kin, be they? No. 'Y golly!" He threw back his head and chuckled. "I got it: your pa was a great feller for fishing, too."

Martin had swiftly unloaded the wagon, and was striding with set face toward the tool-shed of the mill.

"I guess you ain't got much time for fishing, have you, Marty?"

"Not yet," said Martin, and slammed the shed door behind him.

Hours later Mrs. Calkins tapped on the tool-shed door.

"Oh, Marty!"

Martin had locked himself in shortly after his return from town. It was nearly eight in the evening now, and he had not emerged, not even at his mother's urgent call to supper.

"Martin Calkins!" Mrs. Calkins's voice rose just a trifle in pitch. "You answer when your mother talks to you!"

The answer came in an irritated mumble.

"Go 'way."

"What! You talk that way to me? Don't you hear—?"

"I don't want any supper," came the voice from within. "Go 'way."

"Jud Hart," snapped Mrs. Calkins, turning about, "what are you standing there grinning like a fool for? You got a knife on you? Give it to me."

Mrs. Calkins took the long-bladed jack-knife which Big Jud held out to her and turned to the door. She knew how that door was fastened. Inserting the knife between the door and the casing, she pushed up the wooden latch on the inside and with a vigorous kick sent the door open.

Martin did not turn around. He was sitting on a box in the middle of the room. At his left stood the engine of a portable saw-mill which he pried out of its storage place in the corner. Before him he had cleared a space on the floor and upon this space he was concentrating all his attention.

"Well!" Mrs. Calkins took one look and exploded. "Driving the floor full of spikes! Now, Marty Calkins, you tell me right straight what you're doing that for."

"Stumps," muttered Martin.

"Stumps? And that fishing reel rigged up there, with the line fastened on them nails?"

An awful fear swept through Mrs. Calkins' mind for a moment, but she was assured by recalling that there was no insanity on either side of the family.

But when Martin got down on his knees and moved the reel back a few inches, and began winding in the line which was fastened to the spikes, and grunted: "Darn it!" when the line broke, her confidence was shaken.

"Marty," she said, "do you think it's nice to let me and Hattie hear you swear?"

"I'll get it," muttered Martin, breathing hard. "I'll get it before I leave this room."

"You certainly will if you don't mind your manners a little. I'll have you know you aren't so big you can do as you want to around me—not yet, young man. You drop that crazy business long enough to turn around and be human."

Gradually Martin became aware that his seclusion had been intruded upon.

"I told you I wanted to be left alone," he said petulantly. "How d'you open that door? What do you want of me? Can't you leave me alone?"

"I'll leave you alone all right," said his mother vigorously. "I suppose I didn't have a right to open the door, did I? Hattie Lee's come up to get some feathers out of that red rooster of yours, and I want you to mind your manners and come help get 'em."

"Feathers—red rooster?" repeated Martin slowly, then in a tone of complete outrage: "What's that got to do with pulling stumps!"

"Oh!" cried Hattie Lee in the doorway. "Is that what you're doing, Marty? Is it really?" She was beside him in a flash, squatting boyishly before the field of spikes. "Oh, I see, I see! Gee, Marty; if you could!"

Martin arose flushed and disconcerted.

"You don't see. It isn't anything. I'm just fooling around with it. Don't go looking at it, Hattie. Probably nothing will come of it. What was it you wanted—feathers?"

"Don't you bother, Marty," she said swiftly. "You keep right on with this. I can come some other time."

"What do you want feathers for?" he persisted.

"We'll go," said Hattie, linking her arm in Mrs. Calkins's. "You keep right on working, Marty."

"Oh, there's no such hurry," he said, shamed out of his absorption. "No, there isn't. What in the world do you want rooster feathers for?"

"She's making trout-flies and selling them for fifty cents apiece—that's what she wants rooster feathers for," snapped his mother.

Martin looked at Hattie with new interest.

"Honest?"

She nodded. "It isn't anything much. That's what I'm going to do this summer, though."

"I thought you were only making them for your father?"

"I started making them for pop last summer. That's how I learned. His fingers were getting too stiff to tie, and he always made his own flies. He always caught the biggest trout, and city fishermen were always pestering him to buy some of his flies. He wouldn't take their money, but gave them all he had, so he always had to be making new ones for himself."

"Jest like Simon Lee," snapped Mrs. Calkins.

"When I began to make them I put a stop to that. I wasn't going to be making flies for pop to give away. It would have been different if they'd been for him, but I was practically making them for nothing for city men who wanted to pay for them, and I wasn't going to keep doing it—for nothing. One day two men came to our house and said they'd heard about pop's flies and offered five dollars for six of the flies he had the best luck with. Of course he told them to keep their money and went after the flies. He didn't find 'em, though; I had them locked up. I had a right; I'd made them, you know. Pop fussed awful and said he wasn't going to have anybody by the name of Lee acting small like that, but ma and I had our way."

"Women ought to have it," said Mrs. Calkins.

Hattie laughed.

"Pop was so 'shamed he went out the back door into the woods; and those men gave me ten dollars for two sets, six each. That's how I started. They had awful good luck and when they went back

to the city they talked about it, and about two weeks later I got a
letter from a sporting goods store in Chicago that wanted some
of the same flies. So I sent two sets, and they wrote back and said
they'd take all I could make and pay me fifty cents apiece for them;
and I've used all the bright feathers I've got and want a few of that
red rooster of yours, but I wouldn't have come, Marty, if I'd known
you were doing something like this, and I can come some other
time just as well."

"Certainly not," said Mrs. Calkins. "Marty, you get right out
and get that rooster."

"Jud can get it," said Martin, turning back to the work from
which he had been drawn. "Tell Jud he'd better walk back with
Hattie, too. They've got a lot of foreigners down at the Falls and
they might drift up this way."

"Should think you could at least walk back with her if you
think it necessary."

"Eh?" He was back on his box. "All right. Shut the door when
you go out. I'm too busy to pick roosters to-night."

He was too busy for anything but the problem before him.
He was too busy to go to bed, though when the hour for retiring
arrived his mother returned to the shed and uttered sundry
commands. Foreseeing such an event, Martin had braced the door
with a board, and she departed in a state of high indignation.

He spent most of the night in the tool-shed. When the lazy
spring dawn came creeping over the lake and Annie lighted the fire
to prepare breakfast he came forth, looking pale and lined about
the mouth, red of eye and very tousled of hair. He looked out over
the broad acres of his holdings, at the myriad of stumps jutting up
through the morning mists, and he swore at them softly through
straight-set lips.

The fight had not been won during the night, but he had
set himself to win it, so there would be no peace until it was

done. Youth-like, he railed impatiently at his own deficiency, at his lack of knowledge of how to do what he had planned. He thought of the years he had spent in high-school as wasted years—years thrown away out of the most precious part of a man's life. What good did it do him now? Then in fairness he turned about and acknowledged that he was wrong. He hadn't gone to school enough, that was the trouble. If he had had one term at an engineering school, he would probably have had his problem worked out long ago. Instinct told him that the solution would be simple—that was why it hurt so not to have had the right training.

"You fig'ring on pulling 'em with the donkey engine, Mart?" asked Jud as he harnessed up for ploughing that morning.

"Something like that."

"Never heard of anybody doing that."

"Of course not," retorted Martin. "I suppose that makes it impossible, don't it?"

As he returned to his work he thought of Hattie Lee's enterprise. He chuckled grimly as he thought of what proud, lazy Simon Lee's feelings toward the matter would be; for Simon himself was primarily responsible for the enterprise, and it was his shiftlessness that had brought it on. If Simon hadn't wasted hour after hour, day after day, on the trout creeks, studying the feeding habits of trout, he would never have developed the flies that had spread his fame as a fisherman, and Hattie would not have been in the business. Of course it wasn't really a business, Martin thought, as he bent over his engine: to him anything that wasn't connected with the land was trifling and ephemeral.

Thinking of Hattie for some reason, inevitable, perhaps, evoked thoughts of Miss Demaree. That was disturbing. Thoughts of Hattie came and went as a matter of course, as they did of his mother, or Jud or Simon Lee, and wrought no distraction. But with the thought of Alice Demaree there came a sensation of yearning, a sense of lonesomeness, of discontent with his lot, and a desire for many things which he had not desired before.

He fought grimly against the desire to think of her. He concentrated all of himself on the problem of the cursed stumps. He concentrated so well that it was not until on the morning that Alice Demaree came up to Crooked Lake fishing, that his yearning to see her again had reached the stage where he had determined to slip down to Camp Bon Air to try to get a surreptitious glimpse of her that night.

IX

By this time he had the engine out of the shed and was experimenting on the stumps. He suffered cruelly from a fear of being laughed at, and knowing the glee with which his neighbours ridiculed anything new, he chose for his experiments a flat lying back from one of the many coves in Crooked Lake. The flat was out of sight from the house, and the banks of the cove were lined with a dense growth of willows, so he fancied himself hidden from the lake. He had rigged up a drum on the engine and with a wire cable pulled the smaller stumps easily one at a time, as he had known he could, and, also, as he had known, at too great a cost of time and labour. This bright morning the little saw-mill engine was snorting busily. Jud did duty at the free end of the cable, fastening it solidly to the stumps while Martin ran the engine, and Jud was lazily delighted.

"Beats chopping 'em out all hollow," drawled Jud. "No bone-labour to this."

"Oh, shucks!" said Martin in disgust.

"'Y golly, Marty, you are the drivingest fellow I ever did work with," chuckled the giant. "We're going along nice, ain't we? Nice and easy. By the time you get to be my age, Marty, you'll be more willing to take things easy."

"By the time I'm your age I'll have all this country in crops—or break my neck," was the swift retort. "How do you suppose the country is going to amount to anything if somebody doesn't hustle? Pulling one stump at a time! Kid's play."

"One at a time ain't enough for you, then?"

"No. Nor two, nor three."

"You want to go through and yank 'em up like a fellow pulling weeds, eh?"

"That's what I do. And that's what I'm going to do, too."

Then Jud delivered himself of the opinion which had been forming in his mind for days:

"Marty, my ideer is that you been reading too many books lately."

And Martin, greasy and sooty from engine-running and very much worn, swiftly told Jud to take his ideas and go where no man wished to go and to remain there until it froze over. But Jud shook his head and said solemnly, no, he couldn't do that, not even for Marty, not yet awhile, anyhow; and the struggle with the stumps was resumed.

"We've got the power," said Martin grimly, during a breath spell. "We've got the power right here in this little engine to pull half a dozen of them at once; and we could take the big engine out of the sawmill and we'd have the power to yank out a dozen of 'em—if we knew how to use it. Mr. Royle said he could snake a dozen logs at a time if he had the power. We can do it with stumps, too. I know we can, but I don't know how."

The problem enraged him. He felt sure that the solution would be ridiculously simple, and he knew he was on the right road.

"We will brace her up, Jud," said he, "and try if we get an up-pull that way."

Accordingly the engine was raised at great labour, the cable hitched about three stumps and the engine started. Slowly the cable wound up on the drum. The leverage was there, but something was wrong. The first stump tipped slowly, toward the engine, and, half-pulled, lay on the cable, absorbing the power which should have been applied to the other stumps.

"Don't work no better," drawled Jud; but Martin had got down from the engine with a new look in his eyes. Slowly he ran his hand along the cable. The tautness ceased at the first stump; beyond it hung slack. Suddenly Martin thrust out his hand, the fingers spread wide apart, and, gulping boyishly, cried: "Jud! Jud—I've got it!"

He stood staring at the slack cable, gulping in his dry throat and breathing in gasps. He had known all along that it would come if he stuck at it, but it had come so suddenly and without warning.

"And so simple! What fools we are, Jud!"

Big Jud looked at him closely.

"You're mighty white around the gills, Marty. Feel faint?"

"Just a little," said Martin.

"Splash of cold water's good for it."

"Yes." The numbing reaction from the moment of sudden triumph had passed, and his head was hot and throbbing with a jumble of emotions. The cold water of the cove was deliciously bracing. He plunged his head and neck into it. In the mirror-like water he saw himself blackened and smudged, and he laughed and rubbed his face and hand with the white sand of the beach, and dipping his head again to rinse it, he stood up to shake the water from his eyes—and saw the white canoe with Alice Demaree in the bow coming silently into the cove, straight toward him.

X

Martin brushed back his wet hair and smiled. It was easy to smile now; and he was quite sure that he had never seen anything so beautiful as the picture that Alice Demaree made in the canoe at that moment. She was a fair dream come true. Arrayed in white duck skirt, thin silken sweater of delicate pink, and a soft straw hat shading her eyes, she sat like a queen enthroned, leaning negligently back against the cushioned canoe-chair. A short casting rod, with a gleaming aluminum bait at the tip, lay idly across her knee.

A few yards from the shore the Indian stopped paddling, and the white craft came drifting in, light and graceful as a swan. In the instant that its bow was about to touch the beach White Pigeon slipped his paddle blade into the bottom and the canoe stopped and rode motionless on the shallow water.

"I thought," said Martin, smiling, "that you were going away?"

"So did I," she replied, smiling back at him. "But there was nobody to take my trunks to town."

They laughed a little in confusion, and were silent. "Have any luck?" he asked as a matter of habit.

"Only one small strike."

He looked at the reel and saw that the line was quite dry.

"Guess you haven't been trying very hard, have you?" said he, and they laughed again.

"No," she said. "They weren't striking. I think it's too boring when they won't strike, don't you?"

"Oh, you've got to keep at it if you want to catch anything casting. I went round the lake once last fall and didn't have a strike until I was almost back at the dock. Then I got two three-pounders in two casts. Bass are funny things; you can't tell about them."

"Do you like to fish?" she asked, looking up at him.

"I should say I do. But I haven't got much time for it."

"Really? you're so busy? I didn't fancy people were so busy in these primeval woods."

"Primeval?" said Martin, smiling. "What's there primeval about them now? We don't hardly look at 'em as woods at all up here. The loggers have taken the primeval woods and turned them into lumber. We're starting farming here now."

"Really?" she said carelessly. "How interesting."

"It is." In his earnestness he moved a step nearer and her eyes followed lazily the strength and litheness of the movement. "If people only knew how interesting it is I believe there'd be hundreds of them doing it where there are dozens now."

She looked around, smiling strangely.

"Do you really? But the hardships?"

"Hardships? Oh, well, I suppose they would be hardships to some, before they got used to it. What would be hardship to me, though, would be sitting cooped up all day in an office in the city; and still lots of men stand it without suffering at all."

She laughed at this, laughed entrancingly, with a backward roll of her head that emphasised the round whiteness of her throat.

"That is really good! I must tell Uncle Keener that; it will shock him deliciously."

"Say" said Martin with a sudden thought, "wouldn't it shock him if he knew you were up here talking to me like this?"

"Nothing that I do can shock him any more. But why should it?"

"He hasn't said anything about his coming up here that night, then?"

"You mean about buying your land? Oh, yes, I heard him say something about it. Business—I move whenever he starts on that."

She laughed again. "So you think sitting in an office would be a hardship for you, do you?"

"I know it. It's all right for those who like it, but I ain't made for it."

"And yet," she said, studying his face, "I agree with Uncle: I think you would do well in the city."

"How do you mean, do well?"

"I think you would make a successful business man."

"Make a lot of money, you mean?"

"Yes. I'm sure you would!"

"Well, you see, Miss Demaree, even if I did make a lot of money, that wouldn't be a success for me. Not that I don't want to make money, and all I can, at that. But I mean if I had to live in the city, no matter how much I made, I'd be the worst failure in the world."

"I don't understand you," she said.

"I'd be—I'd be no better than dead. I'd feel that I wasn't living at all. No matter how much money I had I'd feel that my life wasn't worth a cent. I'd feel I hadn't done anything with it, not a thing."

"You say that now," she said archly, "but after you had won success I imagine you would have a different point of view."

"But I'm telling you it wouldn't be success for me."

"You would think differently after you had done it."

"I couldn't do it. I couldn't stand it. I'd go wild, and bust away and come up here."

"To—this?" The wave of her white hand expressed gently the derision she would not permit to show upon her face.

"Exactly."

"It seems a pity you should feel like that. It really is a pity—that you should waste yourself up here. I am sure if you were where big things are being done that you would do something big."

"I am doing something big," he began, but she smiled a little and his conviction weakened. "Well, I suppose it doesn't look big to you. Maybe it isn't big. But it seems big enough to satisfy me."

"If you got away from here, to the city, and saw really big things you would be broadened and see with different eyes. Then probably you wouldn't be satisfied."

"Well," he said, grinning, "maybe then it's a good thing I don't go. If it's only a question of point of view, what difference does it make? If I'm so ignorant that this satisfies me, why ain't I lucky in that?"

"But you're not ignorant, and that's why you should not be satisfied with this. You could do big things, and you should, as a duty to yourself."

"Duty? Well—I've got this land to break up, you know."

"Not necessarily. Why should you be the one? Somebody else—it isn't a task for brains."

"Isn't it!" he cried. "That's the trouble; they've tried to do it with their hands and haven't mixed any brains in the job. That's why it's gone so slow."

"Are you planning to hurry it by mixing brains in the job?"

"I'm trying—a little." He tried to suppress it, but the note of triumph rang in his tones like a boast, and she looked at him swiftly.

"Really? Are brains applicable to this—brute labour?"

She had done it now. He had not intended to start the engine again until she had gone, but she should see. He stooped swiftly forward and drew the canoe up on the beach, while her eyes lazily followed the lithe strength of the movement.

"Come and see; I've just got it; something new. Just going to try it."

She rose, lifted by the force of his young eagerness. She held out her white soft hand, and took his hard brown one, and as he helped her from the canoe she brushed his arm.

He led the way swiftly through the willows onto the flat where the engine stood, and got to work at once. He seemed made of steel and driven by superhuman power. His energy infected even Jud, and the big fellow leaped clumsily about to obey swift, staccato orders.

"I've got it now, Jud—run the steam up a little, will you? Just saw how it should be done on the last pull. Pay out some more cable, a whole lot. Simplest thing in the world. More cable, Jud. Don't see how we missed it so long. That's enough. We certainly have been blind. Here we are; five loops. That's right; drag it this way. Now we go; a hitch around that stump; that's right. Another. Come on."

"Marty," protested Jud, "that's three we got it on now—"

"Come on; two more. Then the free end back to the main stem. Five at a time. Now let's anchor the engine better because there's going to be an awful strain on her. Come on."

They anchored the engine securely, and Martin drove up the steam and reached for the throttle. The cable now had five loops at its end, each wrapped around a stump, and each loop running back to the main cable, like fingers to a hand. The main cable ran back to the drum. So engrossed was Martin in the great experiment that he had forgotten Miss Demaree. Slowly and steadily he drew back the throttle. The drum began to wind. It wound until the main cable was as taut as a thin steel bar. With parted lips he turned on more power. The roots of the stumps creaked. The dirt about them began to crack and loosen. The roots broke, the stumps broke loose, and, as the cable was wound up, one stump after another was wrenched free from the ground until all five had been pulled in little more than the time formerly required for one.

Martin shut off the power and leaped to the ground.

"Simple, isn't it?" he said, with fine modesty.

Miss Demaree nodded, his enthusiasm bringing to her lips an amused smile.

"Yes," she said, and then she continued casually: "We saw the foreign workmen doing it down on the Company's land along the river below Rainy Falls the other day. You know Uncle Keener and Mr. Starin have formed a land company, too. They had a much larger engine than yours, though, and it was on wheels, so they could move it around. Do you really like this sort of work?"

XI

It was Jud who recovered first. The discovery was not his, nor the stumps, so Miss Demaree's careless words did not deal him the lightning stroke they did Martin. He tried half-heartedly to maintain his gravity while freeing the cable from the stumps, but soon gave up the effort and threw his great head in the air and bellowed:

"Whoop! 'Y golly! Haw, haw, haw!"

His laughter brought a titter from Miss Demaree, and Martin, trying to smile in cheerful accordance, achieved a wan and ghastly grin.

"You say—you say you've seen stumps pulled that way before?"

"Why, yes. Haven't you?"

"I—I can't say I have. Just like that?"

"Yes, so far as I can see," she replied. "Of course I don't know anything about machinery, but I know they used an engine and a long rope like that with a lot of little ropes at the end. Was it supposed to be a new idea?"

"Well, no; not exactly new," stammered Martin. Then the important fact in her revelation rushed into his mind. "Where did you say it was? Down below the Falls on the company's land? What company? Not the Paper Company?"

"Why, of course," she said, wondering at his excitement.

"They're doing this—breaking land—down there?"

She merely nodded.

"They're breaking a lot—they've got a big crew?"

"It seemed so. I think I heard Uncle Keener say that they had several hundred workmen which they were using down there until they were ready for them at the dam.—Oh! there are some violets."

"Yes; we call them swamp violets." He had recovered his self-possession somewhat now; he was grateful to her for dismissing the painful subject.

"How beautiful, how wonderfully coloured!"

"Aren't they!" he agreed. As if nothing had happened to shake him he went down on his knees and cut out a square of clean white moss with a cluster of the modest little flowers growing in the middle.

"They'll keep fresh a long time that way," he explained.

"Can I transplant them?"

"I don't think they would stand it."

She made to take the plants which he held in his hands, but looked at the black dirt about the roots and at her white hands and stopped.

"I must take them with me, but I must have something to put them on," she said, looking around. "Oh, there's a birch tree; we can get some birch bark and put them on."

"It's about the only one on the lake with any bark left on it," thought Martin ruefully as he looked at the beautiful silver trunk of the tree, but she was standing beside him and the struggle was short if bitter. As his knife sank into the virgin bark he felt a throb of shame, as if he were betraying a friend, but the knife was not stayed.

"There." Even as he held the bark out to her and placed the plants upon it he was asking himself why he had done it, what had changed him so in a moment. The sight of a mutilated birch always had pained him; now he had cut one himself; but the sense of crime vanished as she smiled.

She went to the canoe holding the gift in both hands, and he must take her soft arm in his hard hand to help her in. As she stepped in the canoe rocked and she screamed a little and leaned upon him. Martin's eyes followed her until the canoe was out of sight.

"Got another hitch all set, Marty," called Jud.

"All right, Jud." He came back to his task with lagging feet, and Jud in his ignorance exploded encouragingly:

"What do we care, Marty, if they've got onto this racket ahead of us down there? She works, don't she? And you worked it out in your own noodle and made it work without anybody's help, didn't you? Then what's the diff'! It's a big thing to do, and don't you forget it. 'Y golly! It's going to make this man's country all over. Come on; tune her up again."

"Tune her up it is."

Martin grasped at his work as a man coming out of a dream grasps at the bed-clothes to feel something real. Now that she was gone it seemed like the stuff of dreams. The look in her eyes, the sound of her voice, the touch of her fingers, even the touch of her person when she leaned against him, all seemed unreal. He looked down at his old, smudged clothes. What a sight he must have been to her! Yet she had come ashore at his invitation, had taken his hand; she had stood beside him and talked; she had smiled. Had she smiled? he asked himself incredulously. That was hardly probable. He would probably awaken in a moment and know it was all a dream. He looked around in hope of seeing her again; and he saw the birch tree with the gaping brown wound in its silver trunk.

"All set, Jud?"

"All set."

The engine throbbed and started, the drum creaked, the cable tightened, and the stumps began to loosen. The job was the thing; it was real.

When they had pulled all the small stumps within the operating radius of the fixed engine they took time to think and talk things over.

"She's good so far as she reaches, Marty; but it's an awful slow job to move her and set her up and anchor her for a fresh pulling."

"Too slow," agreed Martin. "It won't do. Even if we took the big engine out of the mill it wouldn't do. We could get more cable and reach twice as far with it, but it would take more than twice as long to make a move with it. I can see it plain enough now: it's got to be a big tractor."

"I reckon that's what the young lady was talking about, eh? A big engine on wheels, she said. That would be a tractor, I reckon, they were using down there—Sa-a-ay!"

"What's the matter now?"

"Didn't she say they was breaking company's land?"

"Yes."

"But what—what the hell! What *they* busting land for?"

"Oh, just because they're good business men. They've got brains enough to see what sort of soil this poor, logged-over, God-forsaken stump country is made of, and they intend to make a killing on the land after they've chewed the woods into paper. Seeing that they're dealing with people who don't go much by books, they buy out the settlers for just what the pulp-wood's worth, so they get the land for nothing an acre. They can break it up for twenty-five an acre—yes, for twenty; and every acre of this country is worth a hundred dollars the day it's ready for the plough. Keener told me they were going to operate on about two hundred sections—some hundred and twenty thousand acres. Take twenty thousand acres out for sand and so on—that's allowing one acre in six—and there's a hundred thousand acres left. A hundred thousand acres at a hundred dollars an acre is ten million dollars. Worth going after even for the Starin Paper Company."

"Sure is," agreed Jud. "That's consider'ble money."

"They've got money," continued Martin. "That's where they have their hold. They've got money, and they've got brains. They use their brains, and the people around here who are too lazy to use their brains will get the short end of the stick."

"You're hard on your neighbours, Marty, durn'd hard."

"Somebody ought to be hard on them. Somebody's got to be hard on them. Look at the way they work; look at the way they get on. They don't get on atall. They don't want to get on unless they can do it the way their fathers did, and their grandfathers before them. And it's their country; it belongs to them; they ought to keep it and get the good out of it when the good times come. Why, I'll bet four dollars to a hole in a spoiled dough-nut that some of those fellows below the Falls who sold their places will wind up as renters on the farms they sold for five dollars an acre. Renters! Working for the money-people who own the land and who sit on their pants way off in some city and don't do a lick, but get the good of the renter's bone-labour. It—it isn't right."

"'Them what has gits,'" quoted Jud.

"Them what *does* gits," retorted Martin. "Come on; let's move her and get going again. To-morrow morning I'll go down and see how they work it down there below the Falls."

"Better we both should go," said Jud after a period of deliberation.

"Why? D'you want a day off?"

"Those Bohunks the other day—I didn't like the way that big fellow eyed you after you let him smell your fist."

Martin laughed easily.

"I guess they won't be running this country for yet awhile."

"They're a sneaky, treacherous set," persisted Jud. "They don't get mad and have it out and shake hands like white men. They carry a grudge and smile and talk nice and jump you when they get you alone. Better the both of us go."

"No," said Martin, "I want you to pile and burn these stumps to-morrow. I'm going to stick spuds in here and I want to get it broken early. You needn't look sore; you won't miss any fun; I'm going strictly on business."

XII

The first hints of dawn had barely begun to pale the stars in the east next morning when Martin started for town. He walked to save horseflesh and soon settled steadily into the driving, knee-bent gait of the woods which carried him along at four miles an hour without any appearance of hurry.

The road was wet and slippery from the heavy night dew. At first, in the darkness, he floundered in hidden pitch-holes filled with water. This vexed him, yet he found in it some degree of pride and satisfaction. Pitch-holes were bad, and pitch-holes full of water were worse, but the fact that the water drained off slowly was a reminder of the fat clay sub-soil that lay beneath.

As the creeping daylight enabled him to see the road for a distance ahead he shook his head. It was a poor excuse for a road, and it seemed to Martin to epitomise the condition of the district.

He passed through Rainy River Falls as the sun was lifting the night-mist from the river and in five minutes he seemed to have stepped from one era to another. North of the town was the straggling, crooked road of the back-woods; south of the town brains and system had taken hold.

The tract upon which the Paper Company had begun its land-breaking operations lay a mile and a half south of the town. Formerly a ragged road along the river, similar to the one north of town, had served the district. The old road still was there, but it was no longer used. From the main street of the little town a new road ran straight as an arrow to the south, and as Martin stepped out upon it his eyes lighted up with admiration. This was a real road; this was the sort of a road a country must have if there was going to be any life in it.

A tractor whistled ahead of him and all other thoughts fled from Martin's mind. He found himself looking out upon a great flat thousands of acres in extent in which a hundred acres in one piece had been cleared. Two large steam tractors were at work. At the farther side of the clearing one tractor was working among the stumps, and on the side nearest Martin one was beginning its day's work of pulling ten ploughs and disks through the heavy virgin soil.

Martin fell in behind the breaking tractor and followed in its wake without a word. The large, heavily weighted gang-ploughs were rigged on a low-hung platform upon which the plough-tender rode, regulating the ploughs with a series of levers. They tore irresistibly through sod and root growth, and behind them the sharp disks cut the turned soil into bits.

The tractor came to the end of the clearing and halted before beginning to turn and Martin, still silent, stood looking back over the wide black swath it had produced.

"Some ploughing, bo, some ploughing."

Martin looked up. The engineer, a short, dried-up looking youth with a red bandanna handkerchief around his neck, his cap far down over his eyes, and a ball of chewing tobacco distending his lean cheek, was looking down from his perch in friendly fashion.

"We'll show you moss-backs something," he continued. "We'll show you where you get off."

"I guess you will, friend," agreed Martin. "That outfit certainly rips her up. One good, heavy dragging and she's ready to plant."

"Do that with this baby, too," said the youth, nodding affectionately at his engine. "But, say, what you doing here, bo? You talk like a white man."

"Habit of mine," laughed Martin. "What of it?"

"Oh, nothing. Seems kind of strange to hear human conversation after training with this bunch awhile."

He rolled his cud about, pursed his lips, and barely missed the plough-tender's feet with a sudden expectoration. "Excuse me, Ignatz; I mistook you for a stump."

"My name Mike," said the man sullenly.

"Listen to him!" said the engineer to Martin. "Mike! Fine chance.—Ignatz, you Hunyak, your name is mud, that's what it is. Get me? Mud—until I can think of something worse to call you."

"Say, they rube'd me right when they hired me," he continued. "Yes-sir, they certainly put it over on Shorty. Me that run a steam-shovel on the Big Ditch working with a lot of Hunyaks! Good job, all right; I like to see the old baby rip up the dirt, but this gang they've got me working with—Blooey! I sleep with a wrench in me mitt."

"How much does a tractor like that cost?" asked Martin.

"Hah?"

"Do you know?"

The little engineer looked his questioner up and down.

What's the ideer?" he asked.

"I need one of them in my business."

Shorty came down off his seat. He was a bowlegged, bright-eyed young man, hard as nails, quick as a cat, and with a chin which jutted out pugnaciously.

"A chip on both shoulders," thought Martin as he returned the other's frank appraisal. He smiled in friendly fashion, but Shorty was more sophisticated.

"You kidding me, bo?"

"Nope."

"You sure 'nough got a job like this on hand?"

"Well—how much are they breaking here?"

"About ten thousand acres in one piece, they tell me."

"I've got only about two thousand of my own to break up," said Martin, "but I want to get my neighbours in on it, and that will twice ten thousand acres."

"White man's job?"

"We call ourselves white."

"I'm your tractor man," said Shorty quickly. "Hire me right now."

"I would if we had a tractor," laughed Martin. "We haven't, though, and it's going to be a hard rub to get one. I suppose they cost like sin, don't they?"

"They cost a lot of money, all right," was the reply. "I guess that outfit there stands 'em about seven thousand beans."

Martin whistled.

"So say I," said Shorty. "If a guy's got seven thousand meg what'n'ell would he want a tractor for?"

"Seven thousand," repeated Martin.

"Oh, you could get a second hand one or a dinky for a lot less, but it takes the real thing to stand up under this gaff."

"Especially on the stump-pulling."

"Sure. Look at the way they're making that baby snort over there. Second hand or light stuff won't last long at that."

"That's what I came to see," said Martin. "I'll see you later."

He crossed the clearing swiftly to where the second tractor was ripping up stumps, and felt a thrill of pride as he noted that the Company's system, devised by experts, was much the same as the one he had evolved out of his experience and native ingenuity. Here, however, the job was done right. The cluster cables were separate from the main cable and had loops for eight stumps. When a cluster of stumps had been pulled the main cable was unhooked from the loops. Meanwhile workmen had been making ready on other stumps; the tractor steamed promptly up to the free end of a new cluster cable, hooked on, and with no loss of time was making a new pulling.

The tractor stopped, and as the engineer prepared to climb down Martin stooped to inspect the coupling on the cable. So had the scene engrossed him that he had not recognised the engineer, and his first intimation that anything was wrong was Shorty's shrill cry from across the clearing:

"Look out!"

Swiftly as he turned, Martin was not quite swift enough. A blow from a wrench glanced against the side of his head, knocking him onto the cable, where he hung for an instant before rolling over onto the ground. A kick, aimed at his face, caught him in the chest as he attempted to rise. He rolled away and lay gulping for air for a few seconds. He saw a snarling, moustached man—the man who had jeered at him at Rainy Falls—coming toward him, wrench in hand. And then, with a wild-cat leap, he was on his feet, his fists up, facing the Austrian engineer. He dodged a blow from the wrench and shot his fist at the foreigner's middle. A grunt and a look of outraged amazement came from the engineer. He kicked viciously, and Martin stepped back and in and drove another punch at the belt line. Three times he landed coolly on the man's body, and then he began to fight.

"Look out!" cried Shorty again, nearer this time, but Martin was beyond caution. He drove his man backward with short vicious blows to the face; he punched him until he had him backed against the cable. He knocked him over the cable, and leaped after him. He found himself in a melée, and he struck right and left and kept after his man. He knocked him down again, and then the pack leaped on his back. They held his arms, and he struggled on, dragging them with him.

The engineer screamed a command, and suddenly Martin saw the man coming toward him, knife in hand. All the Anglo Saxon's race-hatred of knife-fighting vented itself in one sharp explosion of energy, and he tore himself free.

"Come on, you! Come on—knife and all!"

"Here, bo!" cried Shorty, close at hand. "Here, bo." Martin looked at the sharp, double-bitted axe that Shorty thrust into his hand. Shorty was at his back, similarly weaponed, and talking softly.

"Don't crowd me, don't crowd me at all, men. Shorty's my name and I'm short of temper. I want lots of room and I'm the boy who can get it. Keep back and gimme air and I'm easy to get along with; crowd me a little and see the fireworks start. I'm small, but I got a bad heart, men; I certainly have got one wicked heart."

Martin threw down his axe, his eyes never leaving the man before him.

"Put down your knife, you whelp!" he muttered. "Put down your knife and fight like a man."

"Nothing doing, boh, nothing doing," warned Shorty. "That ain't their system. You trimmed him; let's beat it."

"He hit me from behind," said Martin thickly.

"They always do, boh, always do. Come on; they're too many for us. Come on—beat it while they're bluffed—Holy Christmas! There's the boss, and the high-mucky-muck."

XIII

Martin looked round. A buggy was driving recklessly over the clearing straight at them. A huge, crop-haired man was doing the driving, and beside him on the seat, his face hard as ice, sat Mr. Keener.

"That's Blum, the foreman, and the Big Works himself," whispered Shorty, in anguish; but to the surprise of Shorty and of Keener and Blum, Martin strode straight toward the buggy, his chin high in the air.

"I'd like to ask you, Mr. Keener, what kind of men you're bringing into this country?" he said indignantly. "This has been a pretty decent country up to now, I'll have you know. Now it seems a man can't come and look on at a piece of work without being knocked down from behind. Do you expect the people up here to stand that kind of men?"

"Who the — do you think you're talking to?" demanded the foreman, vaulting out and coming close to Martin.

"Don't you worry about what I think, my friend," said Martin, stepping closer. "And don't you think you can run over me at all. If you think you can—try it right now."

"Blum," said Keener quietly. His eyes were like twin slits of ice when he turned them upon Martin.

"Who invited you to look on at this work?" he asked. "Do you realise that you are trespassing? I advise you to be considerably less obstreperous."

"And I don't give a damn for your advice," retorted Martin hotly. "Do you hear me? Not a damn. This is a free country, and I don't have to boot-lick for anybody, no matter how big or rich they are."

"I advise you to leave this property at once."

"Suppose I don't? What will you do, have some of those dogs jump me and put me off? Is that why you brought that kind into this country—to try to scare us out? If so, hop to it; there'll be something to clean up when the dust has settled."

Mr. Keener's eyes gleamed a threat with the consciousness of overwhelming wealth and power behind it, but the eyes that looked steadily back at him were not in the least intimidated.

"I order you to get off this land," he said slowly.

"All right. That's fair enough. I'll go. But"—Martin came close to the buggy and shook his finger in the great man's face—"you keep off my land, too, Mr. Keener, d'you hear? Rich as you are if I ever catch you setting a foot over my line I'll kick you off the minute I lay eyes on you."

"Blum," said Keener.

"Yes, sir."

"See that he goes."

Martin went slowly, conscious that the big foreman followed a few paces behind. When he reached the road he stopped and turned about.

"Come out here in the road," he said quietly.

The other had stopped inside the Company line and stood glaring at the youth.

"Come on, let's see if you can run over me.—You won't come, eh? All right; and now let me tell you something, Mr. Blum; if you even think you can run over me just remember one thing: you'll have to kill me to do it."

"Keep off this land; that's all," said Blum. "You'll get in trouble if you don't."

"I guess I'll get in trouble anyhow," replied Martin. "But I'm not running away from it a bit. Not from any of it."

"I am," chirped Shorty, running up with a bundle under his arm. "Good-bye, Mr. Blum; you'll find your tractor half way down the furrow."

"Huh? What's the matter with you?" demanded the foreman.

"I'm crazy with the heat," said Shorty. "I'm throwing up a perfectly good job just because there's only about a hundred nice little Hunyaks waiting to slip a knife into my back. Got three days' pay coming, too. Well, easy come, easy go. So long, Blum."

"Don't talk to me," he said swiftly as Martin sought to expostulate. "I don't know much, but I know where I ain't well off. Those Hunyaks would have pretended they'd forgot all about my slipping you the axe, and then some time when the chance was good—Blooey! Like that guy tried to hand it to you—in the back of the head. Say! Did you see the lamp you gave him? Zowie! You're there, boh, you certainly are there. Well, come on, let's travel; what you waiting for?"

"For Blum to come out in the road."

"Don't be a hog!" snickered Shorty.

But Martin was of the temperament which is hard to rouse and still more difficult to soothe once it has been roused; and the quick, stubborn pride of the American landholder was rooted in his bones.

"Ordered me off his land. What does he think I am?"

"Well, it's his land, you know."

"I know that. He had the right to. It was the way he did it. Like I was nothing. Like—like I was one of his slaves. I'll show him I'm as good as he is any day, with all his money."

"You showed him, boh, you showed him. You balled him out right. And you certainly beat that Bohunk to a frazzle. Lemme see your head." He stood on tip-toes and inspected the cut in Martin's scalp. "A monkey-wrench is one wicked weapon. Kind-a sideswiped you. They're the worst kind. Come on; there's a spring in the brush here; let's dope you up."

While Martin was cleansing the cut in the cold water of the spring the engineer produced from his scant bundle of clothes a tin tobacco box containing sticking plaster and salve. As he dressed the wound he talked.

"He's one bad hombre, that guy Bielzky who sloughed you; he's got the whole camp eating out of his hand. He's a real wicked bird. My guess is he's wanted pretty bad some place or he'd never be up here. Keep an eye peeled for him. He'll be out to get you, and there ain't any low-down, desperate thing he won't do to get even."

Martin's anger had simmered down by now, and as they fell into step and struck out on the road he turned remorsefully to Shorty.

"My name's Calkins—Martin Calkins," he began diffidently.

"Dewar—Jim Dewar's my monicker. Shorty for everyday use."

"I guess I cost you your job, didn't I?"

"Cost me nothing! I was hunting an excuse to quit."

"What are you going to do now?"

"I should worry. How's the fishing around here?"

"It will be better in a week or so," replied Martin absentmindedly. "How much were they paying you back there?"

"Four and board," said Shorty.

They trudged on in silence for awhile.

"Come on up to my place and try the fishing," said Martin suddenly. "I'm not trying to pay you for helping me out of that jam, but I've got a boat and tackle and a spare bed, and I wish you'd come up and use them, I do for a fact."

"Oh, I ain't busted; don't think that," protested Shorty, diving into his pocket

"No, no! I didn't mean it that way. I intend to make you pay for your board by going over an old engine I've got. I'm trying to pull a few stumps, too, you know."

"Tractor?"

"No. Sawmill engine."

"A tractor's the only dope," said the engineer.

"I know it. We've got to try to get hold of a tractor, somehow."

"Who's 'we'?"

"All the settlers north of town where I live. I don't want to just break up my own land. I want to get them all in on it. Our land's better than what the Company is breaking back there, but we'll never get it broken up as long as we keep nibbling away at it each by himself. We've got to get together and cooperate, and then we can do something and the whole crowd of us will get the benefit of it. That's what I'm after."

"Hard luck for you," laughed Shorty.

"Why?"

"If you can get a bunch of farmers to work together without breaking up in a dog-fight you're a cuckoo."

Martin laughed in appreciation of his companion's shrewdness.

"That's right," he admitted; "they're too much each man for himself to pull well together. But they—we've got to break ourselves of those old ways. We've got to learn to pull together. If we don't the big fellows with a lot of money and brains will be crowding us off the map, and the small farmer will become a renter, working for somebody who's bought a bond in some big farm company."

"They've started that already out West," volunteered Shorty, the roamer.

"I know it. Farming's the one big line that the money-men haven't gobbled up and it's up to the farmer himself to see that they don't."

"They'll have to go some—the farmers. When those big guys go after anything they usually bring home the bacon. They got the dough and they got the nut."

"That's it. The farmer has got to use his nut or he'll be swamped. We've all got to put our brains together and work together." Martin's pace was increasing impatiently. "I've got to show them that we've got to co-operate and get a tractor, and keep on co-operating till we've—Well, we've got to get a tractor; that's the first thing to think of."

"Well, you don't have to get it in such a rush, do you?" protested the panting Shorty.

Martin slowed up with a laugh.

"When I get started on that I never know when to stop."

"They're for sale, you know; all you got to do is to buy one."

"That's right. And all you need to buy one is the money. That's a scarce article up here; but it won't be after we get our land broke."

"Huh! Lot of good that does you now, eh? You got a gold mine under your feet and no shovel.

"'If you ain't got no money.
Why, you needn't come around!'"

"Where did they buy the outfits they've got back there?" asked Martin after some distance had been covered in silence.

"Oh, they do all their buying right in the main office in Chicago. I guess you don't have to go that far to get one, though. The Lawston people have got agents all over the world. Probably got one somewhere around here, haven't they?"

"Yes."

There was an agent for Lawston implements at LacClaire, the country seat, in the southeastern corner of the county. By wagon roads, and very bad roads they were, LacClaire was only twenty miles from Big Flat. By railroad it was close to fifty miles. To go by rail one rode from Rainy River Falls on the old logging railroad—now owned by the Paper Company—twenty miles to the southwest to the Junction with the main line of the Great Lakes Northern. From the Junction to LacClaire was a ride of thirty miles to the east on the G.L.N. Martin had already decided to go to LacClaire to see the Lawston agent, and as he contemplated his prospective journey he saw for the first time how truly the Paper Company held the Big Flat district at its mercy. The old Logging Company, owned and operated by frontiersmen, had always gone out of its way to borrow a few box-cars to hitch onto its log-trains to haul whatever produce the settlers had to ship out to the Junction. But Keener's Company was after the settler's land, and in its make-up there was none of the human friendliness of the frontier. What would it do when shipping time came in the fall?

"I tell you what, Dewar," said Martin finally, "you put off your fishing for a while. It will be better then, anyhow. You come up to my place and run the engine for me. I want to get a lot of stumps pulled so the neighbours can see what can be done, and I can't stay at home to do it. I've got to go down to LacClaire and see what kind of a deal the Lawston agent down there will give us on a tractor."

XIV

A few days later the morning found Martin seated in the day coach of the two-car passenger train which made one daily trip between Rainy River Falls and G.L.N. Junction. He had entered the smoker when the train started, but a glance inside had prompted him to knock out his freshly loaded pipe and retreat to the coach. There he was soon joined by the thoroughly disgusted conductor, Duncan, an old lumber-jack whose left leg had been pinched while top-loading and who was ending his days as a railroader.

"The country's going to the dogs, Marty, going plumb to the dogs, that's all there air to it," said Duncan, as he dropped into the seat beside Martin. "Time was when a white man could ride in that smoker, but, phew! Now I guess there's nothing for us to do but to move out and let the Bohunks have it."

"Is it always like that?" asked Martin, laughing.

"Purty near. We call it the live-stock car now. They go down every morning to the gravel-pit where they're getting gravel for the dam. They've started mixing concrete up at the Falls. They certainly have spoiled this country for white men."

"If they have it's the white men's fault, Dunc'. If the settlers had been up to snuff they'd have farms cleared and broken and the Company wouldn't have had the chance to go into the land business. Then these foreigners would have been used only while the dam was being built, and the country would have been rid of them when it was done. Now it will be nip and tuck. The settlers aren't getting anything out of their land, and a lot of them have sold out. If the white men are crowded out they deserve it. If they lose it's because they haven't had brains enough to make the best of their opportunity."

"It was a good country until these foreigners come," maintained Duncan.

"It was, but the people in it were asleep."

At the Junction a close connection was made with the eastbound morning train on the Great Lakes Northern, and Martin soon settled himself for the ride across the southern end of the country of LacClaire. The G.L.N. ran through the developed part of the country. On both sides of the right of way lay broad, open fields. The stumps were gone. The country was made.

Martin noted the trim, white-painted farm-houses, the big red barns and the fat cattle. This was his dream of what the Big Flat should look like, and here the dream had come true. He opened a window and thrust his head out the better to see the soil that a plough-man was turning over in a field near the track, and he settled back with a sense of pride and contentment as he saw how light the land was. If they could do this down here with light land what couldn't be done with the Flat where the land was black and heavy! The stumps were out down here; that was the difference. Then, as the locomotive tooted for a crossing, he was reminded of another important fact—they had a real railroad here, too.

When he descended from the train at LacClaire he gazed about the neat little town with the feeling that it was a proper culmination of the rich country through which he had been riding. Main Street with its homely monotony of two-story brick store buildings, its brick-paved street, its awnings, lowered on the west side of the street against the morning sun, spoke of solidity, prosperity and permanency. The cupola of the high school which he had attended looked down from an eminence at the end of a maple-shaded street. Beyond Main Street he caught sight of the tree-lined streets and lawns of the homes; and above the intersections of streets hung the bowl-like globes of the electric street-lights.

The branch house of the Lawston Implement Company was on a back street near the depot and adjacent to the livery stable. It was a long one-storied shed with wide doors, and in one dark corner, underneath a covering of canvas, stood a tractor similar to the specimens that were at work in the Company clearing. The shed was deserted and Martin removed the canvas and went all over and under the tractor before any one appeared.

"Looking for Simp?" called a man from the stable. "You'll find him over'n the court-house. Sold a wagon this morning and had to go over and fix up some papers."

Simpson, the agent, a lean, lanky man, was seated upon the railing before the county clerk's desk telling a story when Martin entered the court-house.

"True's I'm sitting here, boys," he was saying, "they didn't have a cent in the house and couldn't borrow any, so seeing as the old woman had her mind set on taking in the circus, what does Pete do but load the kitchen stove and haul it down to Barney's. Got the price of two tickets, six glasses of lemonade and a sack of peanuts for it, and when I sez to him, 'Pete,' sez I, 'what you going to cook on now?' he sez: 'Dunno, Simp, never thought of that; but, gul dung it! the old woman was *bound* to see the circus.'"

Simpson and the farmer, who had just filed a chattel mortgage to secure his wagon, laughed uproariously. The clerk and Judge Holcomb, a politician, looked at one another and shook their heads.

"Simp," drawled the Judge, "why don't you remember better? Last time you told it it was the bed they sold; wasn't it Seth?"

"Uh huh!" said the clerk. "And time before that 'twas a sack of flour they'd just bought."

"Well," said Simpson, as the farmer went chuckling from the room, "don't make no diff'rence what it was; it makes 'em forget what they signed; that's all I'm after."

To Martin's surprise the announcement of his errand was received with a sudden show of interest on the part of Simpson and Judge Holcomb. The agent uncurled himself from the railing; the Judge smoothly assumed his most impressive bearing. Judge Holcomb was a man of massive physique and voice, arrayed in Prince Albert coat and silk hat.

"Well! I do believe you are the son of my old friend, Homer Calkins!" said the Judge in his deepest voice, holding out his hand. "How do you do? I remember you as a boy going to high school here. Well, you certainly have grown up into a strapping specimen. I remember well when you graduated I said to Mr. Sawyer, the banker, that there was a boy who would amount to something. Now we hear you are the moving spirit of Big Flat."

"Well, if I am, I'm not moving it very fast, I'm afraid."

Judge Holcomb laughed richly, a little too richly, Martin thought. "Patience, my boy, patience! Big Flat will boom and wax flourishingly in time, have no fear."

"Thought the Starin Company was buying all you fellows out," said Simpson crisply.

"Not north of town."

"Not north of town, eh? Hm. That's Big Flat, where you live, isn't it? I see. I heard something about it."

"About what?" asked Martin. He liked Simpson's directness, in contrast to the Judge's pomposity.

"About your leading the Flatters on not to sell. Well—I don't give a hoot for Starin or Keener or anybody else. I sell tractors. Let's go look her over."

"There's no need to look the tractor over; I've done that already," said Martin as he and Simpson left the building. "I want to find out if we can buy it."

The agent named the price.

"How much would you have to have down?"

"Thousand."

"If I can scare up a good note for a thousand dollars will you deliver the machine to me?"

"I'll drive her up and start her working myself."

"Well, there's no use taking up your time, then," said Martin. "My next move is to see Mr. Sawyer and try to get the money."

Mr. Sawyer, the president of the LacClaire County Bank, occupied a small office in the rear of the one-story bank building near the court-house. He was a neat, slender old man who in his youth had been one of the few sober men to ride the drive over the Rainy River Falls and live to tell about it, but now, in prosperous old age, his countenance wore a constant expression of diffident mildness as if deprecating the deeds of his young manhood. He arose halfway from his chair as Martin spoke his name.

"Is it Homer Calkins's boy?" he said diffidently, with his gentle smile growing wider. "Martin? I—I felt sure I knew the face. You went to school here, didn't you? Wish you'd sit down."

They sat, and Sawyer benevolently studied his visitor for so long a time that Martin wondered what his next words would be.

"I think you favour your ma," said the banker at last.

Martin told briefly of his plans for the Big Flat region and of the purpose of his visit to LacClaire. Sawyer listened with his head on one side, slowly twiddling his thumbs. When Martin was through the old man looked at him thoughtfully.

"What made you think of all this?" he asked mildly.

"About making the land?"

"About co-operation."

"I don't know. The land, I guess. Something ought to be done with it, and it can't be done without getting together. There's so much to do. Stumps; new road; we ought to have a railroad even."

He paused a moment and leaned forward toward the banker.

"Mr. Sawyer, why don't you build that railroad? You know what that country is, up there, and what it's going to be when it gets going. It's going to be one of the biggest potato districts in this country. Five—ten years from now there's going to be a million bushels of potatoes to haul out of there every Fall. There's going to be oats—we can tie anybody in the world for oats. Timothy seeds itself and goes so heavy it's going to be a champion hay-country, too. There'll be sheep by the thousands, pasturing in the summer and eating all that hay in the winter; and there'll be a dairy herd on every farm, and a bunch of western feeding steers on lots of them. There's going to be a big town up there, too, bound to be. Figure it up: somebody is going to make a lot of money hauling that stuff down to the main-line. The railroad ought to come from here. It makes a short line. The one we've got is thirty miles out of the way, and—well, the Starin Company owns that."

"So they do," said Sawyer, pensively, "so they do. They are doing lots of work up there, I hear?"

"They are trying to gobble the whole country."

"Pshaw!" said the banker softly. "They shouldn't do that." He twiddled his thumbs awhile and looked up.

"I guess I can find you a thousand dollars if you can organize your co-operative company among your neighbours. Of course, you will have to bring me good names on the notes."

Martin looked at his watch and leaped up.

"I can just catch the west-bound," he said, "and get home to-night. I'll be back Monday. Thanks, Mr. Sawyer. Excuse my hurry."

XV

On Saturday afternoon Martin got his neighbours together. He had worked from daylight until dark each day, and at night he had walked or driven to the settlers' homes and delivered his urgent invitations. Most of those whom he visited showed a disposition to grumble. Spring work had to be done; they couldn't afford to waste half a day. His argument, mildly advanced, that they couldn't afford to plug along without stopping to use their brains, usually met with a cold reception; they knew what they were doing, they'd been farming before he was born; they didn't need anybody to tell them what to do; the old way was good enough for them. Controlling the impatience that this attitude always aroused in him, Martin made his plea on a personal basis.

"Come on down just to be neighbourly; I've got it all fixed up, and you don't want to disappoint me."

That was different.

"Well, since you put it that way; don't want to be unneighbourly, Marty, guess I'll manage to be down, maybe."

To his great surprise, the one settler who received his idea with the light in her eyes which he had hoped to see in the eyes of the younger men, was a woman. She was a widow, old at forty-five, a Norwegian, with a row of six tow-headed, apple-cheeked youngsters running from a six-foot boy of twenty to a girl of ten. Her quarter-section was old pine-land, with huge, never-rotting stumps, and in some heart-breaking way she had managed to clear, break and work thirty acres.

"That make it easier for the children," she said after she had thought over Martin's words. "My boy Iner will come."

That gave Martin a new idea and he went straight to Hattie Lee with it. Although his thoughts were often with Alice Demaree,

he had no hesitation about using Hattie to further his scheme, for
he had grown up with her and took her friendship as a matter of
course. As he talked of his plans there came into Hattie's eyes the
same light that had shone in the eyes of the widow Gunderson, the
light that came from a vision and a hope of better things.

"And I can help?" said Hattie eagerly. "Honest?"

"A great deal. I never thought of it before, but now I believe that
the women are more alive to new ideas than the men. You go see
the women, Hattie. Mrs. Gunderson said: 'It will make it easier for
the children.' I think that's a good line to work along, don't you?"

"Splendid."

Had he been less busy, less totally absorbed by his problem, he
might have observed that the light in Hattie's grey eyes had turned
to something infinitely significant. To a softer light that spoke of
something more important even than pulling stumps, something
more beautiful even than the rich, smiling farms he saw in his
vision. But he was blind, blind with the blindness of a young man
wrapped in his work. And, besides, there was Alice Demaree.

The settlers from the nearby farms began to appear at the
Calkins clearing soon after the noon hour on Saturday. Later, those
from farther off began to arrive, and at three o'clock there were a
score of men present. The majority of them came in the sceptical
and condescending frame of mind of the backward-minded toward
a new idea. Some were even in a surly mood, ready to resent at the
slightest opportunity that intrusion upon their slow, fixed scheme
of thought. Martin knew his neighbours. He realized beforehand
that this would be their attitude, and he knew that anything short
of a spectacular success would evoke sneers and jeers and, perhaps,
permanently ruin all efforts to install progressive innovations. He
knew also how to handle his men and he went at it with a will.

"There's that tall, lop-sided Sand Hill crane, Pete Cartwright,"
he shouted as a gangling, grinning youth of his own age came

riding an old grey mare into the clearing. "Pete, you old bean-pole, you look kind of frisky. Get off that old crow-bait and I'll run or jump you for fun or marbles."

The picturesque equestrian threw a long dangling leg over his mount's neck and sat sideways looking down, grinning preposterously.

"Jump over a fence with you, Marty," he said finally.

"I'll go you."

"Standing or running start?" asked Pete, sliding off his mare.

"Both."

They jumped. At the standing jump the long-legged Cartwright cleared the fence rail an inch higher than Martin, but in the running jump Martin waiting until Pete had done his best then commanded the rail-holders to raise the bar a full foot higher, and with an easy, loping run came up and cleared the obstacle with inches to spare.

Big Jud Hart, feeling blood stir at this exhibition, essayed a jump and, falling short, crashed through the heavy rails as if they had been so many dry twigs. Seeking to retrieve himself in the face of the gale of laughter and chaff, he invited any man in the crowd to lift stones with him. A boulder of proper size lay nearby and Simon Lee and several of the other men managed to raise the great weight level with their knees. Iner Gunderson, the twenty-year-old son of the widow Gunderson, was thrust forward by the Scandinavians, and after much urging and blushing, so his apple cheeks were fiery red, the boy bashfully took hold. With no apparent strain to his undeveloped body, and with no alteration in his bashful grin, he picked the stone up and laid it on his shoulder.

"'Y golly!" said Jud.

He repeated the feat and, spreading his great legs to brace himself, raised the boulder above his head and hurled it a dozen feet away.

"Go head, Iner; beat him!" rose the call; but Jud caught the boy by the arm.

"No, siree. He ain't going to strain himself jest to show off. All right for an old fool like me; but he ain't got his growth yet."

"Well," said Martin after a while, "let's go pull some stumps."

He had prepared carefully and was confident. Under Shorty Dewar's expert supervision the big engine had been removed from the mill and set up in the Flat by the lake. Shorty had overhauled the engine and cables to the last valve and hitch and the steam was up. With the skill which they had achieved through much practice under Shorty's coaching Martin and Jud looped the cluster cable around six small stumps. Shorty's heart was in his work and he went down the cable, inspecting each loop and particularly the hitch to the clusters.

"And now," said he, returning to the engine, "just a simple twist of the wrist."

The sceptical chaffing of the crowd ceased as the cable tightened. When the roots of the first stump cracked under the strain put on it the men looked at one another and drew nearer. They followed down the cable as stump after stump was pulled. And when it was over, when they had seen a half day's work done in ten minutes, they suddenly recalled themselves and drew back.

"Purty expensive rig to pull stumps with," said one.

"Might be all right if we all had saw-mills."

"Engine might bust any time. Don't go much on engines myself."

"Can't see how it's going to do me any good."

The latter sentiment was the popular one.

"We ain't all got saw-mills or engines, you know, Marty."

Martin made no reply. Without any necessary waiting he and Jud knocked loose the cable and made a new hitch. When twenty-four stumps had been pulled he turned to the crowd.

"It's a poor rig," said he, "but it shows you what an engine can do. The power of that engine is just a little less than the power of a tractor, which can move around, and which is the machine we've got to have if we're going to do business. With a tractor and two cables we can make eight pulls in the time it took us to make four now. That is the speed at which we've got to break up our land; we can't afford to do it any slower. Every day that we let an acre of ground lie idle is money out of our pockets, and every day we put in with a team and the old pullers is a clean loss. Now, there can't any single one of us buy a tractor. There is only one way for us to get one, and that is to get together. We can get one if we do that. We can have one up here next week, working, if we can raise a thousand dollars. I saw the bank in LacClaire, and we can get it on our notes. Now, here is my idea: let us form a company among ourselves, and let each man go good for as much as he feels he can afford. Suppose ten of us go in; each one will be entitled to use the tractor one-tenth of the time. The machine will pay for itself by Fall; it will break enough land this spring to raise crops enough to pay its full price. What is our land worth now? You know what we've been offered. Well, every acre we break from now on is going to be worth a hundred dollars. We can't afford to let all that money lie under our feet without going after it, and this is the way to go after it and get it in a hurry. This is the way the Starin-Keener Company is going after it. They are up-to-date, and they know what is what. Now we know, just as well as they do. We've seen it work right here. We have got to be up-to-date. We are as good as they are. Our land is better. But we have got to get together or we won't better ourselves at all."

Long before he finished his talk he sensed that he had failed, but he planned to make this speech and he went on to the end as if blind to the reception it was meeting. At his first urging of more speed in land-breaking he saw that it would not go. He was proposing something so new, so revolutionary, that it aroused in these entirely individualistic settlers a resentment springing from the dislike, even hatred, which their kind held toward any innovation. He was, in substance, telling them that their old ways, the ways of their fathers, were not good enough. That was treason. His pleas for co-operation fell upon probably as barren ground as could be found any place in the world.

Martin had deemed that the stumps constituted the greatest problem in the progress of Big Flat; now he realized that the greater obstacle lay in the stubborn mental bent of his neighbours. They didn't want it, that was the trouble; they didn't want it because it was new. And even as he walked with them from the Flat, chaffing good-humouredly and requesting only that they think it over, he had made new plans, and the aim of these was to convince his neighbours.

He was back in the bank at LacClaire on Monday, as he had promised Mr. Sawyer. His mother was with him. She had fought indignantly against the idea, at first, but Martin had insisted patiently and grimly. He would show them, he said through set lips. Then she understood. All her family pride flared up to side with him. It was necessary that she accompany him to the county seat for she held a life lien on the property, and he mortgaged his land to get the tractor.

XVI

At daybreak, a few days later, Nels Borg, who owned the first farm on the Big Flat road north of the town, was the recipient of a great shock. As he came forth to harness his team for the day's work the blast of a whistle down the road shattered the silence of dawn, and a few minutes later Martin Calkins came walking up the road and turned into Borg's clearing. Responding briefly to the settler's greeting, the young man took hold of a stone-boat which Nels had left in his drive-way and drew it to one side. A couple of potato boxes also were tossed out of the way, while Borg looked on bewildered.

"Vat you do that for?" he demanded.

"Don't want to smash 'em for you, Nels," responded Martin, and went back to the road.

The whistle-blast broke the silence again, and presently Jud Hart appeared, carefully picking the safest path in the road, and immediately behind him came a large, new steam tractor with Shorty Dewar, and Simpson, the agent, driving. It came to where Martin was standing at Borg's driveway and turned in. Without pausing or hesitating, and without a word being spoken, it followed as Martin led the way up the driveway to the clearing where Nels was wont to slave among the smaller stumps. Before it had come to a stop Martin and Jud had hold of a cable and were pulling it off the drum. At that Nels Borg carefully put down the watering pail he was holding, shut his fists and came to the fore with slow, positive steps.

"I like to know vat demn nunsense you trying vit me?" said he slowly.

There was no reply. Jud and Martin and Shorty were occupied with laying out the cable; Simpson was busy getting up steam.

"You h'ar me?" said Nels, with a growl in his voice.

Apparently no one did hear him. The cable being paid out, Jud dexterously began dropping the cluster cables over the stumps nearest the tractor.

"Hol' on!" Borg took a step forward and stood on the big wire rope. At the same moment Jud gave an impatient tug at the main cable and Nels was forced to leap or be tumbled onto the ground. He leapt. Instantly he began to rave.

"You ken't make fool of me; you know dat?" he cried, shaking his fist at Jud. "You ken't come on my land and make fool of me, I tal' you dat!"

Shorty Dewar snickered.

"You demn liddle v'ippet!" said Nels, turning upon him. "Vat you leffing at?"

Simpson, at the engine, smothered a guffaw. Borg took a step toward him, took another back toward Shorty, and stood dumfounded.

"Va' in hell is dis?" he demanded at last. "I en't hire anybody to pull stumps, I tal' you dat."

By Martin's orders nobody said a word to him until the first pull had been made and six of Nels's stubborn stumps lay roots up on the ground. As the settler viewed the results and shrewdly counted the advantage to himself his anger diminished.

"How much do you charge an acre?" he said finally.

"Million dollars," replied Martin.

He had directed the placing of a second cable, and immediately after the first pull had been made, Simpson threw in the drive gear and came steaming up to the new hitch. At the end of an hour's work the cables were swiftly wound back on the drum, the tractor backed out of the clearing into the driveway, turned and went puffing out into the road.

"So long, Nels," said Martin, and as he left the clearing he looked back. Nels was standing as if rooted in the ground. He looked at the pulled stumps and then he looked at the tractor. He tried to speak, but his wide-open mouth was incapable of uttering a sound. And the crew of the tractor held in until they were out of sight and hearing before they went limp with laughter.

Before they had arrived at the next place, Curt Harmon's, they had recovered the earnest, silent demeanour which had so puzzled Nels, and they went to their work with the bearing of men who had much to do and little time to do it in and who were by no means to be stopped or dallied with. Harmon, a young married man of Martin's build, was wrecking his harness and ruining his light team by ploughing a piece of ground still full of roots when Martin came stalking into his place.

"Morning, Curt," said Martin briefly.

Harmon slowly turned his head to follow as Martin went swiftly over the cleared ground to the smaller stumps behind the cabin.

"Morning," said Curt at last.

Martin returned to the road and a moment later the tractor appeared and gave a blast of warning. Harmon's horses trembled at the terrifying sound. When the great puffing monster appeared in the road they began to prance, and when the tractor deliberately turned in and steamed across the clearing they made one concerted leap, jerked the reins out of Harmon's hands and went careening away for the barn with the young settler in pursuit.

As if nothing had happened the tractor and the crew went to their work. Harmon caught his horses, tied them, and came racing around to the rear of the cabin.

"Hey, Calkins," said he ominously, wiping his hands on his hips as he came toward Martin, "what are you trying to do?"

The snorting of the big machine and the hum of the drum as it tightened the cable drowned the rest of his words.

"Look out, Curt," said Jud Hart, dragging the second cable out for use.

Harmon took a step toward Martin and found Jud pushing by in front of him. He turned and took a step toward the giant. He stopped. He was not afraid—there is nothing in trousers that your American backwoodsman is afraid of—but he was puzzled. It was a large part of Martin's plans that he should be. Martin knew his neighbours, knew how proud and stubborn they were, how slow to act, how unresponsive to the argument of words, and how quick and shrewd to appreciate the propaganda of demonstrated action. Therefore, he and his men worked as he had planned and ordered, swiftly, efficiently, silently, and entirely disregarding the attitude of the man whom they were benefiting. Even as Nels Borg had seen the light, so Curt Harmon realized that something big was happening, and, as Nels had spoken, he said cautiously:

"I ain't hiring you to do this, remember that."

"The team didn't break anything when they ran, did they, Curt?" asked Martin.

"Not to mention; but—"

"All right boys; one more pull."

The last pull was made, the cables coiled, and as the tractor began to turn preparatory to steaming away, Martin hurried swiftly to the road to escape Harmon's inevitable questions.

"Got Curt woke up, all right," said Simpson shrewdly, looking back as they struck the road. "He's got his wife out there. They're figuring."

Martin gave a sigh of relief when they were out of sight of Harmon's clearing. It had gone as he had planned and hoped, and not as he had feared. He realized the seriousness of the iconoclasm he had committed. He had not merely driven uninvited onto Curt Harmon's land, had not merely frightened Curt's team: he had deliberately and ruthlessly crashed through the cocoon of insularity and prejudice in which the American settler loves to shroud his life. He had committed sacrilege. At Nels Borg's, Martin had not been apprehensive, for Nels was of a practical breed and not too firmly fixed in his pride and prejudices. The test of his idea had come at Harmon's, and Curt, with all the sensitiveness and the pride of his kind, had been won.

They stopped at Simon Lee's for lunch, and Martin told Hattie how he had got the tractor.

"It isn't just for breaking up my land and making a lot of money. Of course, I'm after that, too, but I doubt if I'd gone in the hole for a tractor just on account of my own land. No, I don't think I'd have had the nerve. I've got a bigger idea than that, and that's what gave me nerve enough to get the tractor."

As he told her of his scheme the grey of her eyes lighted up with interest.

"But I thought you had given that up since last Saturday, Marty."

"No," he said soberly, "that made me more determined than ever to do it, because I saw then as I'd never seen before that the settlers would never do it themselves—they'll never do anything until somebody wakes them up. I happened to have this idea, and I know it's what the Flat needs; so, of course, it's my job to get them interested—more so than ever now. They'll take it up. You should have seen Nels and Curt when they saw what we could do!"

He talked on, waxing enthusiastic with the confidence of youth, and the light in her eyes grew brighter, and she clapped her hands together from joy.

"Oh, Marty! It's fine, it's fine! I can almost see the Flat the way you see it in the future, with big farms, and good houses, and roads; and there'll be better schools for the children, and everything." She paused timidly, as if she feared that she had been too bold,—as if she feared she had betrayed some tender secret that nestled deep in her heart. "You'll make something out of this country, won't you, Marty?"

But he was blind and he replied merely: "I will, if I have any sort of luck."

For three days he stayed on the road with the tractor, forcing his missionary work upon his neighbours.

Then one soft spring evening after returning home, as he and Jud lay stretched upon the dock, smoking an after-dinner pipe, presently there came a voice from the gloom, behind him:

"That you, Marty?"

"Hello, Curt," Martin replied casually, but his heart leaped. He had hoped and believed that Curt Harmon would be the first settler to call upon him after the demonstration with the tractor, and the drawling sound of the young man's voice was like music to his ears.

"Taking a rest, you fellows?" drawled Harmon, easing himself down upon the planks of the dock and producing his pipe.

"Nice night, Curt," said Jud.

Harmon did not reply. He sat cross-legged, puffing out over the still water, seeking a way to begin.

"Tractor cut up your road pretty bad, I see, Marty," said he at last.

Martin nodded.

"That's the trouble with 'em," continued Harmon, yawning; "they're so heavy. Can't hardly use it on your low land, I suppose?"

"She's down on my low flat there now," said Martin carelessly. "We start pulling in the morning."

There was a long silence.

"How much you figure on breaking?" asked Curt.

Martin chuckled.

"That depends on how good-hearted Simpson is. Of course, I couldn't buy the thing outright, and I don't know how long he'll let me keep it on the payment I made. I figure on keeping her working six days a week until he takes her away from me."

Harmon puffed on.

"Hm. Figure on working her on your own place altogether, do you?"

"Got to," said Martin, "to get the worth of what I put into her."

"You see," he added casually, after a long pause, "I figure I make about seventy-five dollars clear every time I clear an acre."

"About that," agreed Curt, and Martin smiled to himself.

"Don't suppose a fellow could hire the outfit for a few days?"

"I don't see how I could afford it, Curt," replied Martin.

In the silence that followed Mrs. Calkins's voice was heard up at the house:

"I think they're down by the dock, Nels; you go down there."

Curt Harmon looked up as Nels Borg came walking slowly out upon the dock.

"No go, Nels," said he. "He won't do it."

Nels made no reply. When he had lighted his pipe and seated himself on the planks he said:

"Yim Green coming, too."

Green and another old settler arrived soon after. Then came Simon Lee and a neighbour.

"He won't do it, boys," said Harmon.

"Damn fool 'f he did," snapped Green. "Wouldn't myself. Now, this here new-fangled co-operative ideer you was talking about last Sa'day, Mart; jest how would you go about it—not promising nuthin', you know—but jest out o' curiosity?"

Martin rose in a way that showed he had been expecting this, but he suppressed the smile of triumph that struggled on his lips.

"Come on over to the mill, gentlemen," said he; I've got the papers all ready."

XVII

Youth's years are the years of struggle. Battles are swift and hard and painfully complicated. Complacent middle-age may concentrate ambition; youth must struggle with the welling form of life as well.

Martin Calkins—no more than any other normal young man—could convert himself into a machine for the sole achievement of his plans. He was young and it was spring, and the life-force was throbbing within him. He was changing. His life up to now had been comparable to the stiff, stark trunk of a young tree, growing in a shaded valley. In such trees the energies blindly concentrate in the push upward for the sun. But a time comes when the straight, bare trunk has thrust itself high enough as the sun touches its top. That is a portentous moment. The tree ceases to push on; it begins to spread and branch out. New branches bring to it many sources of life, new wants and needs. The tree changes. Sometimes the new branches seem heavy for it; sometimes they are not well balanced and the tree seems to lose its purpose; it leans erratically; it seems not to be the same straight tree at all.

Martin held to his purpose. The great call had not come to him until his jaw had set, firm and hard so he stayed on the job. But now he realised that the job, formerly so all-engrossing, did not satisfy him entirely. He wanted to make a farm out of the stump-land of his tract; he wanted to see the district converted into teeming fields. But his wants did not stop with this now. He was not quite sure of what else he wanted, but he had a firmly rooted impression that Alice Demaree was concerned in it.

The Co-operative Association demanded much of his time, as he had expected. The tractor, under Shorty Dewar's charge, was on the road working for each member of the Association the number of hours agreed upon. The order of its movements had been determined by drawing lots. Martin had waived his right to its use until the last, having more land broken than the average of his neighbours, and having his mill-engine for use in case he wished to break more. Despite the fact that Dewar ran strictly on schedule, showing no one an hour's favouritism, there soon arose a mild grumbling among the members at the list of the drawing.

Martin had foreseen this, and he spent his time eagerly in soothing the disgruntled and assuring the suspicious. At the same time his spring work must be done. He had hired four Indians and was planting twenty acres to potatoes. It was an amount of acreage unheard of for that crop among the settlers in the district, and he had determined on it partly as a means of encouraging his neighbours to greater efforts and confidence. He realised fully the risk he was running; for a crop failure or a poor price in the autumn would seriously hamper the missionary work which he was attempting.

When he preached his doctrine that the Flat was destined to be one of the richest potato districts in the country he was met by sceptical grins. The settlers, planting among the roots of stumps and cultivating half-heartedly, had grown firmly convinced in the tradition of the district that cut-over timber land was no soil for potato growing. Martin knew there was no oral argument that could convince them that they were wrong, but that the sight of a good-sized field in digging time with large, clean potatoes filling the space between the rows and selling at a good price was what was needed.

One day old Jim Green, returning from town, drove into the Calkins place with a bit of news.

"Marty, d'you know what the Company's doing on their land south of town? Durn'd if they ain't sticking in four hundred acres of spuds!"

"Too bad," said Martin, kicking his planter into the ground. "Everybody knows you can't grow spuds up here."

Green waited in silence until Martin planted up the row and returned for more seed.

"Four hundred acres! How they ever going to get 'em dug?"

"With horse-diggers," said Martin, filling his sack with seed. "The same as we'll all be digging with soon."

"The old hand-fork is good enough for me," said Green.

"No, it isn't, Jim," laughed Martin. "And you know it isn't. If you really felt it was, you'd never have gone in with us on the tractor. You're getting waked up. It hurts at first, I know, but you'll get used to it and when you do you'll begin to like it."

Green's visit brought a sense of relief tinged with elation to Martin. The Starin-Keener Company had the best agricultural advice in the country at its command. The company's agricultural enterprises were based on scientific knowledge. Newly broken land was never at its best until at least the second year; and the company was planting its land to potatoes the same year it was broken. The land was so good—and the Company knew it—that even the partial crop which a new breaking would yield was a paying proposition!

He chuckled as he thought of how this news would affect his neighbours. They might, and would, sneer sceptically at his own venture; but the fact that the great Company, with all its brains and money, was working along the same line would make a deep impression. They would awaken to the fact that their land was full of dollars, would his neighbours, and it would be harder and harder for Keener to buy them out.

When he thought of Keener he recalled his last meeting with him and his thoughts began to wander in unbusinesslike fashion. He remembered the hot-blooded threat he had made to kick Keener off his land if ever he caught him on it. Keener probably had told Alice about that. What would she think of him? What could she think of him except that he was a rough, reckless backwoodsman?

He kept stolidly at his task until the last hill in the last row of his twenty-acre field of potatoes was planted; then, in moments of temporary idleness, his thoughts began to invent excuses for going down toward Camp Bon Air. He had no wish or intention to visit the camp itself, but the lure of life was upon him and it was from that direction that it called.

It was that time of the spring when the sun's rays penetrate down into the cold waters of northern lakes and stir the pugnacious black bass to voracious activities. Now that he had time and eyes for such matters he saw that the bass had begun striking, and on the morning following the end of his planting he rigged up his casting rod and untied his skiff from the dock. The fog still lay in wisps over the water along the shore, but farther out the lake was glinting from the sun. Above a weed-bed within casting distance from the shore a school of minnows, rushing frantically for shallow water, went into the air with a glittering flash of silver, and an instant later the cause of their flurry, a two-pound bass, leapt an struck in their midst with a show of clean, white belly.

Martin had decided upon Clear Lake, where Camp Bon Air was situated, as his fishing ground. He had found his excuse for going down that way. The smashing leap of the bass almost at his own door reminded him that the fishing up there was much better than down in Clear Lake. His mental processes were too direct to hold patiently with self-deception. He went back, hung the rod on its hooks in the mill and set out, paddling with long, deliberate strokes for Camp Bon Air.

XVIII

He paddled without pausing out of Crooked Lake into the Narrows, a shallow channel which joined it with Clear Lake, and went through the channel, shoving hard with his paddle on the gravel bottom. As he slipped between the twin clumps of tamaracks which, on either side of the creek, stood as verdant portal to Clear Lake, he resumed the long, deliberate strokes of his paddle. From the verandah of the camp Alice Demaree saw him coming and, observing the unswerving course which he held for the docks, judged it to be an Indian. When she recognized Martin a smile of triumph flashed for a moment over her face and she rose swiftly and looked outside. Then she came walking indolently down to the dock and reached it as Martin stopped the bow of his canoe upon the beach.

"Uncle Keener isn't here," she said, with a playful smile upon her lips. "He's down at the Falls every day now."

"I know that," said Martin quietly.

She laughed lightly, looking at him through her heavy eyelashes.

"Aunty Keener is inside. Shall I call her?"

"What for?"

"Oh! Then it's Maggie? But you shouldn't come now, you know; she's busy with the morning cleaning."

He sat still, looking at her steadily, and her eyes, toying, playfully, reached to the roots of his heart. At last he said:

"I came to see you."

"Really? But, no; you're merely trying to flirt, like all the men. I thought better of you. Come to see me? Ridiculous! You're too busy to come down here for such a trifling purpose. And why should you come to see me? Don't fib, Mr. Calkins, I know—"

"I came to see you," he repeated.

For an instant she was sobered; a glance at his set face had told her how she had stirred him. She who had played with many men, who was an expert in appraising a man's betrayal of his emotions, knew that never before had she aroused such feeling as this youth betrayed in his quiet words. For a flash she was frightened. The force of him struck her as a warm wind. She retreated a step, then the thrill of it swept her on. She glanced over her shoulder at the cottage and without a word started walking along the beach. She looked back at him playfully, and as he shoved away from shore she disappeared around a tamarack covered point.

When he came paddling up to her in a hidden cove the playfulness was gone from her mien, and she faced him with a serious, forbidding expression.

"You should not do this, and you know it well," she said swiftly. "You know that Uncle Keener does not want you here—after your threat to him."

"That was what I wanted to see you about," said Martin.

"To see me about? Why, pray?"

"To explain. I don't want you to think I'm a tough." He looked at her. "You do think that, don't you?"

With the toe of her tennis slipper she drew a line in the sand and erased it.

"Why do you care what I think, Mr. Calkins?" she said swiftly. "What difference can it make to you?"

"It shouldn't make any difference," he said unsteadily. "A man does what he has to do, and if it's square it hadn't ought to matter what people think about it. But about this—with you—well, it makes the difference—that I feel ashamed when I think of what you probably think of me. You see," he ended lamely, "you've only heard Mr. Keener's side of it."

She turned away to pluck a twig from a tamarack branch, saying carelessly: "Are you sure of that?" And when she turned back the twig was between her red lips. Then she began daintily to pick the green needles from the stem.

"I have heard your side of it, too."

"Where? Who from?"

"Oh, a little fairy whispered it to me." She laughed at the conceit. "An odd little fairy; a funny, homely, freckled little fairy in a worn little gown—who makes troutflies for a living."

At the uncomfortable blush that rose upon his cheeks she smiled and went on: "You know, that little girl, Hattie, who lives in that old tumble-down house on the road? Well, she's a wonderful friend of yours. You should hear her defend you. Surely you must know that you're quite her hero."

"You mean Miss Lee," said Martin. His thoughts and emotions were in a jumble. Somehow he did not like to hear her speak of Hattie Lee.

"Whatever her name is. I met her in the road while out walking the other day." She laughed with a showing of white teeth and throat. "Oh, she made Uncle Keener out quite a scoundrel, and you—you were a great hero. I'm quite willing to believe that version, too," she went on, laughing again. "It—it's most amusing. The squabble men do get into over business! But, seriously, don't you think you were, well, a trifle crude? How could it pay you to kick my poor uncle off your land? Oh, you should have heard him when he told about it! Promise me one thing: if ever you do it you let me have a seat in the orchestra to see the deed done!"

She had turned it all into a farce; to her it was a joke, a thing for ridicule and laugh. He was resentful, but he was also baffled and helpless. He was beaten.

As he looked at her, standing before him like a realised dream of young womanhood, there burst from his lips the confession:

"You are the most beautiful thing I have ever seen. Don't laugh at me, please!"

He trembled when he realised what he had said, but the scene had suddenly turned from lightness to gravity. They looked at one another for one fateful moment, then each looked away.

"No," she said faintly. "Oh, no, no, no!"

"Miss—Alice!" he whispered huskily, stepping toward her.

"No, no!" she gasped. "No. Please."

She stood with her fingers pressed to her lips, her eyes staring blankly out on the lake, and her bosom rose and fell in unison with his swift breathing.

"I must go away," she said haltingly. "I must go back to the city."

"If you do," he whispered, "I will go after you."

"Oh, no. Oh, no, no! You must not—you must not think—Please," she pleaded, "please go."

"I'll go to the city. I won't be a clod all my life."

"Don't!" she pleaded, pressing her hands to her ears. "Don't—please don't."

"Not now," he whispered, "not now. I understand. But I'll try to amount to something. You won't forget? You won't, will you?"

"Don't ask me—don't ask me anything. I won't—I mustn't listen. I didn't realise. Can't you understand? Please!"

"Promise me that you will let me know when you go to the city. Just promise me that. I'll go then; you want to be rid of me."

"No, I don't. Yes, yes; can't you see I want you to go?"

"Promise me you'll let me know?"

"Will you go then?"

"Yes. Promise?"

"Yes."

She threw off the spell, or pretended to throw it off, as soon as he had pushed out from shore. She laughed, waving her hand at him.

"You wretch!" she called and sped out of sight around the point.

The daintily green tamaracks swayed and nodded in the warm spring breeze; a king-fisher, from a perch in a dead pine, hurled itself into the lake with a splash, and, missing its prey, flew screeching back to shore. Straight ahead a hell-diver stuck its head up from the water and promptly dived at sight of the canoe; and Martin, to whom these sights and sounds usually were as music, paddled along as oblivious as an automaton.

He neither heard nor saw. His paddle rose and fell with feverish swiftness; the canoe somehow found the channel into Crooked Lake; but he knew no more of how and why than a man in a dream. He was in a dream. Or was it that he had been dreaming until now and suddenly had been awakened? He was in the midst of a raging storm. And the raging of the storm blinded, deafened and numbed him to all that had spelled life to him before.

Life? He felt that he had not lived before. This was life. He understood that vaguely, though the storm of the senses precluded any attempt at reason. What had gone before was merely preparation, growth; the germination of life forces. Now came Life, tempestuous, omnipotent, ruthless. He had come through the channel less than an hour before, yet now, as he returned, he looked back upon that time as one looks back to a nearly forgotten period in life, or to a dream. And he was not happy. He was even resentful. Was not a man master of his own life?

The city! He had said he would go to the city if she went. And the thought of it shook him; he saw himself a traitor, a self-indulgent shirker of his duty.

When he had emerged from the channel into Crooked Lake he stopped paddling and laid the paddle across his knees and tried to think calmly of what had happened. And then the memory of her last light words came to his aid.

"You wretch!"

And she had laughed carelessly. That was what he remembered most clearly now. It blotted out for the time being the memory of all the rest. Had she been merely playing with him?

The thought was like iron in his soul, and about it his jumbled thoughts and emotions gathered and solidified, like bits of steel upon a magnet. It saved him, perhaps, from the futile mental wanderings and the cessation of ambition which we are wont to diagnose as love-sickness. If she had only been playing with him, and he had taken it so seriously, then he was nothing but a plain fool.

He appraised the whole situation as judiciously as might be, and considering the difference in their circumstances, he came to the humiliating conclusion that such was the description he merited: a plain fool. All right. He was to blame; he had gone out of his way to make a fool of himself. Good enough. But, he thought with a grim tightening of eyelids and of lips, he would be careful to see that it did not happen again. From this time on, no wavering, no nonsense, no thoughts of her. He was young, and full of the confident conceit of youth, and he really believed it could be done.

XIX

The inevitable bickering and dissatisfaction among the members of the Co-operative Association were growing steadily. The settlers who had been unfortunate in the drawing of lots and who therefore were far down on the tractor's schedule began to rue their bargain. They saw the land of their more fortunate neighbours being broken while their own land lay untouched. The spirit of true co-operation was still to be understood by them, and they kicked. They had put their good money into that tractor and they didn't see how they were getting any good out of it. Suppose the thing broke down before it got around to their place?

Martin spent several days on the road, appraising the sentiment among the kickers, and returned home with the fact impressed upon him that under the present schedule the Big Flat Co-operative Improvement Association was doomed to a smash-up. Judging his neighbours in the fair but unflattering scales of familiarity, he calculated that the disruption was due in about a month. Wherefore he did not use the Association's money to pay off the mortgage he had given to secure the tractor, as the agreement had been. Instead he allowed the machine to remain charged against his own land, and kept the Association fund intact in the treasury. He knew he would have need of it.

He had estimated the margin of safety for the Association's existence at a month, and therefore he made his plans so as to have a week's leeway. It was well that he did so, for three weeks later Shorty Dewar, to keep up with his schedule, sought to move by night to the next job. The great weight of the tractor on the soft road discovered the existence of an unsuspected spring beneath the road-bed, and the heavy drivewheels sank gently down and imbedded the machine up to the fire-box.

Martin's conduct then drove the waiting settlers to a display of Curt's unrestrained Anglo-Saxon invective.

"I want men enough to swamp out a road around that spring-hole," said he calmly. "Come on; don't stand around swearing at me. Get your axes and get busy."

He set the example himself and was instantly seconded by Big Jud. Jud was as much in the dark as any of the settlers, but he was greatly pleased. He had been tending tractor until, as he said, he had almost forgotten that an axe was made for anything but cutting roots. Now there was a chance to return for a brief period to true axe-work, and under Martin's lead he slashed heroically into the thicket on the high ground beside the road.

"Shorty," said Martin, "you ain't much good with an axe so you hop in the rig and go and tell Iner Gunderson to come here on the jump. Then go to my place; Simpson got there last night. Tell him to get up steam and drive what he brought up here at once. Hustle now; I'm talking turkey."

By the time young Gunderson had arrived and proceeded to chop like a fiend, the others had begun to take hold. Once they had done so they were caught in the cold, grim blast of energy with which Martin was putting through the job. As always in the face of an emergency he seemed to grow to meet it, and he knew this was an emergency of more import than appeared on the surface. Unless the settlers could be made to work together and, when occasion required, under unquestioned leadership, the co-operative movement was bound to grow shaky and rattle to pieces. It was a test. They would never work together unless they were led, and, in emergency, driven to it. No one else would seek or accept the responsibility of leadership. Therefore, the case resolved itself into a test of himself. Presently the opportunity presented itself. One man stopped work, demanding the road be cut where he wished it.

"You'll cut where I've swamped her out, or you won't cut at all," said Martin. The man was a young settler, who, accustomed to being absolutely his own master, was too much the egoist to labour in unprotesting unison with the others. "You hear me? There's got to be just one boss on this job, and I'm elected."

"Who elected you?"

The gang stopped work for the moment to watch the scene. They had been surprised at Martin's sudden vehemence, but now they saw by his deliberation that it was not due to senseless anger but to a set purpose. He turned on them sharply.

"Stopping for lunch?" he demanded. "Go on with it; keep chopping. Every minute we lose is costing the Association money."

"That's right," said some one. "A tractor's an expensive thing to have idle. Tie into it, boys."

"Now," said Martin, turning to the protesting one, "are you going to fish, cut bait, or get out of the boat?"

"I ain't kicking if the rest ain't," said the man, sensing his isolation.

"Come on, then," said Martin; "you swamp with me."

By the time Simpson and Shorty appeared, driving the second tractor, the one which Martin had secured with the Association's money, there was ready around the spring-hole a new and solid road over which the new engine rolled slowly forward to a position from which cables could be run to the mired machine. An hour was required to drag the latter onto solid ground, and then it was found that it had suffered minor damages which would require a day or two to repair.

"All right, Shorty," said Martin, "get on the new one and drive to the next job and get to work. Simpson, I want you to stay with me. Let's get at it and get this one running."

"Let's have an understandin' before we go any further with this," protested Jim Green. "D'you mean to tell me, Martin

Calkins, that you've gone ahead and put the Association in the hole for a second machine without consultin' any members about it?"

"No, Jim, I don't mean to tell you anything of the sort. I put our subscription fund in the bank; I didn't use it to pay off the mortgage I gave to get the first tractor. I got the new one with that money. The Association is in the hole for one tractor, as our papers read. I'm in the hole alone for this old one."

"Speakin' for myself," persisted the old man, "I can't say I like that kind of dealin'."

"What kind of dealing?"

"It's sharp. It ain't neighbourly."

To control and conceal the exasperation which was within him Martin picked up a wrench and slipped under the tractor to hold the nut on a bolt that Simpson was unscrewing. Lying on his back he could look up through the spokes of the drive-wheel and see Green's bearded chin wagging vigorously in the mastication of fine-cut, and when the beard suddenly ceased wagging he knew what was coming.

"D'you hear?" snapped Green. "I think it's sharp dealing."

Martin gripped the nut and braced himself against the wrench.

"All right, Simpson," he drawled, "I've got a hold."

He had a hope—entirely unjustified by his knowledge of the old man's character—that Green would go away; but when the bolt was free and he came crawling out the old man was waiting.

"We was figurin' all the time," said Green, significantly, "that we owned this puticular tractor."

"You are going to get the use of it—the Association is—as if you did own it."

"We figured," persisted Green, "that it was our'n."

Then Martin turned on him and looked him through for several seconds.

"Let us go on record right here, Mr. Green," he said slowly. "Do you think I am square, or don't you?"

"I ain't sayin' that, Marty, I ain't sayin' that."

"Do you, or don't you?"

"Of course, course. Everybody knows your stand-in'; but—"

"Do you think I'm fit to manage the Association's business?"

"Ain't sayin' you ain't, Marty, but—" Green hesitated.

"But—what?"

"Well, I don't see through it, quite. I never heard of any such dealings before. Why—why in Sam Hill'd you do it? That's what I want to know."

Martin laughed with relief.

"I did it because I saw that one tractor wasn't going to be enough. It was doing the work just about half fast enough to satisfy everybody. I knew you fellows wouldn't come in with another assessment to buy a new machine, so I had to work it the way I did. Considering your case personally, Jim, it just means that you'll get your job done twice as quick as otherwise. Does that mean anything to you?"

"'Twon't cost me any more?"

"Not a red."

"But this machine's your'n," said the old man suspiciously.

"Yes, but it's going to work for the Association just the same."

Green pondered awhile and then looked up swiftly.

"Why you doin' it?" he snapped. "'Tain't business."

"It's the best business in the world," replied Martin. "It's the only kind of business that will pay us up here. I am doing it because every acre of ground broken on the Flat will help raise the value of the land of every man on it, and I've got twenty-five hundred acres. It isn't worth much now. Neither is your section. But when the whole Flat is broken up we'll all be rich, and not until—not until the whole Flat is broken."

While Green was silently assimilating this Martin drew from his pocket a much folded sheet of foolscap.

"We're due at your place two weeks from to-day, eh? Got a pencil, Simpson?" He pencilled an alteration in the schedule. "Be ready for us a week from to-day, will you, Jim?"

Green realised that he was defeated, but he retired stubbornly.

"I'll get ready," said he sceptically, "when I see you comin'."

XX

"It seems to me, young fellow," said Simpson, "that you've taken a pretty stiff job on your hands."

"Darn stiff," agreed Martin. "They're the salt of the earth, but they are stubborn."

"Yes; and that on top of the Company makes quite a load. I suppose you know how they love you?"

Martin nodded.

"You got Keener dead set against you. He thought he had a chance to make a big killing on cheap land here. I've heard that they've been up north and west of the Flat trying to buy up more land and didn't have any more luck than with you Flatters. You kind of woke up the settlers all over this corner of the country and they ain't selling at what the Company figured to pay. So they don't love you, son, and they'll put the screws to you if they get a chance. For God's sake, watch your notes, and don't let any of them fall into the Company's hands. They'll be freezing you out if there's any way to do it."

They worked in silence for a long time.

"Simpson," Martin broke out at last, "the Company could freeze me out alone; they could freeze out half a dozen or a dozen settlers together, probably. But all of us—together—you see, we'll be as big as the Company in time."

"Well—not quite as big," said Simpson after a pause.

"What?"

"You were darn lucky to get this tractor; you know that, boy? Mr. Keener has been to see the Lawston Implement Company. It will be hard for you to get another machine like this if you should want it."

Martin worked in silence for a long time.

"Money!" he muttered finally.

"That's it. Your Association will have a long ways to go before it's as big as the Company. It's the biggest, finest thing ever started in this section, but—"

"Say!" the agent suddenly tapped Martin on the shoulder. "You realise that you're the whole Association, don't you? You're elected for the job of holding it together if it does hold; and if anything happens to you it fails."

"I guess you're right."

"Well, then—I don't want to appear to be telling you your business—but I was fixing the Company's machines the other day, and that Austrian you licked, Bielsky, I heard he's up here in your neck of the woods now. They've got a camp down on Big Squaw Island. Damming up the east channel, you know, so as to shoot all the water down the main stem. That man Bielsky is straw-boss of the gang, and let me tell you, Calkins, he's one—net."

The news was like the clang of an alarm to Martin and to conceal his disturbance he climbed onto the tractor, whistling in such an apparently contented strain that Simpson was deceived.

"You think he'll give you a wide berth after what you gave him, do you?"

"I don't know," said Martin.

He was not thinking of himself, nor even of his job. He was thinking that the farm nearest to Big Squaw Island was Simon Lee's, and that the distance separating them was a scant half mile.

XXI

Once when he was about eight years old while gathering kindling wood in an old slashing Martin had stooped to pick up a great pine chip and had seen the brown, slimy skin of a water-moccasin coiled beneath. It was on a hot mid-summer day and the snake was dozing. Martin, trembling and crying, had gently lowered the chip back in place, then had moved back ten feet or so to get a running start, and, leaping high in the air, had landed with both feet on the chip. The snake never knew what hit it.

At the news that Bielsky was in camp with a gang on Big Squaw Island, his memory harked back to that hot, long-past afternoon in the old slashing, and the same sensation throbbed through his nerves. Since that Saturday in town he had remembered the leer on Bielsky's face as he sneered at the women on the street, because he had never seen such a look on a man's face before—not even among the toughest lumber-jacks; for, though the old-time American woodsman was, at his worst, probably the wildest, toughest creature within the bounds of civilisation, he was never slimy.

There were two Bohunk saloons in Rainy River Falls now, and, while it was common knowledge that they had more than alcohol to sell, the Company had closed its eyes to the nature of these establishments.

"They don't care a darn about the country or the people in it," thought Martin. "All they care about is making money."

That was the trouble with the Company, that was why it was inimical to the settlers. It saw in the great fertile land of Big Flat only an opportunity to make an extremely profitable investment of capital. The productivity of the section meant big crops, and such crops meant dollars. In the most valuable crop of all, strong

115

citizens, which, in spite of its lack of development, the Flat was
rearing even now, the Company had not the slightest interest.
On the contrary, it desired to drive out this independent breed of
settler, and the presence of scores of foreigners would assist in this
process.

That evening after the day's work was done Martin started
for Simon Lee's. When he came to where the road swung near to
the head of Clear Lake, he paused for a while and listened for the
music from Camp Bon Air. But there was no music to-night. He
wondered if Alice Demaree had gone away. At the thought of her
he flushed, recalling their last meeting. And even as he moved on,
urged by a most complete impulse for the protection of Hattie Lee,
he was conscious of the lure that Alice Demaree's beauty had laid
upon him.

He passed swiftly by the Lee clearing without stopping, and
struck off through the narrow stretch of timber lying between
the road and the river. When he emerged from the woods he was
opposite the head of Squaw Island, and, peering across the flood,
he made out the lights of Bielsky's camp. In the darkness he sought
and found a boulder which he knew well and sat down. In another
moment he was up and retreating from the rock, for where formerly
there had been a clean sandy beach the water now was ankle deep.
That puzzled him. It was long past the high-water period of spring.

"They must have had a big rain up North," he thought.

But it would have taken a cloudburst to raise the Rainy River
to that level at this time of the year. He stood for awhile, listening
to the brawling of the swift river, his mind busy with conjectures.
Was it possible that the east channel had been dammed, and would
that make such a difference in the main stream? He went up to
the little bayou where Simon Lee kept his river-boat, but the boat
was gone. He did not relish a long swim in the dark, but he had
determined to see what was being done on the island; so, placing

his clothes on a high, dry boulder, he entered the river and began the swim to the island.

He had calculated that the current would carry him about half-way down the island before he could land, but the instant he struck the full force of the stream he realised that his calculations were amiss. There was a new force in the river to-night, and though he swam powerfully it was not until he was at the foot of the island that he won across. He circled the lower end of the island, and found the east channel. It was now a bed of mud, empty save for a trickle of muddy water in the middle. Moving cautiously, Martin followed the empty river-bed to the head of the island. A temporary dam of piling had been driven across the east channel where it diverged from the main stream. Behind this coffer-dam work had been begun on a concrete structure which was to shut off the east channel permanently.

A hot unreasoning resentment welled up in him as he regarded the alteration wrought by the Paper Company's will. He did not then foresee the ultimate sinister significance of this small dam, the first in the Company's great scheme, but such an intrusion into his home country hurt. And the Company had foreseen that such resentment would arise among the settlers and had prepared accordingly. As he stood in the darkness of the river bank he saw two fires, one near the main channel, where the crew had its camp; the other, a small fire, near the coffer-dam. By the light of the large fire Martin saw the gang's landing place, with Simon Lee's boat tied up at the landing; the smaller fire revealed a short, heavy-set man near the dam, peering into the darkness where Martin crouched.

"Hey, Bielsky!" called the guard toward the camp, "any of your guys butting around the dam?"

"If dey be, shoot dem!" called back Bielsky with a harsh laugh. "It iss an order. We expect attempts to bus' dis dam. Your business is shoot, and let deh Company lawyer attend to deh rest."

"'Tain't none of your bunch then, eh?"

"What matter? Dey are ordered to stay away from dere by night. If dey don't obey, shoot dem. It iss an order. You see somebody?"

"Thought I did. One of them damn hayseeds nosing around, I guess."

"Den you must shoot."

A red flame from the guard's pistol ripped through the night and a chunk of lead went whining through the brush near the dam where Martin had been. He was not there now. He was swimming cautiously around the head of the island to the landing place where Simon Lee's boat lay. By the time the guard had got down to the dam, Martin was drifting easily down current, pushing Simon's boat before him. When he judged it safe he clambered into the boat and paddled across to the mainland. He hid the boat in a bayou farther upstream, and donned his clothes. And then for a brief moment the rage which he had controlled broke forth and mastered him, and he stood lowering across the water at the lights on the island with out-thrust chin and clenched fists.

"Guns!" he growled. "Good God! I wonder what they think this country is; I wonder if they know what they're starting?"

<h1 style="text-align:center">XXII</h1>

He was outwardly calm again by the time he had walked back to the Lees' house, where he found Hattie engaged in wrapping a package.

"Trout flies?" he asked carelessly.

"Yes. It's going in the mail to Chicago in the morning," she said. "I understand you're going there, too, Marty?"

"I—am?" he stammered. "Why do you say that?"

"I heard so," retorted Hattie casually.

"Who from?"

"Miss Demaree. She happened to be over here and she mentioned it to me."

"Well," he said, slowly, "it isn't so."

"She said you told her so."

"I am not going away," he repeated slowly. "And I wish you wouldn't talk about it."

"Haven't mentioned it to a soul, Marty," she said, whisking up the package. "But, land sakes, don't get so flustered about it," she flung back as she left the room. "It's nothing so terrible—nothing to me at all."

While he stood staring after her Simon Lee came into the room chuckling.

"Marty," said he, "I can't get over the way you fooled us on that tractor business."

"Come outside a minute," said Martin.

"Eh?" Lee's smile vanished and his steel-blue eyes ceased twinkling.

"Want a little talk with you—alone."

The older man led the way to a seat on a log outside the house.

"What's up, Marty?"

"I just brought your boat back from Squaw Island," began Martin. "Did you loan it to the Bohunks?"

Simon Lee began to swear. He swore slowly and methodically and with a vocabulary which testified to many winters spent in the woods.

"Did I loan my boat to the Bohunks? I wouldn't loan 'em a boat to row 'em out of the hottest furnace made. Mean to say they had it over on the island?"

"That's where I found it. I figured you wouldn't be over there, so I brought it back. I took a swim over there to see what they're doing. They've got a dam across the east channel, and a guard on it, and he took a shot at me for daring to go near it in the dark."

Simon's natural garrulity and boisterous good-nature dried up suddenly. He sat silent for several minutes.

"Let's have it all again, Marty," he said softly, and when Martin had related his experience on the island, Simon slowly began to finger his beard.

"All right," he said at last in a mild tone. "All right. If that's the way they want it, why, there's nothing more to be said. They can't go doing things like that up in this man's country and expect people to take it and shut up."

"No," agreed Martin, "but we can't afford to have any trouble now. If they come over and begin troubling you, send word and we'll all come running."

"I can take care of my own hen-roost!"

"I know you can. But this is a nasty business and we've got to try to get it settled without letting it break out into serious trouble. Don't say a word to a soul. If the boys hear about the shooting they'll get excited. We don't want that. We've got to try to fix it up sensibly."

XXIII

There was only one way that seemed to offer the possibility of such a settlement, and next morning he swallowed his pride for the nonce and set forth to try it. He knew that it was Mr. Keener's custom to drive in the morning from Bon Air Camp to his office in Rainy River Falls, and while the dew was still wet on the grass Martin posted himself in the road where Keener must pass. When Keener's car finally appeared the young man wished he had chosen some other morning for his attempt, for even at a distance he made out that Alice Demaree was at the wheel. But he did what he had planned—stepped forth into the middle of the road where she must stop or run him down.

He stood there, waiting patiently and grimly while the machine came to a stop. Mr. Keener glared, but Miss Demaree, sensing the embarrassment to both men, was delighted.

Her laughter shattered the silence, but it did not in the least relieve the tension. Then Keener spoke impatiently: "Get out of the road!"

"I have got to have a talk with you first, Mr. Keener," replied Martin.

"Get out of the road!"

A white speck showed in the taut-held muscles on the young man's jaws. He did not trust himself to speak. He stood and looked at Keener, and finally the latter broke out: "I want nothing to say or do with you, Calkins. Our last conversation was final."

"I have got to have a talk with you, and the only way you can get out of it is to run me down."

Keener made as if to alight from the machine, but instead he paused and looked at the young man in the road. Martin stood with his hands on his hips, resting his weight carelessly on one leg;

but as Keener looked he saw that the young man spoke the truth—
he would stay there until he was run down or appeased.

"What do you want? Speak quick!"

"It is about your dam on Squaw Island, Mr. Keener."

"What about it?"

"I want to notify you to have me arrested. I committed a
trespass by going over there last night and looking at your dam."

"What are you talking about? You keep away from that dam,
that's my advice to you."

"Have me arrested."

"Nonsense."

"I demand it."

Keener snorted contemptuously.

"You mean that you make your own law there," said Martin,
"with an armed guard who shoots when he hears a noise in the
brush?"

"I don't know what you're talking about."

"I have come to appeal to you to take that fellow away and to
stop such dangerous methods," he continued. "There is no need
of them, in the first place. This is a law-abiding community. I
will personally guarantee that no settler touches that dam. In the
second place, if you knew the settlers up here, Mr. Keener, I don't
think you'd go using guns."

"I know nothing about all this."

"Keener," broke out Martin impetuously, "I appeal to you as
man to man. You're human, so are we. Take that fellow away and
there'll be no trouble. Leave him there, and if he shoots at anybody
again, somebody is going to get hurt—a lot of men are going to get
hurt. You don't need him, and you nor any other man can afford
to take the responsibility of starting the kind of trouble this will
produce."

"Much obliged," snapped Keener. "Your advice wasn't asked for."

"Man! can't you see what you're starting? Are a few dollars more to you than human lives?"

"Will you please get out of the road?"

"Not until I have your answer."

"My answer is that you may go and see Mr. Bielsky. He is in complete charge of that job. Anything done up there is on his orders, and his orders go."

"Bielsky!"

"He's the man to talk to."

"Bielsky!" Martin stepped to one side. He was through talking. The car swept past, Alice Demaree looking straight ahead. Her cheeks were flushed, her lips slightly parted, and her eyes were aflame with excitement.

XXIV

He stood looking after the disappearing car and saw her turn for
an instant and flash him a look that should have thrilled him, but
now the rays from her eyes fell upon him with no more effect than
sunshine upon white-hot metal. He was half-stunned by Keener's
words. In his heart was the same instinctive anger which would
be aroused in the heart of most of the settlers when they came
to hear about the shooting guard on Squaw Island and Bielsky.
It was an anger of race-pride, an anger of narrow-mindedness,
perhaps, but an anger essentially American. For the root of it was
the stinging thought of Bielsky, a Bohunk, a foreigner, in a position
of authority, giving orders to the settlers, telling them where they
must not go!

Martin went home slowly. First of all, he knew, he must
conquer himself. Recognising the impulse in himself which
had urged him to swift, drastic action, he sensed the manner in
which the less thoughtful of the Big Flatters would be moved
when the news came to them. He had no illusions concerning
his neighbours; he appreciated them for what they were and no
more, and he knew that caution and forethought were not their
strongest points. The day of the logger, of the hunter and trapper,
the day when force was the only argument recognised, was too
recently past in the section for that. There were the Cartwright
boys, long-limbed and yokel-like, who would drive half a day for
the chance of a fight, who shot deer for the market through the
winter, and did it openly, and with whom no game-warden dared
to interfere. Pete Cartwright, thought Martin, would like nothing
better than to drift down the river some night in his batteau to
Squaw Island, draw the guard's fire, and knock him off the dam
with a load of buckshot. And the fact that the Company had issued

orders for the settlers to keep off the Island would have the effect of making many settlers feel that a visit thither had become one of the necessities of life. Martin knew it would, because he felt that way himself.

He was surprised a few days later to find Mr. Sawyer and Judge Holcomb at the house when he came in from his work at noon. They had come up to try the bass-fishing but Sawyer soon drew Martin to one side.

"How is your co-operative scheme coming on?" he asked with keen interest "Are the boys coming in?"

"Oh, yes," said Martin.

Sawyer, recalling the enthusiasm with which Martin had told of his scheme a short time ago, looked at him sharply.

"What's wrong?" he asked.

Martin hesitated. It went against him to seek help from an outsider, but it occurred to him that Sawyer was not an outsider; he was one of the old-timers; and presently he was telling the banker of the situation at Squaw Island. As he hurried through the brief tale the gentle smile on the old man's face vanished by degrees and when the conclusion came Sawyer sat looking pensively at nothing. For he was woods-bred, too, was the banker, and he knew the temper of the men of Big Flat, and he loved them.

"Shoo!" he said softly. "Now they shouldn't do that! no sir-ee, they shouldn't go and do that."

"Have they got a right to shoot at people, Mr. Sawyer?" blurted Martin. "You know the boys will finish it if anything starts."

"That's so, the boys won't be careful—if anything starts."

"Keener doesn't know what kind of people he's dealing with, that's why—"

Martin came to a sudden stop. Sawyer had suddenly looked up at him.

"I am sorry to say you are wrong, Martin," said the banker. "He does know."

"What! He knows that—that this means trouble—bad trouble—and still does it?"

"Yes."

Sawyer cleared his throat softly.

"Mr. Keener has discovered that the Big Flat Co-operative Association is going to keep him from making a lot of easy money—if it keeps going. Consequently he doesn't want it to keep going. Now, he knows how the boys up here will feel about getting shot at if they go near that dam, and he knows that if a lot of the members of your Association should happen to be arrested and indicted and so on you'd have a pretty hard time to keep going, don't you see? Especially—especially if you should be one of those to—well, get in trouble."

"I see."

"I don't believe he is actually trying to start trouble," continued Sawyer. "He's got a right to put a guard there, you know that. But he isn't mistaken about what kind of people he's dealing with up there, or how the boys'll take it; I know that for a fact."

He leaned forward, tapping Martin's knee.

"Calkins, you've got to keep out of trouble."

"Can't be done; when the boys hear—"

"No, no. I don't mean the boys; I know them. I mean yourself. Whatever happens, you've got to stay away from the ruction. Now, don't get hot and tell me you'll be damned if you will: you've got to. In that Association you've started something big. Something bigger than anything ever started up here, something that's bigger than you or any other one man up here. A year from now, if it's still living, it can go on by itself. At present, you're the Association. If you get mixed up in a row something may happen to you, and bang! goes the Association. While the pieces are being gathered up

Mr. Keener will be gobbling the land. That's why you have got to be careful."

"Why," said Martin in surprise, "that's the way Simpson was talking the other day."

"I told him to," said Sawyer. "I didn't come up here just after bass. You're up against a tough game up there, tougher than you know. You're bucking big people, big money. So big that I am not big enough to help you. And if you make one mistake they'll be smart enough to jump in and make the most of it."

"Why can't you help us?" persisted Martin. "Aren't they human? Won't they listen to you?"

"No, they won't listen to me. They know I'm one of the boys up here; I've let them know it. But I've been thinking: there's Judge Holcomb. I'll let him set in this game. They might listen to him."

Martin was not surprised at the prompt manner in which Judge Holcomb responded to the banker's summons; for he knew that Sawyer held a goodly sheaf of the Judge's notes. Martin repeated his story, and at the end Holcomb looked toward Sawyer for instruction.

"Guess you'd better go talk with Keener, Judge," said the banker casually. "We don't want hell to start popping up here on the Flat. The day for that sort of thing is past."

Judge Holcomb bowed in his best manner.

"I shall do so. I shall consider it a duty, a high privilege, to acquaint Mr. Keener with the seriousness of the situation, and to reason with him. As you say, Sawyer, we don't want the fair name of LacClaire County sullied with—"

"Yes, yes," snapped Sawyer. "You go see 'em anyhow."

Holcomb turned solemnly upon Martin.

"Next Tuesday is the Fourth of July," said he impressively.

"So it is. I've been so darned busy I never took time to think of it."

"I presume the good people of Big Flat will celebrate the great day at Lee School-house as usual."

"Yes."

Judge Holcomb sat waiting expectantly, an ingratiating smile upon his large loose mouth. Martin was puzzled. What was he expected to say? He glanced sideways at Sawyer. The old logger's hand was at his ragged grey moustache, hiding the smile that struggled on his lips, but the significant twinkle in his eyes he could not hide. Suddenly Martin understood that Judge Holcomb, also, had come up after something more than bass.

"Judge Holcomb," he stammered, "we haven't got any speaker of the day, and if you—"

"He accepts," drawled Sawyer. "He accepts the duty and the privilege."

XXV

At one o'clock on Fourth of July afternoon the school-house clearing presented the disorderly spectacle of a picnic ground just after a meal. Settlers had begun trickling into the clearing at ten o'clock, but the population of Big Flat was widely scattered, and not until twelve had the last team clanked its way to the hitch rail in the shade of the sombre pines. Many of the celebrants had been driving since daylight. They would now experience for a few hours the novelty of being with a number of their kind, and drive home in the dark, arriving at their clearings in time to start the next day's work. As they wended their slow, jolting way into the clearing—the average conveyance being a lumber-wagon with boards laid across the box for seats—the men shouted greetings at one another, and tied and fed their teams and commented upon the dry spell and the danger of fire, while the women promptly produced the baskets and spread the picnic meal. Now the meal was over, the debris was being cleared up and the celebrating was to begin.

"Where's the Judge?" was the question. "He ought to start things."

Judge Holcomb had not arrived, so Jim Green was chosen master of ceremonies. The Cartwright boys won the foot-race. They won it in a body, each claiming to be in the lead, and in the ensuing discussion Ezra acquired a black eye. But Ezra always did get marred on the Fourth, so the accident was accepted as a matter of course. The tug-of-war was the great event. Jud Hart picked four men to pull with him and young Iner Gunderson did likewise. When the ten men thus selected stepped forward and took hold of the rope old Jim Green, appraising them shrewdly, said: "I cal'late they weigh 'bout a ton"; and if anything his estimate was too low.

It was a long, hard tug. At his end Jud Hart lay on the rope, his heels driven deep in the ground, patiently waiting for the other side to weaken, and at the other end Iner Gunderson did the same. A minute passed. The rope quivered, but the handkerchief tied in its middle moved not to one side or the other. Two minutes. The man in front of Iner was very red in the face. Three minutes. His grip weakened. Instantly the handkerchief flew a foot toward Jud's side, and there it remained until time was called at the end of five minutes.

"Next year we get you, Jud!" cried young Gunderson, jumping up and grinning cheerfully in defeat.

Jud was swelling a little from his victory, but he appraised the young giant seriously.

"'Y golly! Mebbe you will, Iner, mebbe you will. By next year I suspect you'll be grown up to be a purty fair sized boy."

Then came the Judge. He came in Keener's car. Alice Demaree was driving, and the Judge sat beside her while Mrs. Keener and two other ladies from Bon Air occupied the rear seat. The car drew up at the side of the road near the school-house, the Judge stepped out, and the ladies raised their sun-shades and prepared to enjoy the novel spectacle.

Martin found a seat at the fringe of the crowd with his back to the road. Presently he was joined by Simon Lee, and Simon was ill at ease and glanced occasionally into the woods in the direction of the river.

"I wish—" said he at last—"I wish, Marty, that those Bohunks down there hadn't laid off today."

"First lesson in citizenship," laughed Martin. "Wouldn't you have 'em celebrate the Fourth?"

"I would," said Simon. "But, dang it all! I wish they'd done their celebrating on the Island and not come over to our shore. The boys can hear 'em from here. Hark to that!"

From the river bank there came floating through the woods the faint strains of a concertina. It rose and fell plaintively, and with it there came the faint sound of a snatch of song.

"Tantalising, I call it," said Simon. "The boys can hear it, and I'm afraid they'll be strolling over there to have a look."

Big Jud Hart, the Cartwright boys, and those of the younger settlers who had not brought their girls to the picnic, had now drawn apart from the rest of the crowd and formed a group by themselves at the edge of the clearing nearest the woods.

"Big Jud's telling them lies," said Martin as the group gave vent to a roar of masculine laughter. "If he keeps that up it will be all right."

"Jud Hart? Huh! The old bear is the worst of the pack. Ever since he heard there was a fighting man on the Island he's been swinging his shoulders. I can tell Jud when he's hoping for a fight."

"Well," said Martin with a sigh of relief, "here comes the Judge to speak. They won't hear that music now."

Slowly and impressively the Judge mounted the flag-draped stand; the chatter, the laughter ceased, and the Judge began to speak.

He began by reading the Declaration of Independence. From that he ran smoothly into Lincoln's Address at Gettysburg, and having done his duty by the Flag, he appealed with trembling voice for loyalty to the Party. By this latter plea he meant that the voters of Big Flat should, as usual, vote the regular ticket that fall, the Judge being up for election to the Assembly on that ticket at that time.

Suddenly Martin sat up. The sonorous periods of the Judge's speech had lulled him to drowsiness; he had been lazily wondering which was the more useful, a petty politician or a dried up cow, and, with the impatience of the worker toward the talker, had decided in favour of the cow, which could be sold for beef, when he became conscious that Judge Holcomb was speaking in a new strain. Simon Lee had noticed it, too, and the pair started almost as one and looked toward the speaker.

"Capital has favoured glorious Big Flat with its munificent attention. The giants of industry, who provide the power without which our great and glorious nation would be as naught, have cast their knowing eyes upon the Flat and have beheld its glorious possibilities. They have seen what we who know and love the Flat so dearly have known for years, that here is the garden spot of the North. With a hundred, a thousand other regions to locate in they have decided to favour Big Flat."

Martin looked at Simon. The old man was stroking his beard and looking at the speaker through half-closed lids.

"They have decided to shower upon your section, my fellow countrymen and friends, the countless benefits that are within their power. And why? Because the soil is rich, the resources great, the opportunities unlimited? No; not that alone. They have come to Big Flat, my fellow citizens, because they know that we are not a backward people. They have come because here they know we fully appreciate the benefits which a great development will bestow upon us, because here we will welcome capital with open arms, because here property is respected, because here we realise that without capital the country is naught."

Martin was slowly rising to his feet, but the Judge did not see him and rushed on. The audience was under his spell for only a few had sensed the trend and purport of his words.

"All hail, say we, to the great men who will make Big Flat thrive and flourish! All hail to the prosperity they will shower upon this district! And as I close, my good friends and fellow countrymen, I can think of no better words to part with than these: A new era, a great era is dawning for our beloved Flat; let us prove by our actions that we are worthy of this favour; let us hold sacred the property and rights of those who bring to us this great gift!"

There was a volley of applause. Had the Judge read a chapter from the Talmud there would have been applause at the end, though afterwards doubts might have suggested themselves. Simon Lee spat. Martin waited until the noise of applause died down.

"Judge Holcomb," said he, "may I ask you a question?"

"A question?" The Judge was startled. It became very still in the clearing.

"The question is," said Martin clearly, "how much did Mr. Keener pay you to make that speech?"

While the Judge was swelling perilously near to the bursting point with astonishment and indignation Simon Lee drawled:

"Well, I'll bet there'll be a few notes paid in Jim Sawyer's bank to-morrow, anyhow."

Jim Green leaped up from his seat before the speaker's stand.

"And I'll make another bet, Jedge," he shrilled. "I'll bet you don't get a single Big Flat vote come next election."

"I was invited here to speak, not to be insulted," said the Judge gravely.

"But you felt you could insult us, insult our intelligence all you pleased," retorted Martin bitterly. "You thought because we are up here in the stumps, and because we don't know much, that you could take us in with that old, high-sounding wind. You know the fight we're up against, and yet you thought you could come here as our guest, as one of us, and speak for the Company, and we'd be fooled. Well, we're not fooled at all. We know where we stand now. We know that we needn't look for help from anybody but ourselves."

With impressive dignity and set countenance Judge Holcomb stalked down from the stand, across the clearing to Keener's car. And in his heart of hearts he cursed that car and knew he had erred in agreeing to Miss Demaree's insistent demands that she be allowed the privilege of driving him to the meeting. As the car started, he heard the sound which drove all other thoughts from his mind—he heard the foregathered settlers begin to laugh.

"What horrid, unmannerly people!" cooed Miss Demaree sympathetically, but Judge Holcomb did not see the smile that lurked on her lips, nor did he reply. He sat like a dazed man, staring straight ahead, with sagging jowls. That laughter back there was unheard of, it violated all tradition, it was sacrilege. It told of the birth of a new spirit, bred of old experience and new knowledge, among the hitherto docile voters. And in that spirit, should it spread, Judge Holcomb sensed the doom of himself and all his soft-living, shifty, and non-productive breed.

Young Calkins, he recalled, was to blame. He glared angrily back at Martin. Miss Demaree was looking in that direction, too. She delayed the start until she caught Martin's eye, and the look in her eyes said as plainly as speech: "Come!"

XXVI

"Well, what do you think of the old fox?" said Martin grimly.

"I tell you," said Jim Green, shaking his head, "I jest been a-thinking. I been going to p'litical meetings and rallies nigh onto forty year now, and looking back and recollecting's well as I can, all I seem to remember is speeches just like the Jedge made now. They sound purty; I like to hear 'em; confess I felt good while the Jedge was pouring it out—kind-a like hearing an organ play in church. Wouldn't a woke up, either, I guess, Mart, if you hadn't asked him that question. But looking back—hundreds of p'litical speeches I guess I've heer'n—they was all jest about like that: a lot of high-sounding words to make you feel good, and then along somewhere's come the nigger in the wood-pile—what they was after."

"Yah; you right, Yim," said Nels Borg, thoughtfully. "He t'ink he can make fool of us. Vell, I shall vote for Lindstrom, deh feller dat run against him."

"Hello!" exclaimed Simon Lee. "The boys are gone!"

It was true. While the group around Martin had been listening to Jim Green the crowd led by Jud Hart had slipped unnoticed into the woods.

"Can't blame the boys, can't blame 'em 'tall," said Jim Green, vigorously. "Fourth of July only comes once a year. Can't blame 'em for wanting a little fun. Now there's no use getting the women folks all het up 'bout it. 'T won't probably 'mount to anything. You men stay right here's if nothing's happened and I'll stroll down and see how the boys are making it."

"I'll go with you, Jim," drawled Simon Lee. "The rest of you stay here and say nothing."

"I guess I go, too," said Nels Borg.

From the river bank suddenly came a bull-like bellow that shattered the twilight silence.

"Big Yud," said Nels, smiling broadly.

"He's seen his man!"

They looked guiltily around toward the women and then, old men and youths, they broke into a run for the river bank, with Martin well in the lead.

He came with a rush onto the pretty grass-covered opening on the bank which the men from Squaw Island had chosen to desecrate, and one glance at the scene sickened him. Empty and filled beer-kegs, empty whiskey bottles and broken glasses lay scattered about on the grass in profusion, and the odour from their contents, polluting the pure air, stank to heaven. Men lay about in the swinish attitudes of those overcome by liquor. And the liquor was not all.

"Steady, Jud," said Martin; "let the women get away."

The miserable women whom the Austrians had brought from town, to the number of half a dozen, were clambering drunkenly aboard the big working barge which the foreigners had used to ferry themselves over to the mainland. The greater number of the Austrians were doing likewise, and in the rush the women were thrust aside, knocked down, crowded into the shallow water even, while Bielsky was well out in the river, alone in a row-boat, rowing for the island.

Jud Hart was walking with a slow lurching movement up and down the open space before a stocky bull of a man in a red sweater who stood sullenly on the river-bank. Jud was quite happy. He kicked a beer-keg into the stream, spat on his hands and rubbed them together.

"So you're the fighting man of the Keener camp, be you?" he chuckled. "'Y golly! Well, I'm the fighting man of the outfit that's logging against you. 'Bout the same size, we be, too. Mister. Ought to make a good fight. Shuck your hat, Mister, and I'll know what you mean."

Martin looked at the man in the sweater and recognised him as the night guard who had fired at him from the dam.

"What's the matter. Mister?" continued Jud, resuming his restless walk. "Think you won't get fair play? All right; there's a little bayou up here jest around the bend. We'll go up there just you and me and by our lonesomes, and may the best man be able to come back."

Halfway across to the island Bielsky lay on his oars and shouted an order to the guard. The man turned toward the barge, snarling hoarsely over his shoulder:

"Come over on deh island, you big stiff!"

But Jud Hart was not to be so easily despoiled of his fun. With a hop, skip and a jump he placed himself between the man and the barge.

"I got to feel what you're made of, Mister," he said.

The guard's right hand slipped beneath his loose sweater and he said:

"Get out of the way, you big rube; get out of the way or I'll blow your head off!"

Jud Hart stood very still. The good humour of his fighting mood vanished, and his face suddenly became a hard, red mask. As noiselessly as an Indian, bent close to the ground and crouched for a leap, Martin glided for the guard's back.

"Pull that gun!" said Jud harshly.

The guard hesitated.

"Pull it! You rat! Pull it!"

Martin leaped. His long, hard arms clipped around the man's middle like two steel springs. There was a curse, a scuffle; Jud Hart had the gun.

The old shanty-man looked at the big blue revolver in his hand, he looked at the man who had carried it, then he looked at Martin.

""Twasn't even, Marty," he said sorrowfully. "Two of us, and you took him from behind."

He shook his head pensively; his Fourth of July had been spoiled. With a jerk he broke the revolver and tossed the six cartridges into the river. As he returned the weapon to its owner, he pointed to the prominent sight on the long barrel.

"You got any files over on the island, Mister?"

The gun-man paused as he was stepping aboard the barge.

"If you ain't, you go borry one, and you take and file that sight down smooth," continued Jud. "Because next time we meet I'm going to make you eat that gun, and that sight'd cut the lining of your throat all to blazes."

XXVII

Night came, a hot, dry summer night. Darkness found Martin in his skiff, paddling swiftly toward Clear Lake, toward Camp Bon Air.

He went the length of the Crooked Lake without changing his stroke, and with a last mighty thrust sent the skiff flying into the narrows. There he stopped paddling, and let the light craft go of its own momentum. It floated like a duck, seeming barely to touch the water, and it floated steadily on toward the farther end of the narrows, toward Clear Lake, while he sat motionless, the paddle crossed upon his knees. One touch of the blade, and the skiff would have been checked; one sharp stroke in the water and its nose would have been pointed back home; but though his judgment urged him to make such a move, as it had urged him against setting forth, he sat motionless. For the time being he was helpless against the instinctive urge that ruled him, against the memory of the look in her eyes.

The skiff drifted on, its momentum decreasing with each yard, cleared the narrows at a snail's pace, crept into Clear Lake, and then he paddled straight for the cove where they had met before, and as he beached the skiff, whistling softly, Alice Demaree emerged from the shadows.

"Well, stranger!" she greeted with a laugh; and in a moment her spell was upon him.

"Why did you want me to come?" he asked.

"Well!" she gasped. "I can't recollect that I said anything to you about coming here."

"No, you didn't say anything. You didn't need to."

She smothered a laugh of mischievous triumph, whisked her skirts and sat down. He sat at a distance from her.

"I'm sure," she said, "I don't see what you came for if it was only to scold me."

"Scold you? I—scold—you?"

She had turned the tables on him and he was helpless.

He stammered: "You know I didn't—I couldn't—"

"But you did. You know you did. And I don't think it's nice, after all I've been doing for you."

"I didn't mean to scold," he persisted. "I don't know what you mean—that you've been doing for me."

"What did it mean to you to see Judge Holcomb riding in the car of your hated rival?" she asked. "What did it mean to your uncouth friends—pardon me, the other settlers? Wasn't it a shrieking advertisement that the Judge had gone over to the horrible old octopus of a Company? Wasn't it? Well, do you think Uncle Keener was stupid enough to place his car at the Judge's disposal? Or do you think that even the Judge was stupid enough to do it of his own free will?"

"Well," said Martin dryly, recovering some of his poise, "I didn't notice that he was tied hand and foot and thrown into the car."

"Do you know," she said, chuckling, "you have a gift for saying things pithily? You aren't a finished talker, but I really believe you would be if you had proper associations."

"Judge Holcomb, for instance?"

She laughed outright.

"If he didn't get into that car of his own free will," persisted Martin, holding to the subject, "why did he do it?"

"He did it," said Alice, "he did it because he is very vain."

"Vain as a peacock. But I don't see why that would make him do a foolish thing like that."

"Judge Holcomb fancies that he is quite irresistible. Really, he must be quite a lady-killer up here, isn't he?"

"I don't know." It was not a subject congenial to Martin.

"Because he certainly is willing to believe on the slightest excuse that he has made a wonderful impression." She laughed. "Poor Judge! It really was cruel of me, but I couldn't resist it."

"I see," said Martin quietly, "you flirted with him and—"

"I wouldn't call it a flirtation," she said calmly. "It was too easy for that, too much like robbing the cradle. How old is the Judge? Fifty? The old fool! He ought to go around with a nurse."

She looked up archly.

"Jealous?"

"No."

"Not even a little bit?"

"I don't think so."

"He's a fine figure of a man, Judge Holcomb."

"Well, you just called him an old fool," retorted Martin, "so I guess—But maybe that's what you call me."

"No, no!" she laughed. "You're not old; far, far from it."

"A young fool, then?"

She grew serious.

"No. You know I don't. I played with the Judge just—just to help you."

"You shouldn't have done it," said Martin swiftly. "You're Keener's niece; you're living with him, in his family. It wasn't square."

"Pooh! Don't talk to me about 'squareness' concerning my uncle. I know him; I know his business methods and his plans. If he was 'square,' as you call it, I wouldn't have been tempted. His schemings and tricks have disgusted me. It's none of my business. Probably he isn't worse than most, but when you talk of being 'square,' that's nonsense. And then this fat, pompous Judge came. I heard Uncle Keener telling Aunty about how the Judge came to see him. 'Sniffing around for a piece of Company money,' he said. The Judge had a livery team and was planning to drive up to your celebration like an honest, hardworking politician—but he made the mistake of stopping at Bon Air for dinner. He began to exert himself at once to make an impression upon all of us. I was the only one who could stand him, so I monopolised him. He must be a great lady-killer, because inside of an hour he fancied that I was quite hypnotised. And all the time I was wondering if you knew what a traitor he was to you so I thought I had better advertise that fact a little, and made him ride in the car with us. And he fancied it was because I couldn't bear to lose his precious company!"

"His speech gave him away."

"Oh, wasn't that stupid! stupid, stupid! If he had done it cleverly, but so clumsy, so hopelessly clumsy. Tell me, how did such a man ever get elected to anything?"

"I suppose it was because we're more stupid than he is."

"Not you," she said sharply. "You shouldn't adopt that attitude; you know better. You put it all over Uncle Keener that day you held us up in the road, and you put it all over the Judge this afternoon. Stupid? No. Clever—too clever to waste yourself up here. But aren't you going to thank me for exposing the Judge?"

"I thank you for wanting to do it," said Martin. "But I'm sorry you did it—that way."

"I did it for you," she said softly. "I did it to help you."

Though he sensed the dangerous ground they were approaching he said: "Why did you want to help me?"

"I want to see you succeed." She was silent for a moment, then added flippantly: "That's all."

But it was not all. They knew that it was not all. They knew that his success or failure had little to do with the matter, and that the conversation which they had been indulging in was nothing but a mask to hide the real reason for her action, and for their presence there together in the night. But Martin sat motionless, the moment passed, and at last she spoke again:

"I don't think you will succeed without help. You think you will, but that is because you don't understand the power and resources against you. I don't know much about it myself, but I know this: Uncle Keener is absolutely confident that he will have the land he's after—all the Flat along the river—within one year."

He heard her in silence and pondered for some time.

"Do you know why he is confident of that?" he asked.

"No. I've never heard him say. He doesn't say; he just smiles in one corner of his mouth. I know that smile; he uses it when he's got a competitor against the wall. But he is confident. He had his broker up from Chicago some time ago, and they drew up plans for an advertising campaign to sell your land—all the settlers' land—to city investors next summer."

"That's pretty good! Like selling the hide of a bear that's still in the woods."

"Uncle wouldn't plan such a campaign unless he was absolutely confident of getting the land by next summer."

"He must have something pretty good up his sleeve, then."

"He surely has. I can't imagine what it is, but I heard him say to Schwartz—that's the broker—that he'd keep you simpletons so busy fighting Bohunks that you wouldn't have time to suspect where the steam roller was going to hit you. He said—"

"Don't tell me any more he said. I don't feel right, sitting here listening to it. I appreciate it, but it isn't quite the way I fight."

"Pooh!"

"Well, it isn't." He sat with his knees in his hands looking out over the lake, and for a long time nothing was said. Her revelations had had the effect of turning his thoughts and emotions from himself, from her even. The thought of Keener actually planning to realise his profit on the land of the Flat was like a great weight suddenly dropped upon his shoulders. What did Keener have up his sleeve? That was all Martin could think of at that moment, and for once he lost confidence. Keener had spoken of a steam-roller, and that was Martin's sensation at the time: a great steam-roller was rolling down upon his neighbours and himself and whatever they might do they would be crushed.

The depression and hopelessness lasted for only a few minutes, and then the fighting instinct of his breed asserted itself, and he sprang to his feet.

"Maybe that steam-roller will hit us when we aren't looking," said he grimly, "and maybe it will roll us down, but we'll try to bite a chunk out of it before we're rolled flat."

She rose, too. She saw her mistake. She had felt the current breaking between them, had felt his interest turning from her to the land; and she hated that land now, hated it as she hated a rival.

"When we met here before," she began softly, "you said you would follow me when I went to the city."

There was no hesitation in his voice when he replied: "Yes. But I didn't know then what I know now."

She looked at him for a long time, her face turned up, and he saw about her lips the light, tempting smile which seemed a challenge; and the impulse to take her to his arms stirred within him, but he did not move.

"All right," she laughed easily.

"I want to thank you for—"

"Oh, rot! You're as bad as the Judge."

She laughed as she turned away and said: "Ho, hum! And I really thought it was a live man!"

XXVIII

"Keener has something up his sleeve; the Association must grow stronger to buck him; and the one way for the Association to grow stronger is to increase land value, and that means pulling stumps."

This was the slogan that Martin now spread among the members of the Big Flat Co-operative Association. He pounded home the idea that so long as the cut-over lands lay unbroken the settlers were powerless; but the instant the land had been turned into farms they were worth money; and money was power.

During the month of July he kept both tractors steadily at work. Simpson had secured a second engineer for the Association, and Martin himself had gleaned sufficient knowledge to enable him to operate one of the big machines in time of emergency.

The treatment which the tractors received was rough in the extreme, and break-downs were frequent. On such occasions Martin would take charge of the sound engine, leaving Shorty and the new man to devote themselves to the job of repairing. For the big stumps the Association purchased horse-pullers and dynamite.

Most of the settlers possessed one team of large logging horses, in fact most of them had gained the greater part of their subsistence by going in the woods with their teams in the winter-time. Four of the teams, including Martin's, were pooled, and a pulling-crew with four stump pullers was organised and put on the circuit in the same manner as the tractors, with the exception that the man on whose land large stumps predominated, and who therefore would have less benefit from the tractors, was favoured.

Jud Hart had handled dynamite in breaking logjams on the river so he was placed in charge of the blasting. To minimise the danger of the terrible blasting accidents which occurred each summer Martin insisted that individual blasting cease, and that the dangerous work be allotted to Jud exclusively. Having won this concession, he insisted upon each settler turning over any dynamite he might possess to be placed in the Association stock, receiving credit for it at market prices.

His example in putting in a considerable field of potatoes had been followed by most of the settlers who had the land available. As he drove about the country he estimated that there were over three hundred acres planted to potatoes, which probably was two hundred acres more than ever had been planted on the Flat before. The crop was doing splendidly. In spite of the dry season the low-lying flat retained plenty of moisture, and by August first in most fields the tops covered the ground. The bugs were numerous and voracious but this had been foreseen and provided for. The Association had ordered Paris green by the barrelful, as well as the most modern spraying machines.

His love and enthusiasm for the soil and the marvellous power that lay within it received fresh inspiration as he saw in his goings and comings field after field of the sturdy dark green tops of the growing potato plants. In chance moments of idleness he would dig carefully into the hills with his fingers, counting and measuring the young tubers by the sense of feel without breaking the delicate tendrils that connected them with the vine, and he found that the fruit maintained the rich promise made by the tops. In many hills there were already as many as a dozen potatoes the size of hens eggs, and Martin estimated that when digging-time came there would be an average of eight to ten marketable potatoes to the hill.

"They'll go two hundred to the acre all over the Flat!" he jubilated. And as he patted the earth back around a hill he said affectionately: "I knew you had it in you!"

The oat-crop was doing well, but the acreage was small. The usual heavy crop of hay had been cut; the barns were crammed; and huge long stacks, covered with boards or canvas, were to be

seen in every farm clearing. The few settlers who had planted corn
had, as usual, only the poorest of prospects to show for their seed
and labour, and Martin ruminated.

"We can't raise corn and we might as well own up to it.
Ensilage, maybe, when we begin to build silos; but we're too far
north to count on corn as a crop. We can't expect everything; we've
got enough as it is."

August came, and then, in the hottest month of a hot summer,
the dry spell set in in earnest. The rains which had fallen during
July had been sufficient only to dampen the surface of things, and
the long dry periods between had served to prepare a foundation
upon which the heat now built lavishly. The sun beat down day
after day from a cloudless sky. The thermometer consistently
hovered about a hundred in the shade. The clay in the roads was
baked to the hardness of bricks, and the slashings and windfalls
were as so many vast accumulations of tinder, waiting only a spark
to send them flaring into flames.

One day a faint smudge of smoke appeared upon the usually
clear northern horizon. It lay there like a long, faint cloud-bank,
a single sinister island of greyness in the clean blue sea of the sky.
The next morning it was larger. Its colour had deepened and
darkened. It grew day by day. It became a sombre pall, stretching
across the northern heavens from east to west. The sun rose in it,
a sullen ball of red, as if angry at being obscured. The sun set in
it, like a thin red moon, its rays sheathed in the smoke. The hills
about Lake Superior, and in the iron range and the copper range,
were burning, and the fire was beyond control.

Now the air on the Flat was never free from the odour of
smoke. A restlessness grew among the people, among the horses
and cattle, among the wild animals of the woods. Men rose in
the middle of the hot nights and walked muttering about their
clearings. Stolid old work-horses broke into a sudden trembling in

the pastures and charged aimlessly about, their tails up and nostrils wildly distended. The stock which fed in the woods and slashings came into the clearings and stood lowing plaintively though grass and water were plentiful. Deer flashed across the clearings, jumping uncertainly, with nothing visible in pursuit.

Martin grew pale and haggard. He could not sleep. He had forgotten about his fight with Keener, had forgotten the trouble with Bielsky's men, in the inborn dread of the menace which now hung over the district. To the natives of the Flat a forest fire was something elemental, a visitation against which man struggled impotently; and in these trying days and nights of fear Martin fell back into the old point of view. There was nothing that man could do; a rain was all that could help; and the sky above was barren of aught save the cloud of smoke.

In the middle of August a new smoke-bank appeared in the sky on the southern horizon. It grew larger and larger, and more menacing than the cloud in the north. News came that the Big Swamp was burning. The Swamp lay on the eastern side of the Rainy River midway between Big Flat and the town of LacClaire, and no fire upon it had yet been able to jump the river, so the danger to the Flat was small. But the dread of the days had been doubled by the new smoke. The smudge spread over the entire heavens, and the sun was dull red from dawn to dark. There was little wind to speak of, but occasionally showers of cold cinders, carried high and by the force of the flames, would drop gently down upon the Flat.

Martin began to walk the river road at night. By some queer whisper of instinct he had become firmly convinced that the fire would come in the dark. Hope that there would be no fire had gone; it was only a question of when and where it would come. As most of the settlers had their clearings and homes along the road the crude highway to Martin became a patrol line on which, after dark, he walked, seeking what he feared to find. Not until long afterwards did he give thought to the fact that most of his patrolling was done on the stretch of road adjacent to Simon Lee's.

One night near daybreak, as he sat on the school-house steps to rest, he perceived that he was not alone in his restlessness. A tall figure, bent far over, came padding softly along the road. It was Frank White Pigeon, the old Chippewa guide from Camp Bon Air, and at Martin's soft hail the Indian turned in and seated himself on the steps.

"I see your track," he said. "One night, two night, three night. Why?"

Martin replied with a question: "What have you been doing on the road for three nights, Frank?"

"Walk for fire. She's come soon. Smell her. No sleep when I smell fire."

"Neither can I. That's why I've been walking."

"You make good Indian," said White Pigeon. "White man is fool with fire. Indian—long ago—Indian don't have big fire. Indian burn woods every year. Burn leaves, burn brush, burn windfall. No brush in woods then, only the big tree. Indian gallop pony through woods all over then; drive pony with travois all over. No brush; nothing for fire to burn when she's come. Now woods all brush. Fire burn all over. White man do that."

"I guess you're right, Frank," agreed Martin. "But some time we'll have this country cleared and broken up and we'll be rid of the danger of fire."

White Pigeon nodded reluctantly.

"But she's not clear yet," he said, sniffing the smoky air. "Plenty left here for big fire."

For two nights more he met the old Indian at the schoolhouse and exchanged a few words. On the third night, on his first march down the road, he perceived a figure on the schoolhouse steps and greeted: "How, Frank."

There was no response. The figure sat huddled up, its face hidden, an indistinguishable lump in the darkness, and Martin turned in and approached the steps. A titter of laughter greeted him, and as he stopped in amazement, the wrap which shrouded the figure was thrown aside.

"Boo!" cried a voice, and he saw the laughing face of Alice Demaree.

"What in the world—?" he began, but she rose to her feet saying: "Frank told me. I've just come to say good-bye. I'm going home to-morrow."

"Going home?" he stammered.

"Yes." Her manner suggested that she intended to be off in another moment. "Going to-morrow."

She looked up at him; she looked away; and then they were silent. The night noises seemed to hush about them. Perhaps the noises did not hush; perhaps it was only that the pair did not hear them. They were in a void, in a primal world inhabited only by themselves; and the darkness was as a cloak that sheltered them both beneath its folds. And this time she did not make the mistake of introducing anything else in their conversation. Her eyes talked, her whole feminine being was eloquent with the old, dominant tongue of sex. He stammered clumsily in his efforts at conversation, and she replied not at all. She only waited.

"Then I won't see you again—until next year?" he said.

She looked up, and she smiled mysteriously. Soon she held out her hand for the parting. She was all confidence. When she felt his hand trembling about her soft fingers she threw up her head, her eyes a-gleam, her lips parted. A laughing sigh, half-triumph, half-contentment, escaped her lips as he yielded to her and drew her in his arms. But at the touch of her he went mad. He swept her off her feet as if she had been a child; his hard arms clasped her like iron to his breast; and he kissed her so she cried out in alarm.

"Oh, no! No!"

But her lips wandered back seeking his.

"Put me down. Do put me down."

He obeyed, and she moved a step backward, laughing softly.

"You devil!" she murmured alluringly. She put her hands to her hair and stood smiling at him, and, responding to the invitation, he placed his arms about her waist and drew her to him again. Her arms went about his neck; and then, in the midst of his madness, his sanity returned. The words of passionate declaration rushed to his lips, but he paused. Was it something that he had heard? Had some one or something spoken to him? He looked over her head into the woods, and the woods answered back with a primitive silence.

"There!" She had released herself in an instant, and sprung away. "Enough is enough. Don't you come near me," she warned laughingly. "I'm afraid of you. Oh, what a wild man!"

"What did you expect—up here in the woods?"

She looked at him a long time.

"I'm going to tame you."

"What?" He scarcely heard her. He was troubled. Had he heard something? What was it that disturbed him?

"Yes; I'm going to tame you; I'm going to civilise you. You're too wild now, but you'll do nicely tamed. Don't follow me, don't you dare."

He had not intended to. He felt rooted to the spot. She held out her hand again, but drew it back playfully.

"No. I won't touch you. You're dangerous. Good-bye."

XXIX

He stood staring into the gloom of the road whither she had sped, and he was like a drunken man who has been roughly half-sobered. The intoxication which she had wrought upon him had fallen from joyous exhilaration to dull pain. He longed for her, longed for her to return, longed to run after her. But he did not move.

The darkness seemed to whisper warningly at him, and the peace of the soil had been taken from him. Peace! There was no peace. The primitive night and the eternal calmness of Nature seemed sibilant with the warning which had checked him when he held her, warm and throbbing, against his breast. He knew that there had been no whisper, no voice that ears could hear, and yet he listened, his senses abnormally sharpened; and only the commonplace night noises of the woods were his reward. There was—Something. Something older than speech, perhaps; something as old and strong as the life-force which had thrown the pair, man and woman, into each other's arms this night, and he began to move down the road, puzzled, dumfounded, but alert.

He went like a man groping in the dark for something unknown, and as he paused, to listen, though he knew there was nothing to hear, he felt his heart beating wildly, and he was breathing in short, quick breaths. He walked on, and paused again, and now he heard something real. The sound came nearer. It was the sound of soft light feet running toward him through the darkness down the road. It must be Alice. What was she coming back for?

A lithe figure flashed across a light spot in the road, a figure running with the spring of a deer, and Martin gasped and ran forward to meet it.

"Hattie!" he called hoarsely. "Hattie! What is it?"

She stopped as a man stops when he meets the bullet that deals him his mortal wound, and caught at her breast, swaying back from the shock of his presence.

"Marty!" she breathed.

He did not stop to reason that coming up the road she must have met Alice Demaree, so he misunderstood her cry of anguish.

"What is it?" he cried. "What's the matter?"

She stood in her stricken attitude for seconds, looking at him with anguish in her eyes, and her mouth worked piteously. Then her strong, light figure straightened with a jerk. She squared her shoulders boyishly and her head went up while her little mouth grew firm.

"Have you been blind, Marty, have you been blind?" she gasped, pointing with outstretched hands to the north, "Look around; look back of you!"

He looked. He did not start or exclaim. At what he saw his senses cleared and in an instant he was his own man again. Straight up the road to the north a glare of red showed in the sky. A second glare appeared to the west of this one. The fire had come, and it had come in the north.

"Broke out in two places at once," he said quietly. "That's funny. How'd you come to see it, Hattie?"

"How could I miss it?" she demanded. And added: "From my window."

"Weren't you asleep?"

"I couldn't sleep. I couldn't get to sleep. I felt as if something awful was going to happen to-night, and—I guess it has."

Martin was estimating the distances to the fires.

"That one straight north will be about in that old slashing back of Gundersons'," he ruminated aloud. "The other one—let's see."

"Oh, Marty!" she cried, "you know where it is; it's up in your young pines."

"I doubt it," he said calmly. "It looks a little too far for that. Across my line over in the Cartwright clearing, it looks like to me. Where's Simon?"

"He's hitched up and gone down the road to get Nels Borg and Curt Harmon."

"All right. When he comes back tell him to get at the one up the road with all the men he can get. I'll go after the one over west. We've got to try to keep them from joining."

"It's in your pines," she murmured, looking toward the red glade in the northwest. "I know it is, I know it. Oh, those beautiful young trees! Don't wait for me, Marty; I know I can't keep up with you, and you mustn't hold in. Hurry, hurry! Don't mind me."

He looked at her sharply. Her expression hurt him; for he saw that she wished him to leave her, that she did not wish him to be near. But it was a moment of dire emergency and no time for pausing for explanation. He said: "All right, Hattie; be careful," and began to run.

XXX

The sensation uppermost in the tornado of his emotions was one of relief. The tension was over; the fire had come. No longer was there the need to live in a condition of suspense, of fear and worry. Remained only the fight. And he was satisfied. As in the quarrels of his boyhood when the first blow struck relieved the suspense aroused by wordy bickerings, so now the sight of the flames relieved the strain he had been living under. In those first minutes when he ran like a racer up the dark road toward the red glow he saw things with a clearer vision than had been vouchsafed him for months. The memory of Alice Demaree was like ashes in his mouth. Whither had he been drifting? And Hattie—!

But there was no time for retrospection now, no time for thinking. Only time for action, for getting one's hands on the task at hand and fighting it to a finish; and being a worker, he knew the peace of the worker with plenty of work ahead.

As he raced into his home clearing he saw the light from the kitchen window reflected in the lake and knew the news had sped ahead of him.

"Where you been?" snapped his mother. "Jud's been gone ten minutes. Frank White Pigeon woke us. They said to tell you they'd gone toward Cartwrights'. The other one's about at Gundersons', ain't it?"

"Just about."

"Do you reckon this one is in our pines?"

"Don't know. I'm going to find out; you'd better go back to bed."

He gathered to him an axe and a rake and ran across his open field toward the fire. From the field he went into the stump land and presently he reached the ridge which ran north and south near the western boundary of his property.

The glow in the sky was larger and fiercer now; he could hear the flames crackling; and for a while he thought that the fire must be feeding on his tract of young pines. Soon he saw, however, the black tops of the trees silhouetted against the fiery glow beyond and knew that the pines were for the moment untouched.

The fire lay to the west of the trees. There were some two hundred acres of white pine in his pinery, young trees, too small to cut, which he had brushed and limbed and was saving. In time there would be a small fortune in the pine if the fire spared them, but though he recalled this fact as he ran on it appeared of small significance to him in the instinctive desire to get at the fire and put it out at all costs.

He splashed through Otter Creek, the small river which bounded the pines on the east, without troubling to hunt the ford, and went through the forest of clean, straight-trunked trees with its carpet of needles unmarred by brush or windfall. Emerging from the western edge of the woods, he saw that the fire lay beyond the big slashing on the Pete Cartwright place; it had burnt over a field of stump-land and was raging wickedly in a stretch of jack-pine beyond the slashing.

"If it ever gets into the slashing we can't hold it," thought Martin, and, leaping from one windfall to another, made his way swiftly to the fire-line in the jack-pine. Men were working frantically at a trench to the west of the timber-strip; others were raking a clear space beyond the trench; others were plying a back-fire to meet the growling flames.

"How about the other side?" asked Martin.

"She burnt herself out that way," panted the new tractor engineer. "Started right in the stumps; too bad, you know, the tractor—"

"All right," said Martin quietly. "How about the ends of her?"

"Stopped," growled Jud Hart. "Pete's spud field stops her on the north. On the south she's reached the west branch of Otter Creek and can't cross. But she's coming east, boy, and we've got to stop her here."

Martin looked at the roaring, tossing storm of fire and nodded. It was not a big fire yet. Its front probably was less than half a mile. Because of the scantiness of the material it was feeding upon it had not yet assumed the hurricane-like menace of a true forest-fire. In flashes, as it licked out and feasted upon heaps of brush, isolated trees, and juicy saplings, it assumed this roar, swirling and thundering up toward the skies, its voice a threatening brawl. Then it would subside, burning steadily, seeming to gather its energies for the next uproar. If it ever reached the jack-pines it would really begin to burn.

Fortunately there was but little wind, so there was a chance. But the smoke was terrific. Because the fire burned mainly close to the ground the smoke did not ascend but rolled along belt-high, impelled eastward by the movement of the flames. The men nearest the fire were coughing badly with the exception of Frank White Pigeon. The old Indian was starting back-fires so close to the big fire that others constantly shouted at him to come back. On his hands and knees, his face close to the ground to avoid the smoke, he crawled before the advancing flames with a burning ember in his hands, cunningly cheating the conflagration of its richest food with his back-fires.

"We'll stop her here," said Jud.

"We'll have to," agreed Martin, and began to work. He saw that the space which was being cleared before the jack-pines was only half wide enough, and with a shout that put new life into every man there he announced the fact.

"Twice as wide, boys!" he shouted. "Throw that brush another rod toward the fire. Jump at it. We've got to hurry."

He estimated the distance and speed of the flames and saw that the trench could not be completed in time.

"Good enough, boys!" he shouted at the diggers. "Throw your dirt farther toward the fire."

He was up and down the line, from one end of the danger line to the other, working, commanding, encouraging. He shouted for Jud, and with him set to work felling the out-standing trees, dropping their top toward the fire.

"Marty," panted Jud, when the timber-line had been hewed straight, "we ain't going to make it."

"What?" screamed Martin. "What do you mean?"

"Old Frank's coming back. Look." Silhouetted against the flames they saw the bent form of the old Indian staggering toward them.

"Get to work!" roared Martin at Jud. "What's that got to do with it?"

"Quite a lot," said Jud. "But I work when you say so, Marty."

White Pigeon staggered, coughing, into the open space.

"Smoke coming," he coughed. "Bad smoke. Close to the ground."

"Faster, boys, faster!" yelled Martin. "Get it cleared, for God's sake get it cleared."

Pete Cartwright, on whose land the fire was burning, had retreated into the jack-pines and was sitting down.

"Let 'er burn," he said. "Whole farm ain't worth killing myself for."

But at the devil that flared in Martin's eyes he rose uncertainly.

"Get up, Pete," said Martin. "Get up and get back there, or I'll break you in two. Your farm! Man, we're fighting to save the whole district. If she gets into this timber she may sweep the whole Flat. Get busy!"

The cleared space between fire and timber grew steadily larger and cleaner. The men were fighting as if at grips with a personal enemy. Smoke clouds drove them back for a moment, then panting, stumbling, cursing, they rushed back to their former positions. The flames advanced, the heat grew unbearable, and they retreated slowly and stubbornly, turning their backs on the fire to save their eyes from the heat. The exhilaration of fighting mounted to their heads, in spite of the deadening heat and smoke, and they cursed and roared at the brawl of the flames.

"We'll lick it!" cried Martin.

"We'll lick it!" rang the jubilant cry. And then the smoke struck them. A man in the act of throwing brush toward the flame caught it first. He dropped slowly and Jud Hart who was near him managed to drag him back to the timber where both fell flat.

"We go now," said Frank White Pigeon.

The smoke struck Martin and Pete Cartwright at the same time. It blinded and choked them and only by instinct did they manage to drag themselves back.

"Boys all safe?" asked Martin, when he could speak.

"All safe," said Jud.

"We go now," repeated the Indian.

Martin tore a dry pitch-branch from the nearest tree, put a match to it and crawled out across the safety zone, and touched off the long brush pile which had been stacked for the back-fire. But now nothing could stop the timber from going.

"No use cursing," he said, when the men were panting in the temporary shelter of the woods. "We've got to fall back and start a new line. We've got to make sure this time. It will have to be in my pines. We'll drop a good big swath of them this way. Then we'll burn 'em and try to keep our fire from getting back on us. If she does come back and get past us, all right; we'll burn the whole patch back to Otter Creek. We can handle that fire there."

"Other fire go down little," said White Pigeon.

They looked to the east. The glow in the sky there had diminished. It was no longer an angry glare, but appeared subdued both in size and colour, as if surrendering to man's will.

"Well, they could get more men up there in a hurry," said Pete Cartwright.

"They had more ploughed land up there," said Martin.

"Hnn-nah!" Old Frank was standing with his face upturned toward the reddened sky. "Now we look out. Wind come soon."

XXXI

Martin lifted his face and drew in a full breath, and in an instant
was coughing and choking.

"Not a sign of wind, Frank," he spluttered.

White Pigeon stood as he was, the light from the flame-lit sky
reflecting upon his dark, moist skin.

"Wind come. Soon daylight. Wind come just before daylight."

"Which way will she blow?'"

"Blow east. Blow hard. That other fire go to river. You see."

"How far will this one go?"

"Till she hit where other burnt."

"No!" said Martin quietly. If Frank's prediction came true the
middle half of the Flat would be fire-swept, with a high probability
that the flames would spread north and south and complete the
job. On the other hand, if the fire could be stopped in the middle
the ends could be taken care of.

They retreated from the terrific smoke and heat of the flames,
and on the higher ground at the edge of Martin's pines they halted,
a panting, harried group.

Jud Hart struck one of the slender pines with his fist and swore.

"Let's try it here," he growled. "Here's the last good pine left in
the county. Let's fight her again before we give 'em up."

"Sure," said Pete Cartwright. "This timber's worth more than
my whole farm."

"No good," said Martin. "She'll fly when the wind comes. We'd
never stop her here, and then we couldn't hold her at the Creek."

"What say, Frank?" demanded Jud.

"No good. Hear wind."

A faint puff of breeze swept through the pines from the west,
and the branches swayed with the mournful sough. It was as if the

trees were singing their own requiem. Martin looked up around at the smooth, graceful trunks, he looked up at the branches, now rosy with the reflection of the fire. He had seen those pines grow from mere saplings; he had expected to see them grow to majestic trees, but to the westward the fire roared with fresh menace, as its advance flames bit into a bunch of windfalls.

"Come on." He led the way through the pines on the run and down to the bank of Otter Creek. There was no time to lose. The back-fire must be started before the wind rose sufficiently to carry its flames back across the creek. The men plunged into the creek like tired cattle, gasping with relief as they wallowed in the ice cold water, and as they rested for a moment Hattie and Simon Lee and Curt Harmon came springing across the stones that served as a ford.

"Go back, Hattie, go back!" shouted Martin. "Simon, you shouldn't bring her here now."

Simon paid no attention. He stood looking westward, his jaw hanging, and Hattie looked at Martin's haggard, scorched face and knew the worst.

"Oh, Marty!" she whispered. "You don't mean—you don't mean that it's driven you back to here?"

"Yes. The Creek is the line now, and we'll be lucky to stop it here with the wind rising."

"But, Marty," she stammered, "your pines—those beautiful young trees! They aren't going, are they? Can't we save them?"

"Come on, Mart," said Harmon gruffy. "There's two more of us now. Let's tackle it west of your pines."

"No use, Curt. She's hit the slashing by now."

A fresh gust of wind swept over the pines, and the soughing song of the tops grew louder, more mournful.

"That settles it," said Martin, drawing out his match-box.

The other men began stringing out along the creek, starting tiny fires as they went. White Pigeon lighted a dry tamarack branch and dragged it through the grass behind him, leaving a trail of fire where he went. A few minutes of frantic running and scurrying and the deed was done. The fire licked nimbly through the grass on the creek bank, then turned westward where more food awaited it. It ran through the dry stuff and the creek bottom and reached the pines. Suddenly its snapping and crackling ceased. There was a lull as if it gathered itself for fresh efforts, as the swift-burning grass and brush gave out, and it began to nibble at the needle-carpeted ground, and at the pitch about the roots of the trees. For a space it seemed as if the fire had lost its lust for destruction. And then, finding the food rich, it threw itself like a roaring, laughing demon upon the pines.

The panting men, on the creek bank, leaned upon their tools, in silence, and watched it burn. The situation was out of their hands; it lay with the new force which they had unleashed. If the back-fire could burn up the greater part of the pines ere the big fire arrived the conflagration would be halted.

The wind was rising now, and the big fire was roaring through the slashing with the noise of a hundred blast furnaces. But the back-fire was gaining too. The solid wall of flames beyond, and the forest itself, served as a wind-shield beneath which the flames ate avidly into the woods to the westward. Some one groaned as the first tall pine fell, with a leaping of flame like a thousand sky-rockets, and Simon Lee said gruffly:

"Come, girl; we'll be going."

They retreated across the creek one by one, and Hattie went on, unable or unwilling to look back at the forest's tragedy. Two great fires were billowing and roaring in the trees now. The first fire had swept the slashing. It flung against the far edge of the woods with a rising note in its bellow. It rose as it struck the trees, as tornado-driven waves rise against an obstruction, and swept on, higher, fiercer, louder than ever, engulfing tall trees as if they were matchwood. Note for note with it, and flame for flame, the backfire flung its seething self higher and higher. Behind it lay the smoking wreck of a good half of the pines.

The two fires seemed to shriek as they met; for an instant there was a pause, as of two waves meeting and breaking and going to pieces. Then the last of the pines went up in a frantic holocaust, the momentum of the greater wind-driven fire triumphed, and the flames came rushing on to the creek. And then they died down with a sudden growl. The back-fire had done its work well. Where it had burned there was nothing left for the mass of fire to feed upon. The flames grew lower and lower, the skies grew dark again, the roaring decreased to an angry rumble, and the smoke began to spread in dense, choking clouds.

Dawn came to the Flat at last, a dawn of smoke choked sky and red sun, and of stretch after stretch of charred, smoking woodland; a dawn such as the Flat had frequently seen before, but such as it was never to see again. To the inexperienced eye it must have seemed that the catastrophe was complete. Through the bitter smoke one could see little else than the ugly signs of the fire's passing. In spots the fire still burned briskly. But the men of the Flat knew they were fortunate. The fire had eaten its way through the heart of the district, but the homesteads, thanks to the foresighted burnings following the Fourth of July, had been saved. Except Pete Cartwright's. He had been too lazy to burn his clearing and had lost everything but the clothes he stood in. Considerable hay had been burned, and some stock had gone mad and dashed into the fire. Thousands of dollars' worth of pulp-wood and logs had been consumed. But the people who gathered at daylight around a figure on a blanket in the Gunderson clearing compared stories and knew that in the main good fortune was theirs.

"Well," drawled Jim Green, looking at the figure on the ground, "I guess he's going to make a live of it, after all."

"Live? Hell, what you talking about?" came a faint voice. "How 'bout the tractors?"

It was Shorty Dewar and he had been badly smoked for persisting in his futile efforts to get up steam and to run his tractor out of danger.

Then the ugly news came out. The fires had broken out simultaneously in the fields where the tractors had been at work, and both machines were now hopeless wrecks. When news came that Bielsky and the night guard at Squaw Island had quit their jobs and left town on the morning train, this mysterious coincident was explained.

Late in the afternoon the last fire was out and Martin sat heavily on his doorstep beside his mother and looked out upon the scene of charred desolation. But he soon turned his eyes to his fields, and he saw the ploughed land, and the crops growing sturdily.

"Well," he said cheerfully, "the land's still there; they can't destroy that; and the people can do without almost anything else if they've got the good old land.'"

XXXII

The much-hoped-for and prayed-for rain came two days after
the fire had been stopped. It was a big rain. It came in the middle
of the night, a soft, steady patter on the roofs, which gradually
grew into a terrific drumming as the long-dry heavens opened
themselves and poured a flood upon the parching earth. By
daylight the Flat was drenched. By noon, when the rain began
to falter, it was soaked, and in the afternoon, when the heavens
cleared and the sun appeared, the brilliant rainbow which
announced the end of the shower was reflected in a hundred pools
and puddles of cinder-clogged water. The creeks, the rivers and
lakes rose, and on the surface of them rode a scum of ashes, of
burnt brush and charred debris.

The burned-over sections of the Flat lay ugly and sinister, black
and grey, after the washing, but the pasture lands which had been
saved, and the ploughed crop fields, seemed to drink in the water
and fairly leap with a shout of gladness into new life. It was as if
the land had all but died, had given up hope for that year, and
then had had new life, green and joyous, pumped into its veins by
Nature's beneficence.

"I guess the good Lord knew what he was doing when he
held off that rain until after the fire," said Martin's mother firmly.
"'Whom the Lord loveth he chasteneth.' I guess he knew that there
are a whole lot of lazy, shiftless people on this Flat who need a good
chastening every once in a while, and He let them have the fire
first and the rain afterwards so they'd be properly chastened and
appreciate the gifts He bestows upon them."

"Well," said Martin, "that may be so; but in this case it doesn't
scarcely seem that the Lord would have had a hand in it."

"He has a hand in everything. Don't you ever forget that, Marty."

"All right. But I suspect that whiskey was pretty much responsible for the fire, and I doubt a whole lot that He has any hand in whiskey. Bielsky and Farrell went to town and got lit up and bragged about getting even with us until Keener had to fire them. He didn't warn us, of course, just fired 'em, so the Company would have clean hands. Then Bielsky and Farrell disappeared from town and weren't seen between nightfall and the time they staggered out of the bush and hopped the morning train. The tractors were about three miles apart, but somehow the fire broke out on both of 'em at the same time during the night. You may be right, mother, but it looks funny to me."

"'The Lord moves in a mysterious way His wonders to perform,'" quoted the little old lady staunchly. "Don't you ever forget that, Marty. Folks around here may be a little more careful with matches after this."

Days of depression and discouragement followed the fire. The actual losses which had been suffered were not responsible for this mood. But the owners of the burnt-over tracts were gripped by the sickening sense of defeat. What was the use of breaking one's back pulling stumps if the fire was to come along every so often and wipe the place out? There were disadvantages a-plenty in the task of making a living on the Flat; the stumps, the short growing season, the long, hard winters. And in every dry spell in summer the menace of fire.

In previous years when a fire had visited Big Flat the old Logging Company, which in its old-fashioned, inefficient way had sought to populate the district, had been in the custom of coming to the prompt rescue of those who had suffered. Lumber to rebuild destroyed barns and houses, new agricultural implements, and supplies of many sorts, had been issued from the Company's stores on an easy-going system of long-time credit. The old loggers who owned the company also had owned a bank in LacClaire—the

Rivermen's Bank—and in those days there were few of the settlers who did not have one or more notes lying in this bank's vault. There was never a case known where the Company Bank had refused to renew the note of a settler who had been hurt by fire.

But that day was gone. The Logging Company had sold out to the Starin Paper Company, and the bank had gone with the sale. The old-fashioned, inefficient ways had disappeared. Competent, modern business men, headed by Keener, were now administering the benefits of Capital to the district.

The first evidence of this administration might have been read in the sudden appearance of a sign over a store building on the Main Street of LacClaire: "Northern Real Estate Company. Cut-Over Lands Bought and Sold."

Shortly after this an agent of this Real Estate Company made his advent on the Flat. He visited by some strange chance only such settlers as had suffered from the fire, and who were unfortunate enough to have allowed their notes and mortgages to remain in the Rivermen's Bank when the Paper Company had taken it over. The agent first drew a sad picture of the future of Big Flat. In the depressed settler he found a ready audience, ready to agree that it was hard to make a living in that country, and that a man was better off any other place, where fires did not occur.

The weak point in the agent's efforts was that after analysing the faults of the Flat and picturing it as about the worst place in the world a farmer could be, he was forced, in order to fulfil his program, to make an offer to buy. Life among the stumps does make a man prone to quick decisions. Despite the agent's convincing evidence that the only sane thing to do was to sell, the settler invariably decided he would have to think it over. Thinking it over inevitably evolved the troubling question: "If this country is such a hopeless proposition, why do you want to buy?" The agent's answer that it was a speculation was scarcely convincing.

Martin was puzzled at first when he heard of the agent's appearance, but he soon understood the significance of the stranger's efforts. By this time he gauged Keener's character quite thoroughly and knew that Keener would not permit a competitor in the field. It would be typical of Keener—good business—to try to buy while the settlers were down on their luck. When he heard that the agent had hinted to such settlers as were heavily mortgaged in the Rivermen's Bank that they might be losing their places one of these days, he saw what the next move would be, and he went to see Mr. Sawyer, the old banker at LacClaire, in an effort to forestall it.

The banker asked one sharp question after Martin had spoken:

"How are crops up there?"

"'We will raise sixty thousand bushels of potatoes on the Flat this year, Mr. Sawyer."

Sawyer's white eyebrows rose in surprise. "'All right,'" he said, "tell the boys I'll do it."

One day soon after the real estate agent had returned to LacClaire without having managed to close any deals, a number of settlers received notice from the Rivermen's Bank that their note, or mortgage, was due, that there would be no renewal, and that steps would be taken in three days to secure payment.

It was a severe shock to Keener when the various notes and mortgages were satisfied promptly. He made the mistake of threatening to ruin Jim Sawyer, detailing the power he possessed to put the old banker out of business.

"Well, all right, Mr. Keener," drawled Sawyer, "but let me tell you something: don't you wag that darn forefinger of yours at my nose like that. I never did like to have a man do that."

When Martin and Sawyer held their final interview on the matter of the notes the banker asked:

"Does your potato crop still look good up there?"

"Yes."

"Is it far enough ahead to be safe in case of an early frost?"

"The crop is eighty per cent made right now, Mr. Sawyer; we got 'em in early this year. I think they'll average close to two hundred to the acre right now."

"Potatoes ought to fetch about seventy-five cents a bushel this year," concluded Sawyer; "but if they don't you know you'll come pretty near to finding yourself in a bad hole. These figures total—"

"Don't tell me, please," said Martin swiftly. "I've got enough to worry about as it is. We've done our darndest, and now it's up to the land."

XXXIII

The destruction of the two tractors had dealt a severe blow to the spirit which had begun to grow among the members of the Big Flat Co-operative Association. The grumblers had their inning:

"There you are. See what happens to those new things. Now we're about ten thousand dollars out, and what have we got to show for it?"

They had, as a matter of fact, more land ready for the breaking plough than had been prepared in five years previous, but this was not allowed to have weight with the chronic fault-finders. The existence of the Association was threatened. It was out of the question to think of buying another tractor until after potato digging, when the settlers would have more money than they ever had before and might be reasoned into making a fresh investment. In the meantime there were several comparatively idle weeks until digging time. This was the time when Martin had planned to drive the co-operative idea a little deeper into his neighbours' skulls. Haying and harvesting were over; threshing done; cultivating was finished for the season; the potato bugs were killed or the plants were too well grown to be hurt; and the settlers had little urgent work to occupy them.

The tractors were gone, but men, and teams, dynamite and stump-pullers remained. The Association rented teams from the settlers owning them at an agreed price. Each man's labour was similarly hired, and if a man could not furnish either team or man, and secured the benefits of the Association, he was charged for the team or man which somebody else supplied in his place. Each settler was charged for what work was done on his land, and in the end little money changed hands.

"Blamed if it ain't just like getting together and working out your road-tax!" said old Jim Green.

"Same idea," said Martin, and let the thought sink in.

The large areas covered with little jack-pine stubs were neglected for the time being and the work diverted to the fields in which large stumps predominated. More dynamite was purchased, and Shorty Dewar worked with Jud in the blasting. It was the new idea, however, which made progress for the movement. Formerly each settler had pulled or blasted by himself in desultory, unsystematic fashion, working when he listed, loafing when it so pleased him. Now the pulling crews worked full days, six days a week; the blasters worked with the speed and economy of skilled men; and the results soon were appreciated.

"And no blasting accidents, remember that," said Martin.

An incident occurred at this time which strengthened the spirit of co-operation. One of the settlers had failed to turn his dynamite into the common store and began blasting on his own account. His fuse in one charge was damp on the outside and appeared to go out. The settler approached to investigate, and the fire in the fuse, which had been burning briskly through the centre, exploded the charge and the man was blown over a fence into a ploughed field. For a miracle he was not killed. When picked up his mouth, eyes and nose were found full of earth, and when the mud had been removed he was little the worse for his experience. It was days, however, before he dared show himself in his clearing when any one passed, and soon he sent word to Martin that the rest of his dynamite was ready any time they cared to send for it.

"Marty," said his mother one day when she returned from a visit to Mrs. Lee, "did you hear about Hattie? She's gone to Chicago to see about that fly business of hers. Just think of it, the Company she sells to sent for her and are paying her expenses!

She's bought the summer kitchen from Camp Bon Air and had it moved to their place and is going to have six girls working for her."

"How'd she come to buy that building from Keener?"

"Oh, she got it cheap. Keener's given up Camp Bon Air and is building a new place down on Pine Island."

"Hm, way down there, eh?" Pine Island lay in the river a quarter of a mile below the Falls. "Well, I'm glad we won't have him for a neighbour next summer."

"And Simon wants you to come down and help him put a foundation under that new building of Hattie's. Says could you come to-morrow morning?"

A few days later, while Martin and Simon were putting the finishing touches to the foundation beneath the fly factory, a livery rig brought Hattie home from the evening train.

Martin looked at her in amazement. She was attired in a new trim blue serge skirt with a white shirtwaist. Her hat was new, as were her tan shoes, and she carried a new hand-bag and a new tightly rolled umbrella of green silk. "Smart," was the word that came to his mind as he looked at her. He wondered that he had never noticed before that Hattie was a grown-up woman.

"Well, you did get it moved, didn't you, dad?" she called, as she leaped down from the buggy and came at once to inspect the building. She went around it, went into it, and came out. "All right. We can start work in there in the morning."

"Hattie!" bellowed Simon, finding his tongue at last; "why— why, you look like a city girl!"

"The difference between city girls and country girls is mostly clothes," snapped Mrs. Lee. "My, Hattie, ain't that the loveliest serge!"

"Doesn't it fit nice, mother?" demanded Hattie. She whirled around, to show how the suit fitted her firm, slender figure. "Oh, ma, you ought to see the things in the stores! I'm going to order a suit like this for you soon's I make some money. We can order by mail—"

"You come right in and have some supper," interrupted her mother, though she beamed with pleasure at the thought. "And don't you go thinking of doing foolish things like that."

"Come 'long, Joe," called Simon to the driver. "Jest in time."

"I saw Hazel in town and told her she could have the school," said Hattie as they sat down.

"What?" roared her father.

"Land's sakes, Hattie! Ain't you going to teach—"

"Can't," interrupted Hattie. "I've got to have twenty sets of samples ready in two weeks. They send their salesmen out then, and each man has got to have a big card of sample flies. Then they'll begin to send in their orders, and I'll know how many I'll have to make this winter. It will be more than I can do, I know that, even with six girls. I'll have to try to get more help."

Simon Lee laid down his fork and looked across the table.

"Mean that you're going to tie trout flies through the winter?" he demanded.

"All the year round, dad," replied Hattie. "They've made a hit. And think of it, father, it's all your doing. Aren't you proud?"

"Well"—said Simon, looking around helplessly—"Joe!" he bellowed at the driver, "why don't you eat!"

XXXIV

Martin was quite dumb, and for the first time in his life he felt a sense of shyness in the presence of Hattie Lee. She had always been his chum; he had looked upon her much as he had looked upon the boys whom he had grown up with. But he knew, as he looked at her now, that he could never think of her in that way again.

After dinner he assisted her in moving tables and chairs into the new building, and when it was time to go she walked with him out to the road.

"How did you like it down there?" he asked.

"Well"—she paused thoughtfully—"down there you can keep busy. There's something to do all the time; you can keep so occupied that you don't have time to stop and think and feel."

"Huh!—Well, if people like to live that way, I suppose they like it."

"I don't know"—she continued thoughtfully—"I don't know but what it's the best way to live. With many things constantly happening, and many things that you're constantly interested in and doing; you get so that you know no one thing is of such terrible importance, and you get in the habit of taking things less seriously. In time I suppose you could get in a frame of mind where nothing much would matter—very much. We—we're so awfully serious up here; take things so tragically hard. That's because so few things happen to us, and every single thing is so important; we take everything too seriously. Down there, in the rush and everything, it seems that things don't matter so much."

"Weren't you lonesome?"

"I was scared at first," she replied promptly. "Chicago's so big and—and furious. It seemed as if it were my enemy. Yes, that's what it felt like; as if it wanted to smash me. But then I thought, the city is composed of people, human beings like myself, and after you become one of those people you wouldn't feel that the city was your enemy. I managed to do that—a little. They were fine to me, the people in the wholesale house. The manager of the sales department is a nice old man, and he took me to his house to dinner, and then all of us, his wife and two children, went to the theatre. You can lose yourself doing that sort of thing. I did—a little. I forgot things a little. Now, when I come back here I find myself again and—and everything." She laughed suddenly. "I don't know but what I'll go back there and stay—some time. I could make more flies there, too."

The best thing he could think of saying was: "Do you like to do that kind of work?"

"Yes," she said positively, "I like to do that kind of work. Certainly. It keeps me busy for one thing. And it makes me independent. That's the main thing; it makes me independent. I don't have to ask anybody for a single thing I want. I don't have to worry about getting somebody else to do anything, or get anything for me. I can do and get things myself. I can do what I want, and get what I want. I—I don't have to be a slave, like the average farmer's wife. Yes, I like it."

Martin stood kicking his heel in the soft earth of the road, thinking.

"There's a whole lot in what you say, Hattie," he admitted. "I never thought of it before. Women—farmers' women—don't have such a sweet time of it, when you come to think of it."

He had never thought of that before. He was farm born and bred, and the world to him was a man-world. Women had their share in it, but the idea that they might want to know the savour of independence; the idea that beneath the patient exterior of the average subdued farm wife there smouldered a spirit such as had dared to break out in Hattie Lee, was revolutionary.

"More women would do it than you suspect—if they could," she said. "Women are human beings, too, you know; though the way some of them are treated around here you'd never suspect it."

"I think the great majority of the settlers around here are good to their wives," said Martin firmly.

"Good to them," she laughed. "Well, I'm glad I can be independent, that's all. Good-night, Marty."

"Good-night."

XXXV

Frost came late that year. It was not until after the first of October
that the Indians began to appear on their old camping ground
on Clear Lake, and the day after their appearance Martin hooked
up and went to town after the potato digger he had ordered from
Simpson.

The Indians appeared on the Flat each year a few days before
the beginning of the digging season. They came in families and
tribes, from the oldest toothless squaw to the youngest back-borne
papoose, and pitched their wickiups in the same spot each year. A
buck would go to a farmer and make an agreement to dig and pick
potatoes at a certain price per bushel. Next morning the farmer
would find his field flooded with copper-skinned help and the
inevitable pack of dogs. The bucks and young squaws dug, the
older folks and the children picked the potatoes into bushel boxes,
which then were counted and dumped. And if a settler watched
closely so that the industrious pickers were not able to indulge their
penchant for increasing their score by filling the bottom of the
boxes with thick layers of potato vines, it was not bad help.

In town Martin loaded his digging machine into the wagon
and strolled across the track to the potato warehouse. The
warehouse had belonged to the Logging Company and with the
sale had passed into the possession of the Paper Company, but now
a small sign over the scale-house read: "Payne Produce Company."

A wiry little man with a clipped grey moustache and a long
jaw, which rested upon a celluloid collar, was directing a pair of
workmen in the preparation of the warehouse for the reception of
the season's crop. Martin asked if he was the new buyer.

"I am," said the man quickly.

"What do you expect to pay when we start hauling?"

"Don't know. You never can tell about potatoes. One week they're up, next week they're down. Haven't got any idea what they'll be worth when digging starts."

"It will start in a few days now," suggested Martin.

"I know, I know," said the man nervously, "but you can't tell; there may be an awful drop between then and now."

"What are they paying now down at LacClaire? They must have started hauling down there; they begin digging earlier than we do."

"Don't know what they are paying down there," was the prompt reply. "I've been so busy getting things straightened up around here that I haven't had time to find out. Have you got many to sell?"

"I've got twenty acres in," replied Martin. "Ought to haul close to four thousand bushels off it."

The buyer shot his visitor a swift, comprehensive glance.

"Oh. You're that—your name's Calkins, ain't it? Mine's Payne—Jim Payne. Well, now I tell you, Calkins, just between ourselves, I think it's going to be a queer year for spuds. A lot of people think it's going to be a light crop. Well, I can tell you privately that it ain't going to be anything of the sort. It's going to be a big crop, all over the country. Just now the price is up—I understand—and I think she'll hold up for a while, until the bulk of the crop begins to come in. Then she'll drop, and the Lord only knows where she'll go to—down to nothing, probably. Now, it's just this way with me, Calkins: I'm a new man here and I intend to locate here permanently. I want you people to have a good year so you'll plant more spuds next year. I advise you to do this: dig 'em and haul 'em just as fast as the Lord'll let you. Get 'em into town while the market's up. Get 'em sold before the big drop comes. Knowing what I do about the crop, if I was farming here I'd dig and haul every spud I had just as quick as I could."

"But you don't know what you'll be paying?"

"No. There's no way of telling. But that's my advice; of course, you'll take it or leave it, as you see fit."

Martin went to the store and called up a warehouse at LacClaire and found that the buyers there were paying around seventy-five cents a bushel. He drove home in high spirits. There would be no foreclosures on the Flat this year, he thought, as he calculated what the lowest returns from the potato crop must be. The settlers would be able to pay their interest, those who had notes coming due would be in a position to take them up, or to renew them. The fact that Big Flat could produce a good money crop in its present condition, with only the surface scratched, would have the effect of increasing its land values. The banks could afford to loan the settlers more money and to renew loans if necessary. But it was the effect on the settlers themselves that would be most valuable. They would gather new courage, new ambition. They would see that the tractors, in spite of their destruction, had paid for themselves in one season, and the task of converting the settlers to modern methods would be immeasurably lessened.

Then came the digging. The heavy frost which shrivelled the large potato tops to the ground came three nights after the appearance of the Indians, and by noon next day the diggers were in the fields.

It was glorious harvest weather. The frost had tinted the leaves of the hard-woods with their brilliant autumn colours, and there was that tang in the air which belongs exclusively to the North in Autumn time. Martin set his machine-digger at work in his lightest land, with four horses pulling it, and had his first acre dug before his neighbours, using the old hand-forks, had managed to produce a load. He had measured this acre accurately, and when he counted up he found it had produced two hundred and ten well heaped boxes containing a bushel each. Some of his field he knew would yield much heavier than this, and some, the new breaking, would run considerably lighter, but he knew that his estimate for the twenty acres would hold good: he would have four thousand bushels and probably more.

A thrill of pride stirred him as he looked down the rows filled with round, white potatoes of solid, marketable size. It was not pride for his own achievement; rather, it was the pride that a man feels when he sees his faith in some dear one amply justified. The marvellous munificence of the soil impressed him solemnly as it always did when he took time to observe and think about it. It seemed to him that the land was a perpetual treasure trove, patiently waiting, waiting through the years to be used, and asking only man's labour to make it eagerly empty its hidden riches into his hands.

XXXVI

The morning that he was starting for town with his first load of potatoes he was surprised by the mail carrier handing him a letter from Alice Demaree.

"I have taken the liberty," she wrote, "of speaking about you to Mr. M.A. Boler, the man who handles so many land development schemes, who happens to be an acquaintance of mine. You will be surprised to hear that you are getting famous. Mr. Boler had heard all about your Co-operative Association and was immensely interested. He said that you had in your leadership of the Association the machinery for making a fortune for yourself. He is out of town for a few days now and will write you on his return. I know you are too clever not to take advantage of the opportunity he is going to offer you. You *must* begin to improve yourself, and do it before it is too late. Maybe it's too late now? No, it isn't."

And she added a postscript: "You know I never quite thought of you as a farmer; I can't bear 'em."

Martin reread the letter, reread it again, and climbed upon his load and tightened the lines: "All right. Come on, boys; take it out of here."

He was angry at first. Had the letter arrived in the days of depression immediately after the fire its final line might not have stirred him so. But now was the time of the year when it was most glorious of all to be a farmer. The tingle of frost-tinged air was in his nostrils, the gay Autumn colours of the North were before his eyes; in the distance the friendly haze of the Indian summer hung about the hills; and in the wagon-box beneath his swaying spring-seat were fifty bushels of the soundest, cleanest potatoes ever grown.

"Can't bear farmers, eh?" he chuckled. "Well, I suppose it takes all kinds of people to make a world."

At Simon Lee's he pulled up again and lay back in the seat with a shout of laughter at the sight of Hattie and four of the girls from her fly factory who were making short work of picking the potatoes that Simon and his men had dug.

"It's too bad the way these farmers treat their women—making them work like slaves," he shouted.

Hattie threw a potato at him.

"Hold up! Spuds are money this year. Simon, I never thought you'd be brute enough to treat women like that."

Simon turned up a hill of potatoes with a twist of his fork and chuckled.

"I hear they're paying around seventy-five cents down at LacClaire," he called.

"Have you heard what they're paying at the Falls?"

Lee shook his head.

"You're taking the first load in, I guess, but they ought to pay about the same."

Martin drove on to town in high spirits. At every farm that he passed he saw crews working in the potato fields, and in every field the crop was good. At Nels Borg's place a shout from that settler stopped him.

"Don' try deh river road," bellowed Nels. "She's too vet."

"Wet! Too wet at this time of the year?"

"Yah. Too vet. I valk down dere last night to see. Ve can't use it at all."

This meant that the heavy potato load would have to go over the Big Ridge before entering town, and added fully thirty per cent to the task of hauling the crop to market. Martin puzzled considerably over the reason why the river road, usually in good shape at this season, should be too wet to use. Was the dam at Squaw Island responsible? In the end he laid it to the big rain following the fire, and turned up the ridge. As he entered the town he saw Payne, the potato-buyer, lounging before the Company store and greeted him with a shout:

"Here we are, Mr. Payne; the first of the season!"

Payne did not respond, either by word or change of expression. He came out into the street without speaking, clambered upon the load, raked his hands through the potatoes and jumped down.

"Thirty-eight cents," he said curtly.

"Seventy-eight?" asked Martin, thinking he had heard wrong.

"Thirty-eight."

Payne was knocking the dirt from his hands. Martin sat looking at him for a long moment

"What's the matter with 'em, Mr. Payne?" he asked.

"Don't make any difference what's the matter with 'em," retorted the buyer. "The price is thirty-eight cents a bushel."

Martin looked at Payne, looked back at his potatoes.

He did not quite realise yet what had happened, but he sensed that something was terribly wrong, so he grew cooler with each second.

"They're good sound stock. They're all right, aren't they?"

"Right as they grow," said Payne. "Give you thirty-eight cents for 'em. Take it or leave it."

"What are they paying at LacClaire?" asked Martin.

"LacClaire?" The buyer squinted up scornfully. "What's that got to do with you? This is Rainy River Falls."

'They're paying seventy-five cents a bushel at LacClaire."

"Mebbe they are, son, mebbe they are. Thirty-eight is what we're paying here. If you don't like it, why—take 'em down to LacClaire, son, take 'em down to LacClaire."

"I see," said Martin slowly, after a long pause. "Keener?"

"Who said anything about Mr. Keener? I'm buying potatoes here, and I'm the only one who is buying 'em, too."

"That's just the trouble," said Martin thoughtfully. "You're the only one who's buying. Keener's got the only rails running out of town. So you offer thirty-eight cents a bushel when the price is seventy-five."

"Yes, and I'll get 'em for thirty-eight cents a bushel, too. You needn't try to get uppety-uppy with me, son. I've heard about you, but this is about the finish of your cockiness. Thirty-eight cents. Want to take it?"

"No!" exploded Martin. "Before I work all summer to let you or anybody else get rich off my spuds I'll feed 'em to the cows!"

"Go ahead; feed 'em." The buyer stepped back to the store. He had the upper hand and knew it. Martin knew it also. Whether Payne was buying for Keener or for himself made no difference; he was the only buyer in town; he was the only one who would be allowed in town, and the settlers had no other market.

"Feed 'em to the cows, son," jeered Payne. "Mebbe you ain't got any notes or mortgages coming due this month, but I guess most of your neighbours have. I'll get all the potatoes I want, and I'll get 'em at thirty-eight cents a bushel."

"You'll never get mine," said Martin. He was still dazed by the sudden dashing of his hopes, but one resolve had established itself stubbornly in his mind. "You'll never get mine for thirty-eight cents."

XXXVII

He rested his team, fed and watered it and turned toward home. At Nels Borg's he drove in and stored his potatoes in Nels's cellar.

"We mustn't sell a load at that price," he said. "If one man begins selling the rest will follow."

"I got to have some money dis mont'," was Nels's retort. He was so accustomed to being cheated by buyers, and to accepting his hard lot without complaint, that the spirit of rebellion in Martin failed to waken any response in his breast.

"We've all got to have some money," said Martin. "And we've got to get it out of our spuds; but we won't be robbed like that."

"I got to have fifty dollar dis veek. Deh store say if I don' pay dey put lien on my crop."

"I'll get fifty for you, Nels. Don't haul any potatoes—promise you won't haul a single load till the Association's got together and talked it over."

He broke the news to every settler on the road. At every farm he met with the same reply, money was needed at once; as usual, the settlers had been only hanging on until the potato crop could be marketed; but from each he extracted the promise not to begin hauling until the word was given. He was tired out and discouraged by the time he reached Simon Lee's.

"It means that they purt' near got us, Marty," said Simon Lee, when the tale had been told. "Damn a one-man town!"

"It means," growled Martin, "that we're going to do our own shipping."

Lee shook his head. "Over Keener's rails, Marty? Think he'd get us cars and give us a loading switch? No, I don't see him doing that."

"Not this season, perhaps, but some day," said Martin doggedly. "We're fools to be working all summer and let a buyer make the money in the end. Some day we'll do our own shipping; that's what this robbery means."

"All right, Marty, all right. But this season—it's a tight hole, Marty, a mighty tight hole. The boys have got to have money. Where they going to get it? Jim Sawyer's as white a man as grows, but he's got to get his money back. What are we going to do but sell?"

"Are you going to go back on me, Simon?"

"No! But—facts are facts, Marty, and the boys have got to have money."

"They've got to wait," said Martin. "There must be a way out. They've got to wait."

"Marty," called Hattie, running after the wagon, "why doesn't the Association lend money to the settlers so they can hold their potatoes for a better price?"

"Lend money?" he stammered. "The Association? Why, it hasn't got a cent to its name."

"Why don't you borrow some?"

"Borrow? The Association?" He laughed bitterly. "We're so far in debt that anybody who loaned us a nickel ought to be put in the asylum."

"I—I've got five hundred dollars in the bank, Marty. I'll make as much more this winter. Take it, and use it to help the ones who have got to have money now."

He looked at her dumfounded, but presently he began to smile.

"Gee!" he said boyishly. "That's fine; I'm glad you're doing so well, Hattie."

"Marty Calkins, did you hear what I said?"

"Yep. A thousand dollars by next spring. Three cheers for you, Hattie!"

"Will you take it?"

"Hoh! Take it? I should say not. Our Association is too shaky. Do you suppose I'd let you risk a cent of your money in it?"

"Marty," she said sharply, "if I was a man I bet you'd take it in a minute."

"Maybe I would," he agreed. "Maybe I'd take it from you if the Association was safe. But it ain't. Money in the bank is safe, and it's a good thing to have. You leave it there."

"It's my money," she said. "I'll do as I please with it. Haven't I got a right to help, too?"

"You bet you have!" he said with new spirit. "You've helped a lot. I was feeling pretty blue, but I'm getting my nerve back now. Don't you lose any sleep about those robbers in town, Hattie. They've got us down just now, but we're going to get up on 'em; I don't know how, but we *are* going to get up!"

That evening and all the rest of the next day he drove around to the members of the Association, and in the end it was agreed that no potatoes should be hauled to town for a week. He won this agreement only through his own efforts. The other settlers took the news dumbly; they were at the mercy of the buyer; what could they do? Martin was unable to instill in them his determination to fight to a finish, but they agreed to wait.

He had prepared to go down to LacClaire to see Sawyer, but in the evening when he returned from his round he found awaiting him a letter from Boler in Chicago, which changed his plans. The letter had enclosed a money-order for fifty dollars as expense money and urged Martin to come to Chicago at once. Martin, said the letter, was the man whom Boler had been looking for for some time. His idea for the Co-operative Association was the idea Boler had long sought. It was the idea investors all over the country had been looking for. Martin had the idea, the Association had the land, and—Boler had the capital. All would benefit mutually, and Martin would get rich, if they got together, as Boler knew they would if Martin came to Chicago. Mr. Boler was prepared to put money behind the Association and do it at once.

The ornate letter-head: "M. A. Boler Development Syndicate," did not quite make the favourable impression which might have been expected from it; he had seen land company stationery before. But a man who backed his letter with fifty dollars in hard cash!

"Hi, mother!" he called. "How's that blue suit of mine? And have I got any clean stiff collars?"

"Funeral, Marty? Or wedding?" queried Jud Hart lazily.

"No," replied Martin, "but I suppose a fellow has got to dress up when he goes to Chicago."

XXXVIII

The Lake Superior Express reached Chicago at eight in the morning, and an hour before that time Martin was wide awake and sitting at a window, eager to catch his first impression of the great city. He was tremendously disappointed. First came a scattering of small wooden and brick houses built in irregular monotony upon what had apparently been prairie land a few years before. Then suddenly the Express plunged into a great maze of railroad tracks filled with snorting switch-engines and rumbling boxcars and lined on both sides with grimy, clangorous factories. A vast gloom seemed to fall upon the scene. Instead of the rosiness of an Autumn morning the world seemed too wrapped in a pall of thick, palpable grey. And the pall did not lift. As the train rumbled on towards the heart of the city the smudge in the air grew thicker and thicker. Then they crossed a grey river, dark and gloomy beneath the murk, and the porter at Martin's elbow called:

"Chicago!"

"Must be going to rain," said Martin as he rose and stretched himself.

"Rain? Why so boss?"

"The sky is so over-clouded."

"Dat ain't clouds," chuckled the porter; "dat's smoke. We's in Chicago."

Martin looked out again at the grimy sky. He saw that he was mistaken; the sky was not thickly over-clouded, as he had thought, for a faint glow of sunshine came filtering down through the pall of smoke.

"Must have had a big fire down here?" he suggested.

"Not no more'n usual."

"You don't mean to say it's like that every day?"

"Why, suah. Every day and Sunday besides. We's in Chicago, boss."

"And people live in that, when there's plenty of open country that hasn't been touched!" thought Martin. He marvelled more and more over this phenomenon as he rode from the smokey station, through dirty, noisome streets, to the hotel. Why in the world did people do it? Why spend one's lifetime cooped up in a place like this, when there was so much of God's sweet earth and a clean sky to choose from?

The buildings seemed colossal—too big to be human, he described them afterwards. They seemed to lean toward him, to bear upon him; and the effect of them all upon his spirit was as the effect of the walls of a prison.

He found the office of M.A. Boler in one of the tall buildings in La Salle Street, not far from his hotel. Boler was a short, round young man with a large smiling mouth, shrewd but benevolent eyes, and a soft, little hand that fairly clung to Martin's bony fingers.

"Well, well, well!" said Mr. Boler. "Here we are, eh? Miss Cohen, I'm with Mr. Calkins to-day. Understand? I can see nobody."

He led the way to a private office, pressed the best chair upon Martin, pressed a cigar, lighted and proffered a match. All this did not help to make Martin comfortable; he was not accustomed to men being so excessively polite—slopping over, he thought of it— to one another. The only man he had seen to compare with Boler was Judge Holcomb.

"Have a pleasant trip?" said Mr. Boler. "First visit to Chicago? Some town, isn't it? Have to show you around. Yes, yes, indeed. Have a little surprise for you at lunch."

"What is the proposition you wrote me about?" asked Martin.

Boler brought both hands down on his knees with a slap.

"Hah! That's the way I like to hear a man talk. All business. I see that you'n me are going to get together quick, Calkins. Nothing slow about you folks up there. Here."

He drew a large sheet of paper from his desk and handed it to Martin, leaning back to contemplate the effect it had on the young man.

The sheet was covered with large letters, printed with a pen:

The Great Northern Potato Farms Company, Inc.
Let Your Money Work For You On Our Farms.
A hundred invested now is worth a thousand next year.
We are practical farmers; we guarantee success.

"What is it?" asked Martin.

"Ad. Rough draft. Heading. How'd you like it? Huh?"

"Well, I don't know what it's about."

Mr. Boler rolled his cigar thoughtfully.

"It's about a hundred thousand dollars in your pocket," said he. "Sounds good? Huh? Have you got any idea of how many people there are in Chicago alone who are crazy to get rich quick?"

"Get rich quick at farming?" laughed Martin. "If they can do it they're corkers."

"Stocks," corrected Boler. "Investments. About ten thousand of 'em in this town alone good for five hundred dollars apiece. And we've got the whole country for a field. It's good. I know it's good. And I know you and me can get together."

"I don't know."

"You will soon. There's about twenty-five thousand acres represented in your Association up there, isn't there? Plenty. Plenty for our campaign. Ten thousand's enough. Can you carry ten thousand acres with you?"

"I don't know what you mean."

"I'll explain briefly. Take it up more fully later. We form a company. Get ten thousand acres as cheap as we can, paying the present owners in stock. That's just detail. What's valuable is *you*. You and the Co-operative Association you've started. Fine idea. We'll get columns and columns of free publicity on that. News stuff, you know. Special articles. Then when you and your idea have got a reputation—Bing! Full page ads, and all we'll have to do is to collect the money."

"You mean," said Martin uncertainly, "it's a stock-selling scheme?"

"I mean that it's a chance for city people to invest their money in the land, to the benefit of all concerned."

Mr. Boler continued to talk. He talked Martin into a daze. When finally it came time to go to lunch the young man had almost begun to see things in Mr. Boler's way.

At luncheon they met Alice Demaree, who was waiting for them in company with an extravagantly dressed young woman named Mrs. Potter. Martin was too surprised to speak at first, but he observed that in spite of Alice's warm greeting she looked at him with a new expression in her eyes, and, as he looked around, comparing himself with the well-dressed, sleek men in the room, he understood. He knew that he was woefully out of place, and that his appearance jarred upon her. He grew warm and flustered and hid his hands under the table. He was uncomfortable; he felt a desire to get away, outdoors.

"Now, dearie," said Boler to Mrs. Potter at the end of the meal, "we'll be on our way. Say, we'll meet you here at six this evening. All right. Calkins?"

"Fine," said Alice.

When Boler and Mrs. Potter had gone she sat for a moment toying with her spoon.

"Well," she said, "have you talked business with Boler?"

"He talked," replied Martin.

"You've got your chance now," she said eagerly. "You mustn't miss it. Boler's one of the cleverest men in La Salle Street. You mustn't fail to take this opportunity. You must not waste your life up there pulling stumps. You don't do yourself credit. You have a chance now to become something worth while. You can make a fortune, and live like a gentleman." Martin did not speak. He was in the throes of wonderment at what was happening to him. For as she spoke it seemed that the bonds which had held him to her were loosening. He saw her with new eyes. He saw her as a stranger, as one who had nothing to do with his life, whose life was apart and almost antagonistic to his.

"Well?" she said. "What are you going to do?"

"I'll think it over," he said quietly. "It isn't a thing to decide in a hurry."

"That's right. Now where shall we go? I must show you around. I've got the car down. We might go out and meet mother—no," she said swiftly, "not now. Not until you've decided."

Martin was entirely himself now. With a boyish grin he said:

"Do you know where I'd like to go? I've always wanted to see Lincoln Park."

"Oh!" she groaned. But in a moment she was agreeable. "Very well. We'll drive out."

The one thing that Martin truly enjoyed during his trip to the city was the visit to the park. It was one of those rare Autumn days in Chicago, when the wind from the east has driven the smoke from lake and city, when the air is crisp, and the blue sky above shows for a short time what it was before progress placed a city there. The leaves were turning, and while they had none of the vivid colouration of the Northern woods in Autumn, the tang of Fall was in the air, and the lake was blue and dancing.

"This is great, isn't it?" exclaimed Martin, as they left the car at the Lincoln Monument. "Whew! I felt like I was in jail downtown."

He stood, tall, thin and brown before the bronze representation of the tall, thin middle-westerner who had made history, and pale-faced clerks, strolling past, looked at him, at his poorly fitting clothes, at his big brown hands, and smiled complacently.

"Oh, let's go on!" said Alice impatiently.

They walked on through the park and came to the animal cages. Before a cage containing a small black bear Martin stopped.

"Poor old fellow!" he said. "You're a long ways from home, ain't you? You ought to be up in the woods."

"Don't you ever grow tired of your everlasting woods?" asked Alice.

"I'm going to get him some peanuts," laughed Martin. He fed the bear out of his hand and laughed at its clumsy eagerness for the tiny nuts.

Alice had seated herself on a bench out of sight, and when he returned, chuckling about the bear, she said:

"Wouldn't you like to take him with you, for a companion?"

Martin laughed. It did not concern him much now what she said.

"I'd like to take him and turn him loose in the woods," he said. "But I bet he'd get scared at the dark and come whining back for his cage."

The car had followed them and they entered it for a drive up the north shore. At first Martin was pleased; the beauty of the lake and the sweetness of the air were exhilarating. Then, in the fairest spot in the drive, there appeared a long stretch of glaring billboards, urging the passerby to use certain brands of cigarettes, gin, whisky, face-powder and other apparent necessities of life.

"It would be great," said Martin, looking out on the lake, "if they had a bunch of Norway pine where those billboards are."

XXXIX

Boler was even more effusive than in the morning, when they met him and Mrs. Potter in the lobby of the Annex.

"Getting to look like a city man already, Calkins," he said. "Well, we'll enjoy ourselves this evening. Talk business to-morrow. Let's see; we'll go to the Kaiser Gardens for dinner. How's that? They've got Maniola's Orchestra this week."

"I'd just love it," said Mrs. Potter. "There was a piece in the paper about that orchestra. They say Maniola's wife is going to get a divorce on account of some actress."

"Singer," corrected Boler. "Sadie Bell. Used to be his soloist. Saw her in vaudeville."

"Is she pretty?"

"Fine figure. Used to be Lew Hertz's wife. You know, comedian."

Arriving at the Kaiser Gardens, Boler called the manager by name.

"Nice fellow, Adolph," he confided, as he inspected the menu. "Smart fellow. Runs it for a brewery. Only been in this country a few years. Good moneymaker. How about a Bronx?"

"I love Bronxes," said Mrs. Potter. "Oh, there's Maniola. Hasn't he got the most wonderful hair!"

The orchestra began to play and Martin looked across at Alice as he listened.

"Huh!" said Boler. "What do they want to play a thing like that for? Something catchy for me. What is it?"

"Grieg," volunteered an old waiter from the next table.

"Hah? What say? Grieg? Funny name for a tune. How do you like it, Calkins?"

"It's great!" Martin was enthusiastic. "It's fine—it reminds me of the pine woods at night, and rivers and lakes with moonlight on them."

Alice drummed on the table. "Don't you ever forget your woods?"

"I heard your aunt, Mrs. Keener, playing at Camp Bon Air—"

"She always plays it."

"Speaking of pine woods," said Boler, clipping his cigar as the meal ended, "there's a great movie about the logging woods at the Climax, just a few blocks from here. 'The Trail in the Pines.' Great. The real thing. Herbert Jameson takes the leading part. Saw him at the Blackstone one night. You ought to see it."

"I'd just love to," said Mrs. Potter. "There was a big piece in the paper about him."

"Oh, it's a big hit," said Boler. "Everybody's seeing it. It's the real thing, made right in the woods, you know."

"I think it would be fun," said Alice. "Jameson's so stuck on himself he's funny."

"Let's go, then," said Martin.

As they seated themselves in the Climax Theatre Boler explained that Schwartz, the man who had built the theatre, used to have a pool-hall on Halsted Street before the movies became popular, and now he had three theatres like this, and had recently borrowed a hundred thousand dollars to build more; Boler knew the broker who had handled the deal, so he knew it was true.

"Ah!" sighed Mrs. Potter.

Herbert Jameson had made his first entrance in the picture. He was a college boy who had been too dissipated and who had gone into the great woods to make good. The woods consisted of a clump of scrub-oak averaging ten inches in diameter; it was midsummer by the foliage, and the hardy lumberjacks who were attacking the noble forest with their brand-new axes wore mackinaws and high hunting boots and fur caps. Some of the hardy fellows wore knives in their belts.

Then appeared Elsie, the daughter of the village postmaster, bearing a letter for the brutal foreman, and the men dropped their axes to gather about her, chuck her under the chin, and otherwise drive her into a state of terror. Herbert Jameson went into action. He hurled the brutal lumber-jacks about as if they were children. The audience applauded. Herbert offered his arm to the girl and together they went on to find the brutal foreman.

The latter, a terrible man with a black moustache, was in the act of choking two of his men, one in each hand, for failing to work swiftly, when Herbert and the heroine appeared on the scene. Herbert saved the two men by flinging the foreman over his head. The audience applauded wildly. The foreman cursed and vowed to get even. The lumber-jacks thereupon selected Herbert to be their foreman, and so on for six reels.

"What do you think of it?" demanded Boler, as the end came. "How'd you like it? Great, huh?"

Martin replied honestly: "I never saw anything like it in my life!"

"And now," said Alice, as they entered her car, we'll go to the Purple Pig."

"Ah ha!" cried Boler, winking roguishly, while Mrs. Potter giggled with delight.

"The Purple Pig?" laughed Martin. "What's that?"

"Listen to him!" said Boler. "Never heard of the Purple Pig!"

"It's the most popular place on the North Side," explained Alice, adding sarcastically: "You seem to be enjoying the sights of the city so much that we must show you all we can."

"Hah?" cried Boler uncertainly. "Ain't enjoying it? Of course he's enjoying it; ain't you, Calkins? I should say so. Who wouldn't enjoy it, unless he was a dead one? This is the life, eh, dearie?" he chuckled, pinching Mrs. Potter's arm. "This certainly is the life."

"Don't do that," said Alice. "Mr. Calkins might object. I saw him look reprovingly at me when I took a second brandy."

"Hah, hah! She's trying to kid you, Calkins."

"I'm not," snapped Alice. She hummed a little, looking out of the window. "I'm going to have two high-balls just as soon as we reach the Pig."

It was midnight when they reached the place—a large, low building, glaring with lights, and with a pig done in electric lights above the motor entrance. Inside they found a single table vacant among the scores that surrounded the circular space left open in the centre of the room for dancing, and Boler began to point out celebrities. A tall man with a thick, broken nose was the big criminal lawyer who had just won the big case that was in all the papers—woman on the South Side who shot a fellow who quit going with her and went back to his wife. The big lawyer was glassy-eyed and drunk.

"Who are the two girls with him?" asked Mrs. Potter breathlessly.

"The blonde is the wife of that Brosteel—you know. Government caught him for using the mails. Don't know the other one."

"There's Mrs. Doan," said Alice, indicating a tall woman across the floor. "Isn't that Billy Smythe she's with? Is she running around with him?" The tall woman and the slight youth at her side were giggling drunkenly.

"Why, didn't you know that?" asked Mrs. Potter. "It's all over about them. They've been going together for weeks."

"Wife of Doan, the coal man," explained Boler. "Swell house on Sheridan Road. There's MacIntosh, Board of Trademan, going out."

MacIntosh was assisting his lady companion as they departed. The task, however, proved too much for him, and it became necessary for a pair of waiters to assist them both.

"What you drinking?" said Boler. "Let's have some wine."

"High-ball," said Alice carelessly. "Scotch."

"We'll all have high-balls, then."

"I'll have a cigar," said Martin.

"If you don't mind," corrected Alice.

He looked at her steadily.

"No, that isn't what I meant to say," he said, his eyes not leaving hers. "I said all I meant to say: I'll have a cigar!"

"Oh, come on, Calkins; don't spoil the party. Have one more drink, at least."

"I said what I'd have," said Martin, and at the glance he turned upon the broker the latter subsided.

Martin felt sick at heart. The atmosphere of the place seemed to choke him. He wished he were outside and far, far away.

"Ah!" whispered Boler suddenly, "here comes Sam."

A dark, heavy-set, short-necked man, with a puffy nose and puffy cheeks half hiding his small, quick eyes, was striding authoritatively down the aisle. He reminded Martin of Bielsky. Waiters stiffened as they saw him coming. Men and women at the tables looked up at him admiringly, and those whom he favoured with a nod and word of greeting settled back with a look of complacent pride.

"Hello, Sam," said Boler with elaborate casualness.

"Evening, Mr. Boler. Evening, Miss Dem'r—Mis' Pott'."

Boler rolled his cigar unctuously, in a great effort to appear bored.

"Who is that Bohunk?" asked Martin.

There was a moment of blank, outraged silence. Mrs. Potter stared, her thin mouth slightly agape. Alice looked away, her eyes hardening, as if she had been in constant fear that her escort would be guilty of some such outbreak.

"That's Sam Tomolski," said Boler.

"Who?"

"Sam Tomolski."

"Well, who's Sam Tomolski?"

"Owns the place." Boler waved his hand at the room. "Owns another place downtown, on Wabash Avenue. 'Nother big place. Big as this one. Started years ago with nothing but a little saloon down on Clark Street. Owns two places like this now. Got a couple of apartment buildings on the South Side. Smart fellow. Great money-maker. Big bond buyer. I handle some of his business."

"They say Marianna, the singer, is dead in love with him," said Mrs. Potter.

"I thought she was his wife," murmured Alice.

"Oh, no; not quite his wife!" Boler leaned back, chuckling roguishly.

After a moment's pause Martin chuckled also.

"Hah! I see you're wise, Calkins."

"What?"

"You know what I mean."

"I wasn't thinking of that," said Martin. "I was just thinking that you folks down here aren't so much ahead of us, after all."

"Hah? How's that?"

"We're getting to have Bohunk saloon-keepers up in our country, too."

"Oh!" said Alice, turning on him petulantly, "can't you ever talk of anything but your old country?"

But Martin had not completed his remarks.

"Of course," he went on, "they haven't got big, fancy places like this, and white people don't go into their places or have anything to do with them, but they're Bohunks, and they're saloon-keepers, just the same as this fellow, Tomolski."

Mrs. Potter was the first to break the silence.

"Why," she gasped, "there was a great big piece in the paper last Sunday about Sam Tomolski!"

"Smart fellow," supplemented Boler sternly. "Great money-maker."

"Well, thank heaven!" said Alice impatiently, "they're going to begin the show."

The lights were dimmed about the tables. On a square in the centre of the dancing floor a spot-light suddenly shot its blinding ray. The orchestra began to play, softly and slowly at first, then swiftly developing tempo, motif and volume to a sensuous blare, and into the space of light sprang a young girl whose adolescent body the merciless spotlight revealed to the last line beneath the flimsy draperies in which she was clothed. She danced eagerly, as if pleased with her task, but the dance was insignificant, a mere perfunctory attempt at justifying the real purpose of the exhibition. The spotlight wavered as it followed her in her skipping before the tables, and for a flash it fell upon the shiny bald head of a fat, leering old man who leaned far over and feasted his blood-shot eyes upon the girl, while the crowd laughed approvingly.

Martin looked at Boler. The broker winked. Alice was watching the dancer with calmly critical eyes. Mrs. Potter was greatly pleased.

The dance came to a sudden, suggestive end; the old man snatched futilely at the girl's draperies as she ran from the floor; the lights went up.

"Oh!" cried Mrs. Potter. "I think she's awful graceful."

"Some chicken!" said Boler. "Some chicken! Bet you haven't got anything like that up in the sticks, Calkins."

"Not now," replied Martin slowly. "Probably won't have, either; we're going dry up there next year. But we used to have it, or something like it, years back, when the loggers were running things and the river towns were tough."

"Hah? Cabarets?"

"I never heard 'em called that, and I can't say I ever saw 'em myself, but from what I hear there wasn't much difference. Only," he added, "of course, women didn't go in 'em up there."

Alice Demaree was looking away and humming to herself with the suppressed energy of a person determined to be calm at all costs.

"I'm tired of it," she said suddenly. "You people can finish the party; I think I'll go home."

"Why, Alice!" protested Mrs. Potter. "It isn't near one yet."

"Well, you can stay," said Alice, rising. "I'll get a taxi and leave the car for you."

"We'll all go," said Boler, with an angry glance at Martin. "Yes; we'll all go."

Out on the walk beneath the glaring red sign, the party waited for a taxi-cab to take Boler and Mrs. Potter southward.

"You made a bad break there, old man," muttered Boler, in an aside to Martin, "but it's all right. See you in the morning, at the office, about ten?"

"No," said Martin, "you won't see me at all."

"Huh?"

"We can't do business, Mr. Boler. You're all right, I guess; but we don't hitch."

He assisted Mrs. Potter into the taxi-cab and bowed. He even assisted the spluttering broker. The cab pulled away, and the Demaree limousine rolled up. Alice slipped in swiftly, and Martin was about to follow, but, looking at her face, he paused with one foot in the car.

"I guess you don't care to have me come, do you?" he said.

"Why?"

"You look as if you didn't."

"What I want to know," she broke out indignantly, "is whether you said those things simply because you don't know any better, or because you thought you were being clever?"

After a pause, during which he looked steadily into her angry eyes, he expressed what the evening had inevitably inspired in him:

"A saloon is a saloon, no matter how much it is dressed up, and—"

"Oh!"

"And a pig-pen is a pig-pen."

Swiftly she searched her vocabulary for the right word, and swiftly she found it. She leaned indolently back against the upholstery and said with easy scorn:

"You—*farmer!*"

"Why, of course!" he said, in surprise, and then, comprehending, he stepped back and closed the door.

"Good-night," she said.

He replied: "Good-*bye!*"

XL

Two mornings later he stepped off the northbound Lake Superior Express at LacClaire. He was stopping at the county seat on his way home to see Banker Sawyer, and his first deliberate act was to stretch himself to his full height and fill his chest with the nipping Autumn air. He blinked from the rays of the mellow morning sun and looked around at the vast blue arch of the heavens, heavens clean and sweet and unsullied by the smudges of man's progress.

Above the far-away ridges hung the faint blue haze of the Northern Indian Summer; the woods were rampant with Autumn colours; and the river water, flowing beneath the railroad bridge, had shed the soft tones of summer and taken upon itself the glint of polished steel, a warning of the approach of the Northland's long winter.

Visitors from cities, or from the softer lands to the southward, might behold that steel-like glint on the water and shiver; but it was so that the stump-landers liked their country best. Now was the time of peace and comfort in that land; the underbrush, the ferns and the clogging growths of summer were down, the mosquitoes, no-see-ums and deer-flies were gone, and the harsh weather of winter had not begun. It was the golden season in the North, and Martin, burdened with the failure of his hopes in Boler, and with Keener's threat of ruin always upon his mind, took on new faith as he looked about him.

"What you doing, taking breathing exercises?" laughed the operator, leaning out of his window.

"No," replied Martin, "I've just got back from Chicago, and I'm giving my lungs a little real air. Feels good," he said, as he exhaled, "to have that in you again."

"How'd you like Chi'?" queried the operator.

"They can have it," was the prompt response. "I'd rather starve here than own the biggest business there. What are they paying for spuds?"

"About the same, I guess; around seventy-five cents."

As soon as the bank opened for business Martin entered and sought Mr. Sawyer, and told him of the blow that had been dealt the settlers of Big Flat by Payne's action in cutting the true price of potatoes in two. Sawyer had heard the news the day previous.

"I couldn't hardly believe it, though," he said. "Still, if we'd used our brains a little, I guess we might have foreseen the danger of it. They've got you copped off up there at the end of their own railroad iron, and if we had thought we might have known that they're the kind of people who'd use such an advantage every time they had a chance. I don't see what you can do; it looks pretty bad for you folks up there."

"Well," said Martin, "we're used to that. Fact is, I can't remember when things didn't look bad for us up there. There was just a few days this Fall, when we began digging, and the crop was fine, and we were expecting to get a good price for our potatoes, that it began to look a little rosy. Then Payne cut the price on us, and so you see things are back to what you might call normal for us, so far as our prospects are concerned."

"You don't feel licked, then?" said Sawyer, with a slow smile.

"No. No, I don't feel that we're licked. As the Cartwright boys' mother used to say: 'We've never died a winter yet.'"

"Thirty-eight cents a bushel won't bring the boys money enough to pay their notes or interest," said the banker seriously. "A lot of them have got horse notes due right now; they'll lose their teams."

"They'll lose their nerve," said Martin, "that's the worst of it."

"I'll do the best I can, of course," said Sawyer, "but I've got to have many of these notes satisfied this Fall. They've run too long now. And there's a lot of interest money on the mortgages held around town that's got to come in at once or the holders will commence action."

"How much more can you get me on my whole place?" asked Martin suddenly. "Everything—mortgaged to the hilt, I mean?"

"Don't do that," said the old man curtly.

"Five thousand more? It ought to be good for that. Would that be enough to stave things off?"

Sawyer looked at his young visitor for a long time, then with a curt nod he began figuring on a pad of paper.

"Yes," he said finally. "And a bad year for you next year would clean you out"

"Get it."

"Anything short of a banner year, with a good price next fall, will clean you out."

Martin nodded and responded. "Get the loan."

He went from the bank directly to a livery-stable and his request made the barn-boss stare.

"What! You want a rig to drive you up to the Falls? What you want to *drive* up there for?"

"Haven't you got a team?" asked Martin.

"Cost you more'n if you went by rail."

"I know it."

"Cost you a lot more."

"Well," drawled Martin, "of course if you haven't got a team in the barn that will stand the drive up there—"

"Jim!" roared the barn-boss to his driver. "Hitch up them buck-skins."

The driver who accompanied Martin on the long drive northward from LacClaire likewise was moved by curiosity, but to his repeated hints that it was a queer thing for a fellow to want to be driven all the way up to Rainy River Falls when the railroad was cheaper and faster, Martin made no satisfying response.

He lounged easily on his side of the buggy seat, his hat drawn down over his forehead, his eyes lazily watching the road. It was a fairly good road for the greater part of the twenty miles. For most of the distance course lay on the flat bottom lands of the Rainy River Valley, and only where it left the valley because of the river's sudden winding did it cross the hills in which the country abounded. Martin saw to his great satisfaction that not a single one of these rises approximated the hard pull presented by the Big Ridge north of the Falls.

"She's a hard one in spots," said the driver as they jolted across a stretch of dried-up corduroy over a marsh.

"Hard?" said Martin. "Not at all—when there's sleighing."

Martin stopped in Rainy River Falls long enough to ask Payne if he still refused to pay more than thirty-eight cents a bushel for potatoes. He found the buyer at his warehouse, and Martin was pleased to note that the workmen about the warehouse, and Payne himself, were idle. A few wagon loads of potatoes were scattered about on the floor of the car on the warehouse siding, but the condition of the switch told Martin that Payne had not yet been able to ship a single car-load.

"Not coming in very fast, are they, Mr. Payne?" he said, looking the buyer squarely in the eyes. "Hadn't you better come up in your price?"

"Hadn't you fellows better haul some spuds and get some money before the sheriff comes up and serves you?" retorted the buyer.

"That's the way you still feel about it, eh?"

"That's the way I feel about it."

"All right. Then you won't get our potatoes."

"Going to feed 'em to the cows, eh?"

"No, I don't think we'll have to feed 'em to the cows; but I know you won't get them for thirty-eight cents."

"Mebbe I won't get yours," snapped Payne, "but I'll get the rest of 'em. They can't hold out, and they know it, and they know it wouldn't do them any good if they could."

This was the attitude of the settlers on the Flat when Martin got them together. They felt they were beaten. Thirty-eight cents a bushel was better than nothing; they were being robbed, of course, but what could they do? Payne would pay no more and there was no other place where their potatoes might be sold.

"That's where you're wrong," said Martin. He told them his plan, and because it was something new they demurred.

"But even if it would work, Marty," they said, "there won't be sleighing till Thanksgiving, and we've got to get some money right away."

"Sawyer is going to provide the Association with five thousand dollars," he retorted. "The Association will loan it to those who have got to have some money to tide them over a couple of months."

One and all they protested. The Association was bankrupt now; each of them owed it too much money to sign any more notes.

"I'm going good for this money," said Martin. "And I know I'm not going to lose a cent by it."

This began to sound convincing. They knew that Martin, for all his love of new-fangled notions, was fore-sighted and hard-headed, and if he felt such confidence in his plan that he could assume a five-thousand-dollar debt on the faith of its success, there must be something in it.

"Look here, Mart," said Curt Harmon, "even if we do haul our potatoes all the way down to Lac-Claire, and do get seventy-five cents for them, where does it make us any money? We can't start hauling till we get good sleighing. And as soon as we get good sleighing we can take our teams and go into the woods for three a day and board for man and team. Have you figured that out?"

"Yes" said Martin.

"Have, eh? Well, then, mebbe you won't mind telling us how much more we'll make by hauling our spuds to LacClaire than by skidding logs."

"Very little," was Martin's reply.

"Well, then," said Curt, "what's the sense in it? That long haul will g'ant our teams up till they ain't fit for logging."

"It will," agreed Martin. "We'll have to rest them and feed them up for a week afterwards before they're fit to put in the woods."

"Then what's the good of it?"

"The good of it is, Curt, that Payne won't get our potatoes for thirty-eight cents a bushel. The good of it is that we'll serve notice on crooked buyers that we won't be robbed, that we aren't helpless just because we're up here at the end of things, and that we've got brains and back-bone enough to stick together and take care of ourselves."

"It will take half the winter to haul the crop to LacClaire," persisted Curt.

"It might," said Martin, "but we won't have to haul it all."

He was right. Payne began to grow worried as the weeks of Autumn passed by and there were no signs of the crop flowing into his warehouse and cars. In expectation of a great stream of potatoes as soon as digging began he had ordered several empty cars to be sent to Rainy River Falls each day. He had a dozen of them always standing empty on the siding and the Great Lakes Northern Railway was commanding him to use them or give them up. Payne had lined the cars at his own expense and could not afford to tear out the lining or let them go with his material in them. He managed to load a few cars in the course of a month, but he was losing money every day, and he had planned to reap a harvest. Keener was doing his own shipping, having built a spur to the great clearing south of town, and Payne's warehouse remained empty. The $5,000 which Martin had borrowed was enabling the settlers to hold out.

Payne had come prepared for some stubbornness on the part of the settlers, but he was confident that they would give in in the end.

"They think I'll come to them," he said, "but I've got 'em by the short hair, and it's them who'll have to give in."

He continued in this strain until the middle of November, when a premature snowfall and cold spell brought good sleighing to the county; and then one morning as he stood before his idle scales, Payne saw that which made him stare. Ten three-horse teams came in procession down the snow-covered street of Rainy River Falls, each drawing a great sleigh-load of sacked and blanket-covered potatoes. Payne's expert eye accurately estimated the contents of each load at close to a hundred bushels. The procession stopped before the store. Two fur-coated, heavily-mittened drivers tumbled off their loads and entered the store. Payne grinned sardonically. So they had given in at last, had they? Well, he would pay them thirty-eight cents a bushel in spite of their stubbornness, *but* he would do *all* the weighing himself.

The two teamsters emerged from the store, distributed the tobacco they had purchased among their fellows, mounted their sleighs; and the procession drove on, out of town, to the south, on the long drive to LacClaire!

The price had risen a little in the meantime, and late that night the men from Big Flat unloaded their potatoes in a LacClaire warehouse at seventy-seven cents a bushel.

Payne held out for two weeks. By that time five thousand bushels of potatoes had gone from the Flat to the buyers in LacClaire, and the settlers were apparently determined to keep on hauling all winter. Payne saw bankruptcy staring him in the face. He held a hurried consultation with Keener, who smiled as the buyer related the story of his defeat.

"I don't care what you do," said Keener. "They think this was the real thing. They think they'll be safe if they get the right price. Pooh! They'll be up against the real thing next summer. Then they'll have to give in. Yes, you can turn over the warehouse to somebody else if you want to. I don't care what he pays them."

The next day Payne went to LacClaire and sold his lease on the warehouse and siding at Rainy River Falls to one of the LacClaire buyers, who was quite willing to pay the same price that obtained at the county seat.

"The poor fools!" sneered Keener, as he beheld the jubilation with which the settlers hailed their victory. "If they knew their true position they'd be shouting a different tune."

And he looked at the great dam, which required only a few weeks' work to make it ready to hold the Rainy River behind its concrete walls.

<h1 align="center">XLII</h1>

By the time the sleighing was gone most of the settlers had returned the money which Martin had loaned them through the Association, and he found himself in possession of the five thousand dollars he had borrowed through Sawyer. On a wet spring day, when the fog of thawing ground hung grey over the land, and the trunks of the trees were black with moisture, Martin stepped off the train at LacClaire and entered the banker's office. He came in response to a letter from Sawyer, and finding a visitor present, hesitated in the doorway.

"Come in, Martin Calkins," said Sawyer.

Martin looked inquiringly in the direction of the visitor, a sturdily built man with the air of a patriarch about his great, white-haired head, who sat in one corner of the room, looking out of the window with a pleased, though pensive, expression. The velvet collar of his overcoat was worn bare about the edges, but Martin unconsciously removed his hat as he looked at him.

As Sawyer uttered the word, "Calkins," the old man cast one swift glance from his sharp eyes over the young man, and Martin felt that in that instant every secret of his life had passed into the stranger's possession. Then the visitor resumed his studying of something outside the window, effectually eliminating himself from the conference.

"Well, Martin," began Sawyer, "I hear you did pretty well with your sawmill this winter, in spite of last summer's fire and everything?"

"We kept it running most of the time," agreed Martin.

"But I didn't think there was any timber worth sawing left up there on the Flat," continued the banker. "I talked about that with a lot of the boys from up there last Fall when they were pinched;

suggested that they try to make something out of their timber; and they all said there wasn't enough left to bother with, and they couldn't make it pay."

"Yes, that's what they all thought," said Martin. "It was a question of getting them together again. The average settler's crew used to be himself, a boy and a team, and he couldn't get much done with that, so they were right: they couldn't make it pay—that way. Same as they couldn't make land-breaking pay the old way. The Association got 'em together, and there were men and teams enough to log right, so we did quite a little business with the old mill this winter, on a co-operative basis. I just ran it for the Association, you know."

"Oh! Then you didn't make so much out of it yourself?"

"Made more than I ever did. Not with the mill, but the co-operation business got out more of my own logs than I ever did myself."

"Did you have to lick any of the boys to get them together?" asked Sawyer solemnly.

"Didn't even have to threaten," laughed Martin. "They're converted to co-operation. They'd be crazy if they weren't."

"Well," said Sawyer in another tone, "since you did so well, and the boys have paid back what you loaned them, I suppose you want to take up that second mortgage."

Martin hesitated a moment before replying.

"Have the loaners got afraid of the security, Mr. Sawyer?"

"No."

"Have they been asking for their money?"

"No. Not a cloud in that direction. But you've got the money here to your credit now. Five thousand dollars is a big mortgage for you to carry. You'd better take it up."

"No," said Martin slowly, "I'm going to need that money."

"Eh?"

"I'm going through with what I planned. I've been thinking it over all winter, and I haven't changed my mind. I've saved the seed, and I'm going to do it. I'll need that money; I'm going to put in a hundred acres of spuds."

Sawyer looked more closely at the young man and he noted the strained lines about the straight mouth.

"Why so many, Martin?" he asked gently.

"It's got to be smash or win with me," replied Martin, drawing his hand across his forehead. "Keener warned me last spring that if I didn't sell out to him he'd ruin me within two years. I don't know what he meant. I thought last fall when it looked like we'd have to sell our potatoes for thirty-eight cents that that was what he meant: that he'd choke us off from a market, but that couldn't have been it, because he let Larson come in and buy at the right figure after Payne quit, and he's so confident I know he's got something up his sleeve. I *know* he has—something big." He clenched and unclenched his hands nervously. "And he knows we're worried. He expects us to go easy, because we don't know where we stand; and that's just why I'm going the limit!"

"A poor year will wipe you out, clean."

Martin nodded. "Yes, but I've got confidence in the land; that won't go back on me."

"A poor price next Fall—"

"I know; I know."

"Keener may not let a fair buyer operate at the Falls."

"I've thought it all over, Mr. Sawyer," said Martin, "thought over everything. And I'm going the limit, because anything short of it would look like quitting."

Sawyer rose to shake hands when it came time for Martin to leave.

"If I knew what Keener has up his sleeve, as you say, I'd do my best to help you," said he.

"I don't know what it is," was the reply, "but whatever it is, it's so big that he's sure he's got us licked."

There was a period of silence in the office after Martin had gone. Sawyer glanced over some papers on his desk; the visitor continued his interested gaze out of the window.

"Well, Lem?" said Sawyer softly.

The man addressed turned his venerable head slowly and faced the banker.

"Jim," he said thoughtfully, "I've been spending too much time in big cities lately. I don't think I'd exactly begun to lose faith in our country's future, but I'd sort of begun to question. So many millions of people in the big cities—people who think that America means a place to get rich quick, and buy a limousine, and get your picture in the papers. Jim, I'd begun to think of our country as a fine, big, beautiful woman who was getting fat and flabby from doing nothing, and eating too much, and who got up at eleven o'clock, and wondered how she was going to get through the day. Oh, me of little faith!—Jim, I've been too much in cities lately, and I thought the old breed was gone from the face of our land."

"Too bad you aren't going to build any more branch lines, Lem," said Sawyer.

"Eh? Oh, that." The visitor rose and shook himself like an old bear. "I said that before I'd seen your young friend. Neil MacNish will probably be around here with his surveyors in a few weeks.

"Jim Sawyer," he said, as they shook hands in parting, "I'm much obliged to you for making me stop off. You've given me a good day. I feel heartened. I feel like bragging a little. We think we've done a lot with this north country. Shucks! It's just begun, just begun. Jim, is there anything that beats the outdoor American?"

"I hope there isn't," chuckled Sawyer. "Particularly that young outdoor American who just left us. I'm worried, Lem, about what that man Keener may have up his sleeve."

"I wouldn't worry—not after seeing the boy."

"I don't know," said Sawyer. "Keener's a small, cowardly man, and since he looks so confident, as young Calkins says, he must feel that he's got something almighty sure."

XLIII

In the damp, soggy days of spring, while the ice and snow still
lay thick in the sheltered woods, though the air was heavy with
the odour of sun-stirred soil, Martin began a careful measure and
appraisal of such land on his place as was available for a potato crop
that year. The determination to plant one hundred acres of this
crop had solidified into a fanatical swat of stubbornness; he would
plant a hundred full measured acres, not the average, indifferent
estimate of such an area.

He was disappointed in the results of the measurement of the
fields that were ready for the plough; he had hoped to find he had
eighty acres, but the measurement showed a scant sixty-five. This
meant that he must break thirty-five acres before planting time,
instead of the twenty he had calculated upon; but he had learned
much about stump-pulling since last year, and the task did not
appall him. A second-hand donkey-engine furnishing power to a
derrick rig took the place of a tractor. Anchoring this outfit in the
centre of a stump-patch and using a long cable, it was possible to
clear an acre of ground before moving. Simpson provided him with
the latest horse-pulling devices, and both teams were put to work
as early as the ground permitted. Ten acres of the area selected
for clearing consisted of large, firm stumps, and here Jud Hart
wrought swiftly with dynamite.

Martin went at his task with a steady blaze of energy that had
in it no mercy for himself or others. He spent himself with no
thought of the consequences to himself, or to others; he spent the
strength of his workmen in the same way. He grew extraordinarily
thin during those hard months of spring; his body became an
arrangement of steel muscles upon a bone frame; he began to stoop
a little, his long arms dangled loosely from his wide shoulders, and

his walk became a weary slouch. To see him slogging heavily across a ploughed field was to behold a tired man, a man who has spent himself till his reservoir of energy is apparently empty, but to see him flare up and jerk a cable end out of the hands of a slow-moving workman, and toss it around a stump was a different matter.

He grew a little hard toward his help, for he had a big payroll for a farmer, and he had a big task in hand. As he himself was swept along with his determination, so he swept others. "The boss is putting all his money on one number," said Shorty, on the day that ploughing began. "He's got a right to be grouchy."

"He's a hard one," agreed Jud admiringly. "I knew he had it in him."

If he had known the nature of the menace which Keener held over him, he felt the strain would not have been so hard. He spent many sleepless nights brooding over this and trying to guess the significance of the Company's threat. In the end he gave it up as a useless waste of time and energy, and devoted his whole being to the task he had allotted to himself. His concentration brought the desired results, and day by day as he saw the job being conquered he came to think less and less of Keener's threat, until on the day that it became sure that he would have a hundred acres cleared and ploughed and ready for planting time, the danger from the unknown source seemed so far away as to be nothing more than a bad dream.

On the day after this Simpson came driving up with a gasoline tractor—the first in the district—to be used in the ploughing, and he had a message from Keener.

"He stopped me just as I was pulling out of the Falls," said the implement man, "and he said he understood you'd done a sight of work up here this spring. Told him I understood you'd got fixed to put in a hundred acres of potatoes. 'Well,' he says, 'I haven't got anything against doing young Calkins a favour,' says he. 'Tell him I'll take his land and his place off his hands and pay him fifty dollars an acre for the broken land and five for the stump-stuff,' says he. 'And,' says he, 'tell him this is his last chance to save a cent out of the wrecking that's coming to him.'"

The message was a harsh awakening to Martin, who had allowed himself to sink into a lulled sense of security. Keener by this time knew him too well to try a bluff. He would not have sent this warning by Simpson unless he possessed the means to back it up.

"That all he said, Simp?" asked Martin.

"That's all, Mart; I've give you his words as near's I can remember."

"Run your buzz-wagon out in the field and give a trial," said Martin quietly. "See if she can rip up that old sod. I'll be with you in a minute. Got to get something from the house."

He went to the house and told his mother what Simpson had told him. He had foreseen the indignation with which the staunch old lady would receive the news, and he checked it promptly.

"Hold on, mother; take your time and think it over. It's terribly serious, more so than we've ever guessed."

"Marty Calkins, are you getting afraid of this land?"

"No, sir! The land will stand up. But you see we don't know what Keener intends to do."

"And I, for one, don't care," snapped Mrs. Calkins. "The good Lord gave people land, and if they do right by it, and work hard, He ain't going back on them, you can depend on that."

"Well," said Martin, "I dunno. Don't you s'pose He's pretty busy sometimes to bother about small fry like us?"

"No, I don't. And what's more, I know He ain't going to do no favours for that devil, Keener, shame on me for putting such a name to any living man. You—you're running things, Marty."

She paused abruptly, and looked away. Martin did likewise.

"All right," said Martin hoarsely. He tried to say more, but in the moment he could not trust himself. "All right," he repeated, and hurried back to Simpson, tingling with pride in his mother and with the line about his mouth set just a shade more grimly.

"Tell him to go jump in the lake, Simp," he said quietly. "Now let's see; how does she handle sod?"

"I knew you wouldn't sell," said Simpson. "Why, she handles it all right, Mart, but the darn stuff's so wet it sticks a lot to the ploughs."

"Wet! What are you talking about? This is our oldest field; dried out first of all."

"Don't make any difference, she's wet now. Look at them furrows."

Martin walked down the ploughed ground, and the soil at the bottom of the furrow squelched beneath his boots. The field was wet, there was no questioning that, but Martin had been facing and overcoming obstacles for many weeks and the condition of the soil did not impress him as much as it should have.

"Go ahead," said he. "Rip her up. I guess she'll dry out before planting time."

He was too busy to stop to think about a wet field. He was too busy to stop and think at all. He worked from daylight till dark for six days a week, and begrudged himself the leisure of the Sabbath.

One Sunday afternoon near the first of June he spent the day in inspecting the lower sections of his land, and he was a little disturbed to find that the soil was far from as dry as was proper at that time of the year. He followed the shore of Crooked Lake down to the narrows and saw that the lake and the creeks that drained into it were still high in water. He determined to have a look at the River, and swung away through the brush for the foot of Clear Lake. He walked steadily, his head down and his eyes on the trail.

At the foot of the lake he found the old tote road which ran to the river, and as he stepped into the road he came to an abrupt stop. A sudden flurry disturbed the brush ahead of him, and in a moment what seemed to be a headless ball of brown came rolling along the ground straight at him. Martin swore. He had been startled out of his mood of concentration, and he did not like it. Then he saw what the brown ball was, and slowly he relaxed, and he grinned boyishly. It was a mother partridge, blusteringly and unhesitatingly risking her own life to save her hidden nestful of eggs or chicks from fancied danger.

"Take it easy, old girl, take it easy," chuckled Martin. "Don't worry, I wouldn't touch your nest for a farm."

The bird strutted about in the road, clucking and ruffling her feathers.

"That's about the bravest thing I've ever seen done," thought Martin. "Go on your way, old girl; nobody is going to touch a feather on your head."

And even as he uttered the words a shot-gun bellowed in the brush to the left of the road and a charge of shot knocked the brave little mother into a bloody mass of flesh and feathers.

"I got you, you little devil!" gloated a voice in the brush, and a man came running clumsily out into the road. He was a young man, pale and fleshy, and Martin recognised him as one of the clerical force in the mill office at Rainy River Falls.

"Some shot!" he said to himself, as he reached to pick up the bird. Then he saw Martin. "Hello, boh!" said he carelessly.

Martin did not reply. He stood dumb and helpless, looking from the man to the shattered bird, from the bird to the man. He was sick and white with disgust and anger, and only one word, one fighting epithet, seemed capable of coming from his tongue. He began walking slowly toward the hunter.

"Hold on!" said the latter. "What's the matter; this your land?"

Martin came on in silence.

"Hold on now," blustered the stranger. "Don't think for a minute you can bluff me. You stay right where you are."

Martin was on him in one leap. They went down with a crash. When they arose the gun was in Martin's hands. He opened it and threw out the undischarged shell. For a moment he stood undecided, then he swung the weapon against a tree and broke the stock. He found a stone and smashed the lock. He pounded until nothing remained but the bare barrels and these he threw far into the brush.

"Go away," he said thickly. "Go—quick!"

The man had backed away in terror at the sight of this silent, Berserk rage. He had never seen elemental anger in action, and the spectacle numbed his very soul.

"I know you," he called from a distance. "You're Calkins. You'll get yours."

"Go on! Keep moving."

"Your goose is cooked. In about a week they'll finish the big dam!"

XLIV

Martin stood looking after the swiftly retreating figure without appreciating the significance of what he heard. The rage which had exploded within him was too intense to permit any words to register upon his mind. Smashing the gun had not satisfied him. He looked down at the pitiful feathered mess at his feet, looked up at the sky, looked down the road whence the man had vanished.

He was no sentimental naturalist; he was one of the best partridge shots on the Flat. But he shot them in the Fall, the open season, and shot them flying; and this bird had been shot in the closed nesting season and—sitting! His feeling was that he had witnessed a cowardly murder. Then he turned away and went on, and for the first time the words of the clerk meant something to him.

"In about a week they'll finish the big dam."

He puzzled over it as he walked along. What had the big dam to do with him? How could it affect him?

He found himself at the bank of the Rainy River with the puzzle still unsolved. The river was high for that time of the year, but he recalled other wet years and knew that it had been higher. Even if the completion of the big dam at the Falls raised the water by several feet he foresaw no danger that the Flat would be flooded. The west bank of the river was high along the greater part of Big Flat. Here and there along bayous approaching small lakes in size, indented the shore, and these would take care of enormous quantities of high water, but Martin resolved that he would keep an eye on the river.

He forgot this resolve in the rush of next week's work. It was plant time now; and the ground was ploughed and disked, draggled and marked, and the seed ready. He had determined to get fifty acres planted so early that in case of an early frost in the fall half of his crop would reach complete maturity, and the task was a strenuous one. He worked from daylight until dark, and at night he cut seed until he fell asleep. And his low land did not dry out, nor did the low land of the other settlers on Big Flat. However, there was some land which lay high enough to be planted now, and Martin was so busy that he did not stop to think of what the unseasonable wetness might signify. He was too busy to think at all. He had his work to do, and he did it, and it sapped all the mental and physical energy in his being.

Next Sunday morning he retraced his steps of the Sunday before.

The water in Crooked Lake and Clear Lake he found had not fallen the fraction of an inch. He followed the tote-road to the river, sought out a watermark and found that the same condition obtained in the stream. The water was at the same level as it had been a week before.

Martin returned to the main road, selected a comfortable log and seated himself and lighted his pipe, and presently a low humming noise rose from down the road, disturbed his thoughts, and a motor car loaded with trout fishermen whirled into sight and slowed down.

"How far is it to Tamarack Creek?" shouted the driver.

Martin replied accurately. The distance was much greater than the fishermen had expected.

"Keener don't know his own country," chuckled one. "He told us it was less than five miles from his place down on Pine Island."

"Maybe we better wait till Miss Demaree comes along; she knows the way," suggested one.

"Nothing doing. It's getting late now. Keener ought to have given us a guide. Say, young fellow, how'd you like to come along as guide? We'll pay you."

"Thank you," replied Martin, "but I've got other things to do. You don't need a guide; just go ahead as I've told you and you can't miss it."

He did not move from his log. He was in his own country, and he was not going to run, even to avoid a meeting with Alice Demaree. He had allotted himself one pipeful on that log, and he was conscious of a sense of relief as the tobacco ran low without her appearance. He knocked out the ashes and arose. As he did so he heard the roar of her car. It came with a rush, but there was a soft spot in the road before the log and she was forced to slow down; and Martin looked at her, untroubled, and there was no lure for him in the gaud of her beauty.

The car came to an abrupt stop, and the young man in the seat beside Alice gave a short laugh.

"'Fraid of the natives, Alicia?" he drawled.

Alice was looking at Martin. Perhaps she hoped to see in his eyes a flicker of the old flame which she always lighted, but she was disappointed, for Martin bowed formally, hat in hand.

"How do you do, Miss Demaree?"

"Hah! He knows the beauteous Alicia," cried her companion. "Been breaking hearts up here, too, Alice."

Alice swept Martin with her eyes from toe to head.

"Still grubbing in the dirt—I see," she said. "Mr. Calkins, this is Mr. Starin—not the real one, only his nephew and heir."

"Alicia!" groaned the young man, languidly. "Oh! Calkins, eh?" He raised his head and looked at Martin curiously. "Keener's wrong," he said, sinking back indolently. "Keener's wrong," he said, sinking back indolently. "It's a shame; he looks like a decent chap. Drive on, Alicia."

The complete calm in Martin's eyes as he looked at her tantalised her into speech as she threw in the clutch.

"So sorry you and Uncle Keener aren't speaking, Mr. Calkins," she said. "I'd invite you down to the Island. Splendid crowd there this week—invited up to celebrate the completion of the dam."

"Oh, why rub it in?" young Starin protested, laughing; then the car went roaring on and out of hearing.

XLV

Monday morning Martin was in the field at daylight as usual. He had made no change in his programme, nor had spoken a word to any one of the fear that lay on his mind.

He went about his planting as if nothing in the world had happened to interfere with his prospects, and only an unnatural quietness and an unnatural swiftness and strength in action betrayed the mood he was in.

An hour before noon Jud, who was planting by hand, drove his planter into the ground, caught the squashy sound that came from the soil, raised the planter and stooped to examine the hole he had made.

"Marty!" he called.

Martin, who was planting like a madman at the farther end of the field, stopped suddenly.

"Better come over here," said Jud quietly, and when Martin arrived he pointed at the water seeping into the hole which his planter had driven in the ground.

"She's wet, Marty."

"Yes."

"Must be wet over where you're planting, too."

They crossed the field and Martin looked stupidly at the ground he had been planting, as he saw that he had been wasting seed in wet ground for the last half hour.

"Well," he said, "we're stumped, aren't we?"

"The rest of the fields are all wet, Marty," said Jud. "Too wet for planting now. Rot the seed. Have to wait till she dries out."

"Yes."

"Ought to dry out in a couple days if it don't rain."

Martin did not reply. He looked into the next field and saw that Shorty Dewar had stopped his team.

"What's up, Shorty?" he called easily.

"Come and take a look at this ground, Boss," responded Shorty. "Looks pretty moist to me."

"Bring in your team," said Martin.

"Huh?"

"Bring in your team. We've quit planting. Come on, Jud."

He and Jud walked in silence to the house. His mother, surprised at his unseasonable appearance, looked at him closely.

"Anything gone wrong, Marty?" she asked.

"Nope. Just taking a little rest. Let's have dinner a little early. I'm going to town."

"What for?" she asked after a moment of silence.

"Oh, business."

"You'd better put it off, I think, Marty," she said quietly. "Simon Lee and another man was in here in an automobile looking for you. They went up the road some place and said they'd be back after dinner."

"Who was the other man? Somebody taking Simon fishing, I suppose?"

"No. I don't know who he was, but I know they weren't going fishing, because Simon looked like he was ailing. And, Marty," she added gently, "I guess you'd better wait till they come back."

"What—what did they say to you, mother?"

"They didn't say anything to me," was the reply, "but I've known Simon Lee for a good many years and I can tell when something's wrong."

Soon after dinner a mud-bespattered car came jolting its way in from the main road with Simon Lee in the seat beside the driver. There was no need to look further than Simon's face to know that something was wrong. The proud, genial man seemed to have grown old. He sat slumped down in the seat, and the twinkle was gone from his eye. The man who drove was a sturdily built man attired in cheap, rough clothes, with a rusty derby hat on the top of his head, and a straggly grey moustache, which never had known a parting comb, curving over his mouth. Martin thought he might be a cattle-buyer till he saw his eyes. Then he rose to greet him respectfully.

"Marty," said Simon Lee in a sickly tone of voice, "this is Mr. MacNish, of the Great Lakes Northern, and he's—he's got something to say to us, Marty."

Neil MacNish was looking at Martin, and he did not trouble to acknowledge the introduction, or to trifle with small talk. He looked at Martin, with eyes that made one forget the incongruous derby hat.

"Leave it to Lem Mills!" he blurted finally. Then without troubling to explain he tumbled from his car and seated himself Indian fashion on his heels.

"Keener," he began, with no preliminaries, "is one congenital hog, net; and, boys, he's done you dirt."

No one ventured to speak, though MacNish was silent for a long time.

"He had no need to put that dam on the east side of Squaw Island. That's what threw the water to the west bank and is keeping the Flat so wet."

He paused again, and still there was no response, and when he resumed his hearers leaned forward to listen.

"Long ago," said Neil MacNish, "quite a few years before people were bothering about newspapers and books and mills to make the paper for them, and before the Rainy River had got its channel cut straight and wide and deep as it is to-day, this Flat here was a great shallow lake. It covered the country at least from the

Range up north to the Big Ridge down near the Falls, and the lakes that remain up here—Crooked, Clear, Tamarack, and so on—were the deep holes in the lake bottom, holes that were deeper than the channel of the Rainy River.

"The Rainy wasn't at all the river it is now, and it was having a mighty hard time of it getting through the gap at the Falls onto the low ground beyond. The Falls weren't there at all as they are to-day. There was probably only a trickle going down through a soft spot in the ledge that ran across the gap.

"But the river was working all the time, cutting deeper with all the pressure behind it and going down till it found the sand under the rock of the ledge and under-cutting the ledge. Then there came a winter with heavy snow, and in the spring a steady spell of rain, and then on top of that, probably an old sockdolager of a cloud-burst. It must have been awful high water and it must have come awful fast, because one fine day that ledge cracked a little, and then a wall of water hit it kuh-splang! and, whoosh! the whole blamed thing went downstream, and the Rainy River Falls and the Rainy River were made.

"The Rainy cut right through everything after that, like a hydraulic monitor cutting through a bank of sand, and pretty soon it was something like what it is to-day, running so straight and swift that it sucked the big lake up here downstream in a hurry. Then the Flat became a swamp. But the river wasn't through with it yet. Its channel lay lower than the Flat and it sucked away the surface water like a siphon. The Flat dried out. It dried out because the Rainy River is the swift, draining stream that it was. It ceased to be a swamp; it became dry land, and saw-logs grew on it. The logs went; it became good farm land. But it will become a swamp again now that the Rainy River is dammed up."

His tale ended, brutally abrupt; and after it there fell a sickening silence, a silence heavy with the atmosphere of tragedy.

So that was it; that was what Keener had up his sleeve. Ruin. The complete, sordid ruin of being drowned out. Death for the fine dreams, hopes, plans.

Minutes passed. The silence became painful and then Martin, stretching himself easily, drawled out: "Well, maybe Keener will take pity on us and give us jobs in the mills."

"By George!" cried MacNish, and smote his thick thigh. "Lem Mills was right!"

And then Simon Lee laughed in relief, and a trace of the old twinkle returned to his eyes.

"Mebbe he will, Marty; never thought of that. Guess I'll put in my application right away."

"Or maybe Mr. MacNish can use us on his railroad," laughed Martin. "I'm a pretty good hand with a shovel, Mr. MacNish."

"Me, too," said Simon. "What'll you pay us, Mr. MacNish?"

They chuckled quietly. They had heard the worst. And knowing the worst, and face to face with it, and being what they were, they jested at the Fate that ruined them. Only Jud Hart was strangely silent, for Jud knew more about the Rainy River than any other white man.

"Now that they've raised the gates down there at the Falls, Mister," said he, "won't that raise the water up here?"

"Certainly," replied MacNish. "It will back up. That will be the finishing touch."

"This year?" asked Martin.

"Well, you know your land better than I do. The water won't go down any more, however. It will get higher."

Martin broke a stick into two pieces, measured them carefully against each other and tossed them away.

"It's hard to believe, Mr. MacNish," he said. "I mean, I can't understand it. You see, Mr. Keener wanted to buy this land. He wanted it badly, the whole Flat. He wants it now. How could he

use it any more than we can if his dam is going to make a swamp
of it?"

"Easy enough," was the reply. "If Keener owned Big Flat that
dam wouldn't be making a swamp of it. He put his wing-dam
across the east channel at the head of Squaw Island, and that threw
all the current into the west channel. If he had owned the Flat—if
he ever does get to own it—you'll see that dam moved. It will be
placed across the west channel, and that will turn the current into
the east channel away from the Flat. The mouths of the bayous in
your west bank will be dammed up, and where the bank is low, or
so soft that the water seeps through, it will be raised or filled in.

"Over on the east side of the river below Squaw Island a little
ways, there is a long marsh, just beyond the bank. It runs almost
parallel with the river. That's where the water would be stored if
Keener had got your land, and Big Flat would be safe and dry.
It ought to be so now; but Keener—he's a hog! He's the curse of
business—the hog who wants everything in sight. I can't see why as
big a man as Dan Starin will have him around."

"Starin's a big man, is he?" asked Martin.

"A very big man. He isn't after your land, you know; he
wouldn't bother with it. That's Keener's private venture, on the
side."

"We might," said Simon Lee, "see this man Starin."

"No!" growled Martin. "Go and beg him—anybody else—to
help us out of a hole? Not by a darn sight!"

"Mister," said Jud Hart diffidently, "ain't there no law that can
give the boys their rights?"

"Lots of it," replied MacNish. "Enough to drown 'em. Enough
to last a lifetime and to swallow fortunes if they take it into court."

"I see," said Jud. His next remarks seemed quite irrelevant to
the subject. "I remember one Spring on the drive, twenty year ago,
I guess it was—high water and a short crew. She kind of jammed

on us down there in the bend at Red Bank—Say, Mister, I guess that's 'bout where your long swamp is, on the east side, ain't it?"

"Just so. Red Bank is a natural dike between the river and the swamp."

"Figured it was. And I remember saying to Jim Sawyer—we was the white-water men: 'Jim, if there was a gap in Red Bank right here in the bend,' says I, 'it would tap the old Rainy and suck off all this high water.' Jim guessed it wouldn't do anything of the sort. Now, who was right, Mister?"

"You were." MacNish's battered derby had slipped far down over his forehead and from beneath the brim his eyes were studying Jud keenly. "You're one of the old ones, aren't you?"

"'Y golly! Guess you'd call me that—one of the old ones. I always thought I was right about Red Bank."

At last MacNish rose to go.

"Hard luck, boys" he said. "Calkins, I understand you are the one it will hit hardest."

"Yes," said Simon Lee in a hard tone, "Marty's the one who'll lose most—because Marty's the man Keener's after."

"Going to ride home with me, Mr. Lee?" asked MacNish.

Simon made to rise, caught Jud Hart's sidewise glance, and sank slowly back on the ground.

"No, thanks, Mr. MacNish. I guess I'll set around with the boys a little longer."

MacNish looked at him sharply.

"You're one of the old ones, too, aren't you?" he said. "Well, so long, boys."

"So long."

<h1 style="text-align:center">XLVI</h1>

Simon Lee and Jud Hart replied as one to MacNish's farewell, but Martin did not appear to hear, or to notice that the engineer had gone. He sat looking straight before him and seeing nothing. The ridges at the corners of his jaws seemed carved of granite. The lids of his eyes drew close together, and in the slits between them there was a glimpse of something calculated to make one start and ponder.

He rose, presently, and his manner was so elaborately at ease that his two old friends glanced at one another apprehensively.

"Going any place, Marty?" asked Simon casually.

"Left my pipe at the house. Going to get it."

"Ain't going to town, by any chance?"

"I'm going to get my pipe," said Martin, and turned toward the house. In the doorway he happened to glance back. Simon and Jud sat as he had left them. They neither moved nor spoke, but sat looking intently out over the lake.

He entered the house and saw his mother, busy at her sewing table; she did not purpose to allow any crisis to interfere with the truly important things of life.

"Bad news, wasn't it, Marty?" she said, briskly biting a thread.

"Yes." He was a little disappointed, and at the same time relieved to discover that he felt no inclination to pour out his heart to her. She was his mother, and he had turned to her naturally, but now he understood that this was the prompting of the boy which was left in him, and he was a man.

"See if you can thread that needle. I declare my glasses ain't what they used to be at all."

Martin chuckled.

"That's right, mother, don't you ever admit that it's your eyes."

"My eyes? Land sakes! I hope my eyes are good for some time to come. Well," she continued as he threaded the needle without a tremor, "I guess the news wasn't bad enough to scare you, anyhow."

"Scare me? No, I guess it didn't scare me. No, not exactly that."

He went out the back door and stood looking at the fields beyond, the fields which in a few weeks would be too wet to plant, and then, choking down something in his throat, he slouched down the slope onto the Flat.

He felt better when the first wind-break hid him from the house and from the lake, and there, in a cluster of fragile birch saplins, he sat down, where his eyes saw nothing but the fields which he loved and which were a part of his dreams. The old look of too much patience for one of his youth came upon his face for a moment, and his head drooped to rest upon his hands, but in an instant he threw his chin high, and clenched his fists.

He rose and in the warmth and sunshine of the bright spring afternoon began to wander about, crossing and recrossing the plots he had planned to plant to potatoes. He wandered among the thick timothy of his hay-land, down old tote-roads, over ridges, through slashings and burnings; and he felt like a coward and traitor; for the old, unshakable faith in the land was not in him.

He recalled a night a year before, when he had first met Keener, and how the touch of the living soil beneath his feet had stirred and strengthened the faith which Keener had sought to destroy. The soil had no such effect now. And the sun in his eyes, and the odour of young things in his nostrils, and the sights and feel of Nature's invincibility all around, gave him no faith.

He had been hit too hard. He was numbed—too numbed to be sensitive to the inspiration of his outdoor world—and for that reason he felt that he was beaten.

He seemed to forget, little by little, the land, the dam, and the story which Neil MacNish had told; and he only remembered Keener.

Keener filled his mind, or such part of his mind as was consciously operating this afternoon, and his interest in Keener was so complete as to exclude an interest in anything else, and he yearned to meet him, as primitive man yearned to meet his enemy from time immemorial.

The yearning grew. He forgot many things; forgot his land, his mother, himself. He smiled in a terrible, bleak fashion and set off through the woods for town.

XLVII

Branches whipped his face, blackberry briars tore his clothes, and he did not feel them. He waded the Narrows, scarcely sensing that he was passing through water, and paid no attention to trails or roads.

Instinct drove him on a straight line toward the main road, which was the shortest way to town. Instinct only. Had he stopped to think he would have recognised the woods he was in and probably have turned away, to the south, but he had ceased thinking and instinct was his master.

The roots of instinct lie hidden mysteriously; for his blind rush carried him straight through Simon Lee's grove of birches, through the under-bush beyond the grove, straight out into the Lee clearing, and face to face with Hattie Lee.

She was hanging up washing in the yard behind the house, and caught sight of him just as she was lifting a sheet onto the line. She remained in the position for some seconds. The sheet dropped back into the basket.

"Marty!" she gasped. "Marty! What is it?"

He made no reply.

"You—" She paused. She shrank back; then impulsively she ran to him. "Marty, Marty! What's happened? What—what are you going to do?"

And still he did not reply; he only started guiltily at her words.

"Marty!" She came close to him, her eyes wide with fright at the look on his face, and put her hands upon his arms. "Marty, Marty!"

And then, as he looked down at her, the primal darkness seemed to slip from him; and he seemed to be returning to the world of light, and sunshine and hope!

"What was it, Marty?" she said presently.

"Why, why, nothing, Hattie. Just—walking. Hasn't Simon got home yet?"

"No."

"Guess he and Jud must have gone fishing."

"Oh, no, Marty! You know better. What is it; what's wrong?"

"Nothing wrong. Simon's up at our place."

"Tell me, Marty; please tell me."

And presently, seated beside her on an old log, he told her quietly how MacNish had revealed the doom of Big Flat.

"But, Marty, they can't!" she cried. "Isn't it against the Law?"

"The Law?" stammered Marty with a guilty start. "Against the Law? Why—I'd forgotten that. Maybe it is."

"Oh, it must be." She was quite positive and confident. "I'm sure it must be. Why, it's like robbing you of your land, Marty. The Law won't allow even a rich man like Keener to do that."

He was not quite so sure about that, but her faith in the Law, her confidence, inspired him. He began to talk and now he seemed to see the situation with different eyes, even as he saw Hattie with different eyes. She had summoned back the youth in him, and as he talked his tale rose from pessimism to hope, until at the end he was saying: "MacNish doesn't know the Flat the way we do, and he doesn't know us. Keener doesn't own this country, not quite yet, and we're not licked, not by a darn sight. It sort of knocked the wind out of me at first, but now I'm getting my breath back, and I tell you, Hattie, I don't believe MacNish is right after all. I won't believe it. That's it; I *won't* believe! The land's too good and the people are too good. We've been in hard fixes before. We'll make out somehow. I'm going down to LacClaire. I don't know anything about law, but I believe it's fair, and if it is it won't let Keener drown us out like a lot of chipmunks."

"You just bet it won't, Marty. Don't give up for a minute.
You—"

"What?"

"Nothing, Marty."

She had looked up at him and now she was looking away;
and he looked at her, her slender roundness accentuated by the
tightness of her checked kitchen apron.

A robin, mounting the sun-touched top of a tall pine,
announced his opinion that the spring day was closing. The
cheerful notes, rippling liquid through the late afternoon stillness,
brought an end to the silence which had crept upon the two.

"Well!" exclaimed Hattie with a start.

"Guess I'll be starting for the Falls," said Martin clumsily.

He hesitated. Then, in something of a daze, he went without
another word.

XLVIII

He went swiftly out of the clearing, down the road and out of sight, without looking back. He heard the liquid notes of the robin thrilling in the top of the sun-crested pine, and he added an inch to the length of his long, swift stride. When he was well out of sight and hearing of the Lee place he gave vent to a distinct sigh of relief, but he did not pause or slacken his speed. He was afraid that if he did he might begin to wonder, and to dream, and this was no time for anything of the sort.

It was a time for action, a time to get something done in a hurry. He was keen again, strong, alert and aggressive. The hours of numbness following upon the blow dealt by MacNish's facts were gone; it was a part of the past; youth had thrown off its effects, had almost forgotten that it had been. He did not even stop to remember why he had started for town or how he had been saved; he was too busy.

His mind had leaped from its mood of desperation to grapple aggressively with the problem. A week longer of the high water and he would be ruined. There was no way out of that. It was a fact as inexorable as the coming and passing of the seasons. He would be ruined, and many other settlers would be in the same situation, and the Co-operative Association and all his hopes and dreams and plans for the Flat would go down in a hopeless crash.

Something must be done in a hurry. His stride accelerated as his thoughts flew on. What could be done? Would the Law help? He believed it would; he had the faith of generations of law-abiding men behind him. But if so, how? He must have a plan; he must find a way himself; the law could only help to bring a just plan into fruition.

The water must go. That was the premise from which he builded. The situation was not natural. Nature had been perverted by the dam. The dam was there to stay, he realised that, but the water must go through it somehow. A way must be found to let the water take its natural course.

Could the Law force Keener to open his big dam and let the Rainy River through? A few days would do the trick. The great river would act like a gigantic syphon sucking the surface water away from the Flat; and the land would be dry enough for planting within a week. The Law ought to make that possible, because it was the square thing, and that was what the Law was for: to give everybody a fair play.

His absorption was so complete that when he reached the auto-livery in Rainy River Falls he ordered a car to take him down to LacClaire without pausing to inquire the charge for the trip. He slumped himself down in the back seat of the little car and drew his hat over his eyes, and he maintained that position in silence during the long, jolting ride to LacClaire and until the end of the drive before the screened porch of Banker Sawyer's modest home.

"Well!" said Sawyer when he recognised the face that peered through the screen door; and when he and Martin were seated on the porch, with the light from the window revealing the young man's face, he said quietly: "Take it easy, boy; take it easy."

Martin did not do anything of the sort. He leaned forward nervously and poured out the bad news which MacNish had given him, went from that to the idea of forcing Keener to open his dam, and concluded by requesting Sawyer to put him at once in touch with a lawyer.

"For that's the only way out of it," he ended. "The water's got to be drawn off in a hurry, and the Law has got to do it for us, and I've no time to lose getting things started."

"I see," said Sawyer. From where he sat in the gloom of a dark corner he studied Martin's face. Particularly did he study the young man's eyes.

"I suppose the rest of the boys on the Flat know about this?" he asked. "The Cartwright boys—and the old-timers?"

"Oh, yes; I suppose most of them know it by this time," replied Martin impatiently, "but that won't do any good. I'm here to get action right away."

"You can't do anything to-night."

"Can't!" Martin started to his feet. "I've got to."

"Sit down, Calkins," said Sawyer. "You've come to me for help, and I'm glad you've come; but you've got to take my advice. We can't do anything tonight, so you might as well take it easy. To-morrow morning we'll see what can be done."

"Something has got to be done," said Martin softly. "You hear me, Sawyer, something has got to be done. It's got to be done, or—it's the end of Big Flat!"

Sawyer waited until the unwonted outburst had spent itself and Martin had returned to his normal mood of calm.

"You're bunking in my shanty here to-night," he said quietly, but in such a tone that it was obvious he had determined to have his way.

"Couldn't think of it. I'll go to a hotel—"

"You'll stay right here." Sawyer's tone was not an invitation; it was a serious command. "That's the best way you can help your case at present, stay right here, in my house, so two or three people can swear you were here. Will you take my word for that—without explanations?"

"Yes," said Martin, after a long pause.

"All right. Now, let's take it a little easy—until to-morrow. Is Simon Lee getting any big trout this spring? I've been intending to come up and try 'em some day. Might go back with you to-morrow; don't know but what I will. Could you give me a bunk, if I should come?"

"A bunk? I guess you know there isn't a house on the Flat where they wouldn't sleep on the floor and give you the bed if you asked for it."

The banker chuckled, and turned the conversation to reminiscences of Big Flat in the old, gone days, when the old-time lumber-kings fought for saw-logs, and rough, desperate deeds were done by the daredevil crews that ran the Rainy River.

"But you never ran up against a proposition like this dam," said Martin. "What would you have done in a case like this?"

Sawyer rose, stretching himself elaborately.

"Ho hum!" he yawned. "We've logged enough for to-night. Let's turn in."

XLIX

Next evening, at nine, Martin stood in the telegraph office at LacClaire with the final answer to his appeal to the Law in his hands; and the answer was that he was beaten.

Wise old MacNish had been right, after all. With Keener's attorneys alertly prepared to meet and forestall every appeal to the courts, there was Law enough in the case to drown them all.

The final appeal, after a day of disappointments, had been by telegraph to the governor of the state, and the character of his reply was inevitable—the conditions at Big Flat did not constitute an emergency which justified official action.

Martin read the telegram which Sawyer had passed to him and handed it back. He was silent a long while, his head bowed, and when he looked up his eyes were not easy to meet.

"That means we can't get the water drawn off in time—by law," he said at last. "Well—I certainly am obliged to you, Mr. Sawyer, for all the trouble you've gone to on my account."

Sawyer, with his eyes on Martin's, said slowly:

"What are you thinking of doing now?"

"Going home. No use hanging around here any longer."

"Better wait till morning. I'll go up with you—going fishing."

"I'm going to-night." Martin's tone was as hard and bleak as his eyes.

After a pause Sawyer said: "I'll go with you."

Martin had turned away, but Sawyer's words caused him to halt and look back slowly.

"Why?"

"I'll go with you." In Sawyer's eyes there was something of the same look as in Martin's, and that look is seldom to be seen except near American frontiers.

"Why?"

"Just once and for all I'll tell you, Martin: because I have come to think a lot of you, and I am going to see this through."

"You don't have to; we aren't asking any more help from any one."

"I know you aren't. That's why I'm coming along."

"What!"

"Just that. You aren't going to get yourself in trouble if I can stop you."

"And Keener isn't going to crow over me," said Martin. "You can put that in your hat, Sawyer: Keener isn't going to crow over me. I know one law that can reach him. I'm going to Rainy Falls, and I'm going at once."

"All right," said Sawyer. "I'll drive you up."

The drive through the dark night to the Falls was mainly a silent one. Here and there Sawyer swung the car from the road and drove up to a settler's house.

"What time is it?" he would ask when the startled settler and family came to the door; and when the time had been ascertained, he would say: "You know Martin Calkins, don't you?" And in the light from the open door the settler and his family would have their attention called to Martin's presence in the car.

It was half past eleven when they drove into Rainy River Falls, and the town was dark and sound asleep, save for the light which gleamed from the office of the little hotel.

"Better keep on to your place, I guess," suggested Sawyer.

"I stop here," said Martin.

In the office of the hotel the night clerk and the town-policeman were listening to a fat little drummer's explanation of how he maintained his health:

"Every night before going to bed I take a good walk. Every night, rain or shine, no matter where I am. Then I take long breaths—so—while I walk. When I come back to go to bed the blood is all out of my brain. I am ready to sleep. I go to bed; the next thing I know is morning. Good sleep; that's what gives you good health."

Sawyer went to the desk and registered.

"Mr. James Sawyer," he said loudly as he wrote his name on the register. "And Mr. Martin Calkins. Martin, step up and register."

Martin obeyed and then went straight across the room and shook the sleepy policeman into full wakefulness.

"Where's Keener?" he asked harshly.

"What? Where's who? Mr. Keener? Down at his cottage on Pine Island, of course. Where'd you suppose he'd be this time of night?"

"What time does he come to his office here, in the morning?"

"Oh, 'bout eight, I guess. Mebbe little later these mornings on account of all the company they got down there."

"Going to bed?" asked Sawyer.

"Not me," said Martin, and seated himself grimly in a chair beside the officer. Sawyer did likewise, and it became so still in the little office that the slow tick-tock, tick-tock of the clock above the desk was plainly audible.

After awhile the drummer returned from his stroll.

"Great, great!" he said, swelling his chest out as he took his key from the clerk. "Swell walk. Great. Say, it's a great river here, by moonlight, ain't it?

"Fine," agreed the clerk, sleepily.

"I specially like a swift river—like to see it, going along there with the moonlight on it. It's great."

"Uh-huh."

"I been down on the bridge below town watching the logs go by," concluded the salesman. "By golly! It was nice. They was twisting and bobbing, going up and down, sometimes in the moonlight and sometimes out of sight. They was just scraping the bottom of the bridge and going so fast. It was great. Well—good-night."

L

The stranger had reached the stairway before he noticed that the room had become queerly alive; that the men were sitting up, staring at him in strained fashion. The policeman's mouth was wide open and the night clerk stood frozen with his pipe half raised to his mouth. Martin was on his feet.

"Logs?" said Sawyer quietly. "Did you say logs, sir?"

"What's the matter? What if I did say logs?"

"Going under the bridge—high water?"

"Say! Say, what's the matter, gentlemen; I just told what I saw."

"It can't be!" protested the policeman.

"Those Hunkies," said the chalk-faced clerk hoarsely. "In bunk-cars—sleeping—on the track below the bridge—a hundred of 'em."

"It can't be!" repeated the policeman again.

"We've got to wake those Hunkies," said Martin quietly.

They followed him out of the hotel, Sawyer, the clerk and the salesman at his heels, the policeman last of all.

There was no need to investigate the drummer's report, for the raw, growling note that rose from the raging Rainy River hurled its tale into their ears.

"Sluice gates wide open!" gasped the clerk. "Wow! Hear her roar!"

"The Hunkies below the bridge?" Martin caught the nod from the clerk and plunged through the darkness down the bank to the siding where water was whirling about the wheels of the bunk cars.

"Roll out, roll out! For your lives, roll out!"

Shouting and pounding, they roused the labourers from their heavy sleep.

"High water! Out, or you'll drown!"

Martin caught the flashlight from the policeman's fumbling hands and leaped into the first car.

"Get out, get out!"

He saw that the last bunk was empty and went to the next car.

The foreigners began to cry out in their own tongue, huddled up like sheep, or ran amuck. They lay dumb in their bunks, and had to be thrown bodily out into the rising water; and they fought back madly. And above the pandemonium of cries and shouts, and the growling of the river, came the grinding shriek of the bridge as it gave way beneath the torrent.

"Look out! The cars are moving!"

Martin was in the last car when the cry came. He thrust a stupefied man out of the door and leaped out into a swirl of water up to his breast. A twisting, shrieking body whisked past him in the darkness and he lunged out, caught hold of a leg and raced for the high bank.

"All safe?" he cried, as he dragged his man to safety. "All make it?"

"All, I guess," came Sawyer's ringing voice. Higher up, boys; she's rising fast."

And then, as they stood panting on the bank, there came from far up the river a colossal rumbling sound, a noise which shook the ground, and which Martin recognised and which turned him pale. As if in echo to the first explosion, came a second and louder one, apparently nearer town. After the two explosions the deafening roar of the unleashed Rainy River seemed like the murmur of a far away brook.

"Dynamite!" The word was out of Martin's mouth, and he wished it unsaid.

"About up at Squaw Island, wasn't it?" panted the night-clerk. "Yeah; 'bout at Squaw Island dam."

"But this—this dam—what happened here—what happened here?" asked the salesman.

"Sluice-gates—somebody's dropped 'em—dam wide open. They've turned the trick."

"Who do you mean they—'they'?" asked Sawyer sharply.

"Nobody."

Martin was running down the bank as fast as his legs could carry him. Pine Island would be flooded, and if the bridge floated it would sweep down and wipe the island clean of buildings.

"The Island—!"

"Yes. Come on!"

He outdistanced his followers in this long run, caught up with the crest of the flood and passed it, and soon saw lights gleaming on the island, and knew those on it were awake. Cries came across the water. They knew their danger. But he thought of the boats— they had only light row-boats and canoes on the island and the river was a leaping torrent.

"Catch holt there!" growled a voice, and the prow of a sturdy river bateau came thrusting out of the darkness up to the bank. Martin caught hold and drew the heavy craft to a resting place on the solid ground.

"Unload 'em—got to go back for more. 'Y golly! That you, Marty?"

Jud Hart was leaning on a long push-pole in the stern of the boat, holding it steady against the rushing water, his great form looming darkly above a boat load of lightly clad women.

Martin reached into the darkness toward the hands that stretched out to him from the dark, and a moment later he had Alice Demaree in his arms, carrying her upon the bank. Four other women followed.

"Get a pole," said Jud. "Men left on the island. Water's rising, and it'll take two of us to push her back."

"Jud," said Martin, as they shoved away from the shuddering women, "how did you come to be here?"

"I was on a little bender, Marty," replied Jud glibly. "Sleeping it off over on the bank. Woke up and heard the river growling and sez to myself, better get those folks off that island."

"This is Pete Cartwright's boat."

"'Y golly! I noticed that, too, Marty. Pete must have been spearing down here below the dam. Hang tough, boys!" he bellowed in response to a cry from the island. "Be there in a minute."

It was many minutes before they had managed to effect a landing on the foot of the island. Half a dozen men leaped for the boat as it touched land, and the first was Keener, but Jud thrust him back with a heavy foot, bellowing angrily: "You come last, Mister. Tried to crowd in with the women when we were overloaded—you come last."

"Keener," said young Starin as the loaded boat was pushed out, "you're too yellow to live. Yes, you're too yellow to stay here after my uncle hears about this."

Then the crest of the flood caught them and flung them downstream. They battled it silently until the current began to master them, and then Keener began to gibber.

"Shove!" said Martin presently. "There's a point—shove hard!"

The leaves of a willow whipped his face and he lunged into the darkness and caught a branch. The branch broke and the boat was whisked downstream.

"Shut up!" bellowed Jud Hart at Keener's blasphemous whining. "Shut up so we can hear ourselves drown."

"Jud!" cried Martin, crouching in the bow as they raced toward another point. "See where we are?"

"Tamarack point. Keener, that's our last chance. There's white water and rocks beyond. Pray, darn you, pray."

"Shove," said Martin.

Jud's mighty strength threw the bow inshore, and Martin flung his arms blindly into the darkness and his hands clipped onto the roots of the old tamarack on the point. In an instant it seemed that his arms must be torn from their sockets.

"Hang tough, Marty!" Jud Hart gave a mighty shove on his pole, and Martin felt the bow scrape and leaped out. For a flash it seemed to him that he had erred, that the river would wrest the heavy boat from his taut-stretched arms and whip him back into the stream. Then Jud Hart shoved again, and Martin heaved the bow up on shore, slipped and fell as he did so, and felt Keener step on his breast as he clambered, gibbering, ashore.

And then, with his life his own again, Keener turned on Martin, shaking a pudgy fist frantically.

"You'll pay—you'll pay, Calkins! You pauper—you criminal—you did this. I'm ready for you. I'll fix you. You'll go to prison! I'll put you away, you—"

Martin knocked him down with a blow square in the mouth.

LI

With morning came a coherent story of all that had happened. A group of masked men had rushed the dam at shortly after midnight and knocked unconscious the two watchmen, the night-engineer and fireman. It was done roughly and in a twinkling, and when the four victims regained consciousness they lay helplessly bound on the engine room floor; the sluice gates had been lowered; and the hoisting machinery had been so thoroughly and expertly wrecked that it would require days before repairs could be effected. And the sluices were built to empty the pond in ten hours.

The police officer and night-clerk of the hotel fixed the time of the two explosions up the river at 12:15. These explosions came from two great charges of dynamite which had been exploded within a few seconds of one another. The first had blown the middle out of the dam at Squaw Island. The second, the larger blast of the two, had torn a gap a rod wide—now widened by the water—in the Red Banks on the eastern side of the river, through which the water now was pouring in a torrent onto the low-lying swamp beyond. And there was not a clue to the perpetrators; not one of the assaulted men could identify his assailants. It was a mystery—so great a mystery that men shook their heads solemnly, and winked on the sly.

Keener was raving. He knew that his grip had slipped and he was clawing and scratching like a cat to hang on, and discharging employés right and left. People were shunning him, and he felt himself the centre of a vast conspiracy of enmity.

"If you're in it you'll pay, too, Sawyer!" he bawled at the banker. "I believe you're all in this—the whole lot of you are in this conspiracy."

"Well, I guess you're right, Keener," drawled Sawyer after some deliberation. "I guess you'll find that the whole county is against you."

"You admit it, eh?"

"Why, yes. We sort of all stick together up here. It went against us hard when you started out to hog the land around here and make it a one-man country."

"You admit it. All right; you're on record. You and Calkins; you're together in this affair."

"That's just what we are, Mr. Keener. We've been together for something like thirty-six hours, now. He hasn't been out of my sight during that time, except for the half hour when he was helping get you off the island, after you'd tried to crowd in and risk drowning your women-folks. I've made it my business not to let him out of my sight; so I can take the stand and swear that he didn't know that this was going to happen, and didn't have a thing to do with it."

"Ah! You knew, then? You knew it beforehand, eh? Good! I've got one of you now; I've got you, Sawyer!"

"Well, I confess I didn't *know* that this was going to happen," said Sawyer, "but I was afraid that something was boiling up. I knew you'd gone too far, Keener. You didn't know the people up here, and you tried your game a little too soon; the country wasn't quite tame enough for your purpose. I couldn't quite see the boys up here letting you drown Calkins out without doing something to help him, because they haven't been brought up like that. I knew they wouldn't let you walk over them, but they're getting to be tamer and more long-headed than I thought. I didn't think of the dam so much: I figured they would kill you!"

"I'll see every last one of them behind the bars, where they belong."

"You'll have to if you put one there. They stick together. If you could put them all in prison, I guess you could make a one-man country, as you're trying to do; but I don't think you're going to be around here long enough to do that."

Martin waited in town to be arrested, and he felt strangely peaceful, relaxed, contented, as a man might feel at the triumphant end of a long struggle. The prospect of prison stared him in the face, for Keener left no ground on which to doubt that: Calkins was the leader of the Big Flat settlers; it was he who had organised them, and filled them with the spirit of hatred toward Capital's beneficent plans, therefore it was he who had stirred them to lawlessness. But for him Keener's plans would have progressed to their profitable ends. Calkins was responsible for the outrage, and Keener was ready to spend much money to send him to prison.

Still Martin felt content. He sat on the porch of the hotel, Jud Hart at his side, waiting to be arrested, and he felt at ease. For before his eyes the mighty Rainy River was doing its full, natural duty to the high water of the Flat. It was acting like the mighty syphon Nature had intended it to be, sucking away the pent-up water, and hour by hour lowering the stored up flood. In twenty-four hours the river would be below normal and the surface water drawn off the Flat, and in a week the drained soil would be dried out and ready for planting. The Flat was saved!

"Have you sent for blood-hounds yet, Mr. Keener?" he asked cheerily as Keener passed. "They say they're a great help in tracking criminals."

Keener's scowl was a trifle less domineering than it had been. The town was filled with people, and except for a few strangers they made way and turned their backs when he approached.

"I reckon he don't need blood-hounds," drawled Jud Hart. "He'll get some of those city detectives. They'll fix us."

"It will be pretty hard on an old-timer like you to go to prison," said Martin. "Young fellow like me, I can get used to it, but it will be tough on you."

"They tell me," said Jud, "that if a fellow is good down there they make him a trusty and let him do 'bout as he pleases."

"Not an old criminal like you."

"Guess you're right there, Marty. Wonder if they'll feed us good?"

"Don't worry; you'll know soon enough."

"Wonder if they'll give me standard chewing?"

"They hang anybody who asks for it."

"'Y golly! They're hard ones, eh? Well, we'll make 'em haul in some provisions if they start to feed us, eh, Marty? Yes, sir; we certainly will let them know they got a couple new boarders."

And the Rainy River went down, inch by inch.

Keener came by, crushing a telegram in his hand. He looked ill.

"Bad news," yawned Jud. "Detectives can't come. We'll have to wait some more to get arrested."

They waited in vain. On the morning of the second day it was noised around that Mr. Starin, himself, was coming.

"Get ready, you old criminal," said Martin when he heard the news. "Here's where we catch it."

"Well, I guess we deserve it, don't we?"

"Certainly."

"I mean," drawled Jud, "we should have left Keener on the island."

A special train brought Mr. Starin up from the Junction at noon, and Keener watched it as it approached; and as he recognised the private car swaying behind the little locomotive he swallowed, like a man whose throat suddenly has become dry. For it was not Mr. Starin's private car that he saw—it was a private car belonging to the Great Lakes Northern Railway, and Neil MacNish and a corps of engineers, and Mr. Sawyer of LacClaire were keeping Mr. Starin company.

In the evening, after a busy afternoon, Sawyer came to Martin and Jud on the hotel porch.

"If we had known what a big man Starin is all this needn't have happened," said he. "He wasn't much pleased to find that Keener was using the Starin Company's dams for his own private land business."

"What are they going to do?" asked Martin.

"Why, they're going to use that swamp for their mill-pond. Mr. MacNish had it all planned and showed Starin that it would be just as good. Lem Mills sent Starin a few words by wire; and I convinced him that a dam that didn't drown out the land would be cheaper—and safer—in the long run. So Mr. Keener is leaving the Starin Company."

"What are they going to do about us?"

"You? Oh, they passed that up," was the reply. "The dams were insured."

Presently Sawyer turned around and shook hands. "Martin, you've won out. I told Starin about your struggle up here; and from now on the Company is with you, instead of against you. You've won—you've done the trick!"

"I have? Why, I didn't do it at all," said Martin. "The others did it—my friends."

"Well," said the banker dryly, "that's a way of getting things done, too. At all events, Big Flat is safe."

After awhile Martin turned to Jud Hart and said:

"Guess we'd better get home and cut some more seed."

He had lost four days in planting.

This was the fact that dominated his thoughts, his action, his life, when he came home and resumed his task where he had dropped it; hence, that summer became the one in which people predicted that Martin Calkins would work himself to death.

But youth—youth such as his—is not easily slain by work in the open, else possibly the predictions might have come true. He worked harder than he ever had before, harder than he ever would again in all his life for such a length of time.

He was four days behind in planting, and all summer it seemed that he was hurrying feverishly to regain the lost time. But now he worked with a different spirit, and though he wore himself down to the thinness of the proverbial fence-rail the springiness of his step, the brightness of his eyes were those of a man who is triumphing over the weariness of toil. The depressing uncertainty and fear were gone. He had only one task to accomplish now; and that was to do his duty to the soil; and during that summer he did or thought of little else.

Said Hattie Lee, at the Fourth of July picnic:

"Marty, I declare you've got yourself so thin I'm nervous when I see you stoop over, afraid that you'll break right in two."

"That's all right," he retorted, a trifle hurt. "As long as I keep the bugs killed off and my spuds cultivated I won't worry about myself."

"Oh! You and your spuds! Don't you ever think of anything else?"

"Not if I can help it. And I don't expect to until my crop is made."

"And then you'll be so set you won't be able to think of anything else. You're getting to be like an old man. You're just like most farmers—you think more of farming than you do of living."

He stored that last shot away somewhere in the lockers of his memory, to recall and ponder over some time—when he had time. For the present he had no time at all for anything but doing the best he could for the soil and the crop that it was growing so richly.

The bugs were bad, the weeds likewise; he was not the easiest man in the world to work for that summer, and of his hands only Jud and Shorty knew him well enough to grin appreciatively at the scope of language which the boss exhibited on occasions. With the new railroad fairly crying for men a man didn't have to work for a boss who was so bull-headed; and as a consequence Martin was often looking for a couple extra men for a week or so.

"Bull-headed, eh?" said he, with a cheerless grin, as he looked over his clean, thriving fields. "All right. Let it go at that—until this crop is safe."

Many farmers on the Flat that summer lost a percentage of their crop because their potato vines were stripped to the stems by the omnipresent bugs, and others because they got behind with their cultivating; but few bugs lived long enough to make more than one meal off the potato tops on Martin's place, and no weeds found room to steal from the soil the nourishment that should have gone into the crop.

In the latter part of August Jud Hart dug here and there in the hills and said:

"Marty, she's going to be the best crop I ever see."

"If we don't get an early frost," corrected Martin.

In September, when the early frost had passed without being sufficiently heavy to hurt, Shorty Dewar said:

"Boss, you're going to clean up big."

"If there's any sort of a price," supplemented Martin.

For he was growing sceptical as harvest time approached, and he could not grow enthusiastic over his prospects; he could not quite believe in them. He had known too much disappointment, and it seemed to him that something must happen to interfere and keep his dream from coming true.

When, at digging time, the price stood at only fifty cents a bushel he said, in spite of his knowledge that the potato crop was short:

"Yes; and it will probably drop when they begin coming in."

But the price did not drop when the crop began coming in. On the contrary, it began to creep upward, cent by cent. It went to sixty cents a bushel, then jumped to sixty-five.

"It won't go very high though," he asserted; but in contradiction of this statement he did not sell a bushel, but stored the crop as it came from the fields.

When the price had reached seventy cents he said nothing, but devoted all his thought and energy to driving his machine diggers and his crew of Indian pickers to the limit, and after dark he worked at the task of turning the old mill into a warehouse to hold the crop.

Larson, the buyer in town, drove out one day and eyed the mountains of potatoes covetously.

"I'd like to handle 'em, Calkins," he said.

"What are you paying?"

"Seventy-five."

"I'm not selling."

The day after the last bushel had been dug and stored, and the crew had bruited the news about concerning the magnitude of the crop, Larson drove out again.

He found Martin nailing tar-paper over the walls of the mill to shut out the frost from the potatoes that filled the old building to the cracking point, and by the way in which Larson tied and blanketed his horse Martin knew that a crucial moment had arrived. He went on with his nailing as if he were alone.

"Nice day," said Larson, looking around.

"Pretty fair," agreed Martin.

"I think this Indian summer is the nicest time of the year myself," continued the buyer.

"'Tis if it don't rain."

"Saw a lot of partridges in the road out there. Been after them any?"

"Not yet." Martin turned around—to look at Larson's horse.

"Say, ain't that Jim Green's old Fanny? Did you swap with him?"

Larson drew off his driving mitt and carefully scratched his nose. He had not come out to talk "horse."

"Price went up a little to-day," he said carelessly.

"Eh—yah?"

"Yes. Eighty cents now."

Martin drove a nail and drawled: "Eighty cents, eh? I heard there was another buyer talking of starting in at the Falls."

"How many bushel you got in there, Calkins?" asked the buyer, abruptly.

"Oh, 'bout twenty-two thousand."

"That's what I heard. I'll take 'em all for eighty cents."

"Guess again, Lars."

"Well, I tell you," said Larson confidentially, "on a big batch like this I can afford to handle 'em on a smaller margin."

"You'll have to if you expect to get 'em."

"I want to get 'em," said the buyer. "I admit it's a nice big batch to handle. I'll give you eighty-three cents."

"Hah!"

"Eighty-five."

Martin drew out a crooked nail, straightened it, and drove it in again and said: "You've bought 'em."

LIII

It was days later before he began to realise how he had failed. For now came Life. It clamoured at him and possessed him with the eagerness of the long suppressed. It told him that if a man in the full blooming of his manhood denies Love, he has damned himself to a life of hopelessness, regardless of whatever material success he may achieve.

He had denied Love. On that fateful spring afternoon when, driven by a primal desire for revenge upon Keener, he had come upon Hattie Lee in the clearing, and she had been a light to guide him out of his dark mood, he had glimpsed the vistas of his paradise; and he had committed the sin of sins and, with tight-set lips and averted eyes, had passed it by. In the blindness of his young strength and ambition he had fancied that the fulfilment of his chosen duty to the land was the fulfilment of his destiny, and that nothing else mattered—that it was Life.

He knew better now. In these days of leisure the scales fell from his eyes, and he began to feel; and looking back on the past months, he realised that he had made of himself a machine, as selfish and harsh as only a machine can be.

Life was taking its revenge. Often, as he sat chatting with Simon Lee to conceal the purpose of his frequent visits to the Lee place, he looked at Hattie with the hungry hope that he might again behold in her eyes the look which he had evoked that spring afternoon in the clearing. He looked in vain. Hattie seemed to have lost interest in everything but her work, and when, by chance, they were alone both became dumb and helpless. The hearty comradeship which had been theirs for so long was gone forever, and with it the ready chaff and laughter; and when he tried clumsily to win back to the old ease he failed so miserably that it was painful to them both.

Hattie spent most of her time in the fly-factory, working steadily, and she began to look a little old. At times as she sat bent over her work there came into her eyes a look of disappointment and pain, and then her hands would drop idly in her lap and she would look out of the window toward the old log by the birch-grove at the edge of the clearing. Sometimes she would smile wistfully as she looked, as one might smile at memory of a childhood dream which Life has taught may never come true. It was Autumn now, and there was no robin trilling in the top of the sun-crested pine.

Once Martin found her so. He had entered the workroom noiselessly, and the first that she was aware of his presence was when she lifted her eyes and saw him attempting to steal out without letting her know he had been there. They looked into each other's eyes, but neither spoke. Presently she resumed her work, and he went out of the room.

He had won material success. There was no doubt of that now. Struggles there would be in the future—who is free from struggle who traffics with the soil and Nature? Disappointments, defeats, discouragement, likewise would come; for these, too, are the inevitable lot of the man in the open, the fruit of whose labours is dependent upon the elements. But from now on his progress was assured. He no longer had a tract of stump-land, he had a farm. Come weal or woe, drought or flood, crop-failure or crop-success, he had a farm. He had a hundred acres under plough. In the proper time he would have twenty times that much. Two years ago he had dreamed of this, and, dreaming, had asked himself: what more could a man want! But he was a boy then and now he was a man.

Jud Hart came to him one day, tugging hesitatingly at the tufts of hair in his ears.

"Marty, would it be crowding you at all to ask you to pay me off?"

"Not at all, Jud; you can have it all to-day if you want it."

"Well, then, I guess I'll take it, Marty, if it's all the same to you. I got a hankering to go out west where Black Jack Doyle is knocking down the big trees. It sort of come over me lately; I want to hear the boys yell, 'Timber!' and hear the big ones go 'Whoosh!' when they hit the snow."

Shorty Dewar came likewise, stirred by the impulse to pursue the will-o'-the-wisp of the roamer's existence.

"I've stayed longer in one place than I ever did in my life, and I'll be darned if I know why I did it, because you certainly are a hard one to work for, boss. Guess it was because I wanted to stay and see you hand it to Keener."

"I didn't hand it to him," said Martin. "Somebody did it for me."

"That's all right, too; but there's more than one way of blowing out a dam, you know. One of them is being the sort of guy your friends will risk going to jail for—even if you are a hard guy to work for. I may breeze back here and run a tractor for you next spring, at that, you can't tell; but I'm on my way now. A guy can't work all the time; he's got to live some, too, you know."

On one of those perfect Indian summer days of the Northland, when each breath of air carries with it a thrill, Martin drove Jud and Shorty in to catch the afternoon train. The departing pair said: Ah! it was like getting out of jail to know they weren't going to work for him any longer; and Martin solemnly enquired of his horses if they had ever beheld two more utterly useless men. Then Shorty volunteered the opinion that a term in jail would seem like a vacation after serving on the Calkins place; and Martin retorted that Shorty undoubtedly knew best where he belonged.

The chaffing was in vain, however, for they had come to know one another so well that each knew the feelings that the others were trying to hide. As they approached the station a silence fell upon them, and when they saw that the train was starting at once they were relieved.

They shook hands casually.

"So long, Shorty; so long, Jud."

"So long. So long, Marty."

But as the train pulled away to the westward two figures, one large, one small, stood motionless on the rear platform looking back at the figure at the station whose eyes followed them steadily until they were out of sight.

LIV

After that he pottered around the house for a few days longer, banking up the foundation with saw-dust, hanging storm-doors and windows, and making ready for the winter, but one morning while he was rigging his gasoline tractor to run the wood-saw he stopped suddenly, hurled his wrench to the ground, and with his chin held high and shoulders squared he went with a swinging stride down the road to the Lee place, and into the fly-factory and straight to Hattie.

"I want you to come outdoors with me," he said. "I want to tell you something, and I don't want to tell it indoors."

"Marty," she said, wearily, dropping her work for a moment, "I wish you'd go away and leave me alone."

"I won't," said he. "I can't."

"You can," she said resignedly. "You've done it so long."

"I can't, Hattie; I can't leave you alone any longer. I've tried. I can't stand to be alone myself. I can't stand to be away from you. I've got to come here, and I've got to tell you this, there's no use of my living if you won't listen."

"It's no use your talking this way to me, Marty! No use, I tell you. It only hurts us both; and—and it can never do either of us any good. Never, never, never!"

"Never?"

"No. Never, never, never!" she said, with her clinched fists against her breast. "I won't listen; I don't care what you want to say. I'll never, never be so cheap as to take Miss Demaree's leavings!"

"Hattie—!"

"Don't! Don't say any more. It hurts me, it hurts me so. Go away; please go away! I'd almost gotten over it. Leave me alone— please leave me, alone."

"Hattie! Do you mean that—honest?"

"Yes, yes, yes!"

"For—good?"

"Marty! That night—of the fire—did you—did you really—kiss her?"

"Yes."

"Then," she cried, her face white with anger, "don't you speak to me, don't you come near me, again!"

But a little anger had risen in him, too, and he did not move.

"You aren't going to drive me away like that," he said, more steadily. "I know I was a fool, but that night cured me. I didn't know I cared for you then; it wasn't until last spring that I knew I cared."

"Yes, and how well you showed it! You scarcely looked at me all summer. You cared more for your old potatoes than you did for me, and now when you're through with them you've got time to come around and talk about caring for me!"

"Oh. I thought it was Miss Dem—"

"Don't mention her name to me again! Oh, Marty, how could you, how could you!"

"Hattie," he said firmly, "I want to say this before I go: it doesn't make any difference about her, and it doesn't make any difference how you feel toward me. I know how I feel toward you, and I know that I am going to feel that way toward you for the rest of my life. That's all. Now, shall I go?"

"Yes," she said, and he went.

A few days later, at supper, his mother said:

"Heard about Hattie, Marty? Well, she's all of a sudden decided to go to Chicago to stay. She wrote her Company and they made her an offer to come down there and start a fly-factory for them; and all Hattie will have to do will be walk around and see the girls are doing their work right, and she'll be paid regular wages for doing it, and a certain amount on every dozen flies they sell; and land knows how much money a week it is that she will be making. But the Lord only knows what made her decide to go and do a thing like that and leave her home and neighbours and go out among strangers, and city folks at that; for it certainly ain't at all natural for Hattie to leave her ma and pa like she was some giddy young fool just anxious to get into city life. Hattie Lee ain't like that, and why she's doing it is something that certainly gets way beyond me."

After supper Martin went swiftly to the Lees'.

"I'm going away from Big Flat," he said.

"*You* are? Why, what in the world!"

"You won't have to go away, Hattie. I'll go, and then you can stay."

"It wouldn't make any difference now," she said slowly. "I have made up my mind to go. I'll keep busy, and I'll be a business woman, and—Well, I have made up my mind to go—on the morning train."

"Will you shake hands, Hattie?"

"Of course."

"Good luck."

"Good luck to you, Marty."

He looked at her, and tried hard to smile, and then he turned away and went back home.

He counted the hours as he lay awake through the night. Now it was eleven, and at seven she would be leaving the house: in eight hours she would be gone. Now it was twelve o'clock, six hours more before she left. One, two, three—the hours seemed fairly to run away. And then it was seven; he was sitting down to breakfast, thinking only: "She's gone, she's gone!"

He went to the tool-shed and fussed prodigiously. He calculated that Simon, after driving her to the train, would stop in town for awhile and reach home round nine-thirty, so at nine Martin was landing from his skiff at the foot of Crooked Lake, where an old Indian trail ran into the timber. At nine fifteen he was hiding in Simon Lee's birch grove, peering out across the clearing to the road whence Simon must come on his return from town. He heard the creak of a buggy down the road, and drew back, waiting breathlessly for the rig to appear. It appeared very slowly, each moment a torture to him—and it was the widow Gunderson driving home with a sack of flour. He waited in vain for another rig to appear, and then, after an hour, he noted that Simon's buggy was in the carriage-shed by the barn. Apparently they had made an early start and Simon had come home and unhitched before he arrived.

He stole slowly away from the clearing, away from the birches, to a bare knoll at the foot of the lake. It was an ancient Indian village site; along the side of the knoll facing the lake ran a primitive effigy mound and on this he seated himself aimlessly. A red squirrel chattered angrily behind him. A stick cracked. He sprang up, whirled around and found Hattie looking down at him from the top of the rise.

"I changed my mind," she broke out impetuously. "I guess I've got a right to change my mind if I want to, haven't I? What were you doing up in the birches?"

He walked up to her, asking: "Is anything wrong? Why didn't you go?"

"I told you, because I changed my mind."

But her eyes drooped, and looking down at her he saw the red blood rising beneath her clean dry Indian-summer tan.

"You had your mind made up last night."

"Yes," she whispered, "until you went."

"Till I went?"

"You looked so—so awf'ly helpless, Marty."

"Hattie!"

"Ah!" she cried, turning her face toward him; and then it seemed to him that all the winds in the universe were driving him toward her, and he trembled.

"I think—I think you ought to go, Hattie."

"Why do you say that?"

He struggled a moment.

"Go away, Hattie, go away!"

"Not now!" she cried triumphantly. "Ah, Marty! Marty, do you love me, Marty; do you really?"

"Love you! Can't you see? You—"

"Say it! Say it!"

"I love you. Hattie, I—"

He put a hand out and touched her; he called her name; and the next instant his arms had whipped her to his bosom with a grip that made her cry out

"But you, Hattie," he stammered, looking down at the little curly head on his breast, "do you mean that you, too—?"

Slowly she lifted her head from its resting place and turned her face up to him. Her eyes were wet with tears, and her lips were smiling. She raised herself on her toes, and he bent toward her, and slowly and reverently they joined in the sacred first kiss of love.

Other young lovers, perhaps, in long-past days had met and wooed in that quiet spot, youths and maidens of dark skin and primal ways. Perhaps the knoll had beheld many such scenes, and perhaps the spirit of ancient loves remained about it. And perhaps, in the past, other angry red squirrels had chattered protestingly, as a squirrel did now, at the complete rapture of two young people beholding the world made a paradise through the miracle of love.

THE END